ALSO BY NELLIE HERMANN

The Cure for Grief

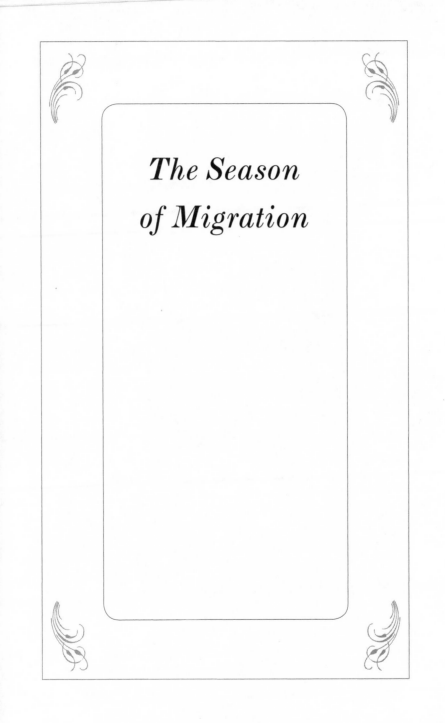

The Season of Migration

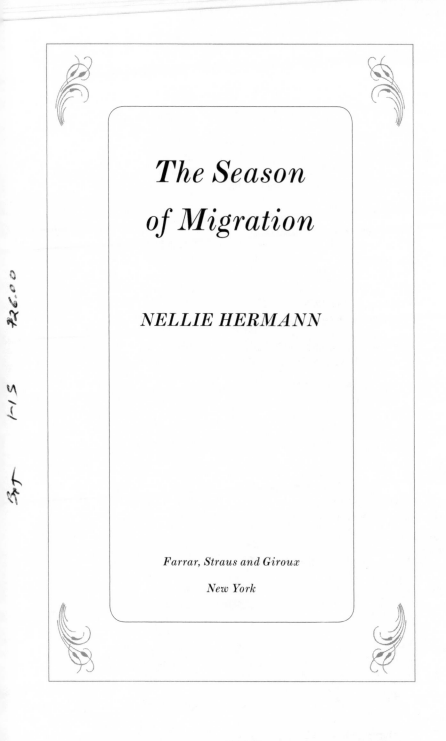

The Season
of Migration

NELLIE HERMANN

Farrar, Straus and Giroux

New York

Farrar, Straus and Giroux
18 West 18th Street, New York 10011

Grateful acknowledgment is made for permission to reprint excerpts from
Vincent van Gogh—The Letters: The Complete Illustrated and Annotated Edition, 6 volumes, edited by Leo Jansen, Hans Luijten, and Nienke Bakker, London/
Amsterdam, 2009 (www.vangoghletters.org).

Library of Congress Cataloging-in-Publication Data
Hermann, Nellie, 1978–
    The season of migration / Nellie Hermann. — First edition.
        pages   cm
    ISBN 978-0-374-25547-3 (hardcover) — ISBN 978-0-374-71173-3 (ebook)
    1. Gogh, Vincent van, 1853–1890—Fiction.   I. Title.

PS3608.E7636 S43 2015
813'.6—dc23

                                                                          2014017263

Designed by Jonathan D. Lippincott

Farrar, Straus and Giroux books may be purchased for educational, business,
or promotional use. For information on bulk purchases, please contact the
Macmillan Corporate and Premium Sales Department at 1-800-221-7945,
extension 5442, or write to specialmarkets@macmillan.com.

www.fsgbooks.com
www.twitter.com/fsgbooks • www.facebook.com/fsgbooks

1   3   5   7   9   10   8   6   4   2

For M. H.

and for "entirely different" idlers everywhere

Though I fall ninety-nine times, the hundredth time I shall stand.
—Vincent van Gogh, November 19, 1881

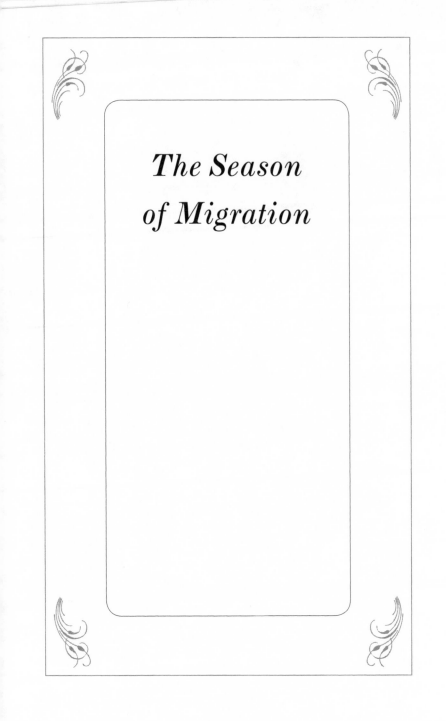

The Season
of Migration

Prologue

September 3, 1879
Petit Wasmes, the Borinage mining district, Belgium

Dear Theo,

It was quite a long time ago that we saw each other or wrote to each other as we used to. All the same, it's better that we feel something for each other rather than behave like corpses toward each other, so I am putting my hand to paper to reach out to you.

It's mainly to tell you that I'm grateful for your visit that I'm writing to you. The hours we spent together those weeks ago have at least assured us that we're both still in the land of the living. When I saw you again and took a walk with you, I felt more cheerful and alive than I have for a long time, because in spite of myself life has gradually become or has seemed much less precious to me, much more unimportant and indifferent. When one lives with others and is bound by a feeling of affection one is aware that one has a reason for being, that one might not be entirely worthless and superfluous but perhaps good for one thing or another. It has been a quite a while since I have felt this way. A prisoner who is kept in isolation, who is prevented from working, would in the long run suffer the consequences just as surely as one who went hungry for too long. Like everyone else, I have need of relationships of friendship or affection or trusting companionship, and am not like a street pump or lamppost, whether of stone or iron.

Since my dismissal as lay preacher in July, yes, you are right, I have been waiting for something, and I don't know what. You call this *idling*; I do not. You say I am not the same any longer; I say perhaps, but what man is? This time I am trying to do things right.

I have been wandering through mining country, a man in exile, a castaway, a snake wriggling out of its skin. I move between my room in Cuesmes at the evangelist Frank's house—with a bed and a desk and a worn carpet on the floor—and the room where I write from now, the abandoned salon in Petit Wasmes, a few miles away, where the floor is dirty and the few chairs are strewn across the space. I prefer the salon to the furnished room; it suits me better, and I appreciate the notion that no one can see me. I walk the landscape, I sit by the mine, in the cemetery, in the open fields covered with soot, unaware of the time, guiding myself only by the movement of the sun. I carry stacks of paper and occasionally sketch on my knees, quick strokes of what I see. Often, after I have done so, I tear up the paper and let the wind carry the strips away.

Yes, this is what I have been doing, Theo, but it is not idling. I have been trying to be patient, to be calm, to make no sudden moves. I am trying to do things right this time, to listen, to hear, to see. Great forces are shifting in me; I must let them take their time. I have been riding the waves of these forces as if I were in the ocean: some nights, they cast me to the floor, where I weep into the dirt; other nights, they are calm, and I feel I can see the land ahead.

As I think back on your visit with thankfulness, our talks naturally come to mind. I've heard such talks before, many, in fact, and often. You said, "Do you not wish for improvement in your life?" Plans for improvement and change and raising the spirits—don't let it anger you, but I'm a little afraid of them, because I have acted upon them before and ended up rather disappointed. How much in the past has been well thought out that is, however, impracticable!

Improvement in my life—should I not desire it or should I not be in need of improvement? I really want to improve. But it's precisely because I yearn for it that I'm afraid of remedies that are worse than the disease. Can you blame a sick person if he looks the doctor straight in the eye and prefers not to be treated wrongly or by a quack?

And if you should now assume from what I've said that I intended to say that you were a quack because of your advice then you will have completely misunderstood me, since I have no such idea or opinion of you. If, on the other hand, you think that I would do well to take your advice literally and become a lithographer of invoice headings and visiting cards, or a bookkeeper or carpenter's apprentice, you would also be mistaken. Supposing it were possible for us to assume the guise of a baker or a hair-cutter or librarian with lightning speed, it would still be a foolish answer, rather like the way the man acted who, when accused of heartlessness because he was sitting on a donkey, immediately dismounted and continued on his way with the donkey on his shoulders.

But, you say, I'm not giving you this advice for you to follow to the letter, but because I thought you had a taste for idling and because I was of the opinion that you should put an end to it.

Might I be allowed to point out to you that such idling is really a rather strange sort of idling? It is rather difficult for me to defend myself on this score, but I will be sorry if you can't eventually see this in a different light. Idling? The word makes me crazy; I wish it were a tangible thing so I could light it on fire.

I went to visit our parents after you left here, just as you suggested I do. They were surprised to see me, Pa answering the door in his suit, Ma standing behind him in her apron, as if they were expecting a visit from a holy angel. I was a disappointment, as usual. It was oppressive to be there, everything in that house reminding me of earlier times, when we were brothers in all the senses of the word, and I kept thinking of you turning your back on me to get on the train to Paris. I left there after only a few days. Our parents handed me an envelope containing money, and they said it was from you, though there was no note. I have not touched the money—it sits in the desk in my room in Cuesmes—but I wonder about it. After a visit like we had, what could you mean by such a gift, and without so much as an acknowledgment of what has passed between us?

If I must seriously feel that I'm annoying or burdensome to you or those at home, useful for neither one thing nor another, and were to go on being forced to feel like an intruder or a fifth wheel in your presence, so that it would be better if I weren't there—if I think that indeed it will be so and cannot be otherwise, then I'm overcome by a feeling of sorrow and I must struggle against despair. It's difficult for me to bear these thoughts and more difficult still to bear the thought that so much discord, misery and sorrow, in our midst and in our family, has been caused by me.

If it were indeed so, then I'd truly wish that it be granted me not to have to go on living too long. Yet whenever this depresses me beyond measure, after a long time the thought also occurs to me: it's perhaps only a bad, terrible dream, and later we'll perhaps learn to understand and comprehend it better. But is it not, after all, reality, and won't it one day become better rather than worse? Sometimes in winter it's so bitterly cold that one says, it's simply too cold, what do I care whether summer comes, the bad outweighs the good. But whether we like it or not, an end finally comes to the hard frost, and one fine morning the wind has turned and we have a thaw. Comparing the natural state of the

weather with our state of mind and our circumstances, subject
to variableness and change, I still have some hope that it can
improve.

There is so much that you don't know. This may be what
hurts me most. It takes a person to explain, but it takes another
person to hear the explanation. If I have changed, it is because
of what I have been through here, and you make no effort to
understand what that has been. In all the hours that we spent
together, how could you not have asked me about this place?
How could you not have asked for the story of what might have
changed me?

I want to tell you the story of what I have been through here.
I am tired already of the silence, but you are not here to talk to,
so I pick up my pen. It will take me a long time to tell you, and
I am not sure if I will be able to tell all of it properly, or if I will
ever actually send this letter or any other to you again, but tonight
I am calling out: Theo! I am here! I am your brother, always, and
despite how you have hurt me, I want to reach you.

I feel a sun beginning to burn in my hands—something is
growing in me that I must coax and tame.

Your loving brother,
Vincent

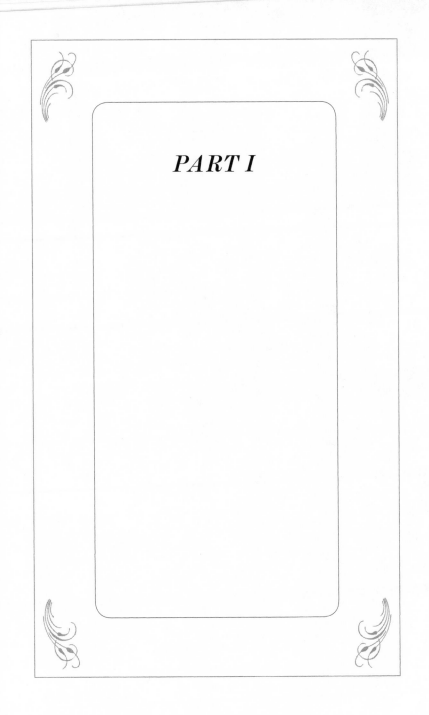

PART I

1880

He walks. Cold water is pouring from the sky, and he tries to hear the rain falling around him, onto him, trickling off the brim of his hat, over his eyes, through the hair of his beard, over his lips. He listens for each drop of water cascading against his skin, into the streams along the side of the road, onto the crows sitting on the thin, bare branches of the trees. The knapsack that he carries is thick canvas, but it must be soaked through. He thinks of the letters tucked inside, tied together with a length of twine, and imagines the words on them turning to water and washing away. He knows he should worry about this, but he cannot muster the strength.

What is the sound of the rain? It is too overwhelming to be a symphony; it is a whoosh, a swallowing, a leviathan with open mouth and lifted tongue. He is inside the cold body of a devil made of water.

His hands are growing numb. He touches the sprig of ivy that he keeps in his pocket, and its contours are blurry to his fingers. They cannot see it, he thinks, his fingers are growing blind with cold. The shape of the ivy emerges in his mind; he sees it rise behind his closed eyes, but his fingers fumble against it clumsily. My mind is not yet numb, he thinks vaguely, and trudges on.

He is going to Paris to see his brother Theo. Theo, at long

last, Theo who abandoned him, whom he hasn't heard from in nine months, since Theo visited him in August. Is that right? Is that where he is going? Suddenly he is confused. His feet are carrying him somewhere, but his mind does not know where. Who will be there at the end of this road; who will greet him when he arrives at his destination? Theo, Father, Angeline? He sees his father's top hat, resting on the table inside the parsonage door; Angeline's delicate hand, her long, slender fingers topped by nails blunted and dirtied by too many shifts in the mine.

He is walking through the rain; he will walk on until it stops. This is all he knows. He is somewhere near the border of France; he knows this because for a long time he was walking along the train tracks. Did he reach France today? Was that yesterday? He is walking. His life is collected in his footsteps; there is no past or future, only one step and then the next. He feels as if he has been walking on this road his whole life. The water has reached his feet through his boots; he wears a suit of ice water under his clothes.

He fights the temptation to lie down in the road. He walks on, a man made of water.

He wakes up in a bale of hay. A blanket that smells like a horse is pulled up to his chin. When he opens his eyes, he is first aware of the warmth. His body is shining heat; the center of him is a sun.

He looks around him: He is lying on a hay bale in the corner of a barn. A floor strewn with hay strands, a rectangle of bright light cast from a dirty window on the wall opposite, a pitchfork leaning against a pile of bales, a scythe cast onto a bale nearby. And in the corner, a stall with a cracked wooden door, through which he can hear the sound of a bull chewing calmly.

He thinks of getting up, but the sun inside him is a weight holding him down. He thinks he must have a fever, and closes his eyes instead. When he opens them, there is a man standing above him. The man looks down at him through a shaft of light coming from the dirty window. He blinks up at the man, the outline of whom, against the light, is bright and fuzzy, particles of dust lifting off like the gentlest insects, floating away into nothing. For a moment, Vincent thinks he must be dead, and that the man is an angel.

"I found you in the road in front of my farm," the man says. He does not look angry; he is only stating the facts. "You were wet all the way through. You can't be feeling good now." The man pauses, looking down. His face is dark and blurry, an image from a dream. He speaks again: "Who are you? Where are you going? How did you get here?"

Vincent opens his mouth and then shuts it again. He looks up at the man with what he feels sure is a dumb expression. It is safer than uttering a word.

"Okay," the man says, and nods. "You can tell me later. Rest now." He turns around and leaves the barn, easing the creaking door shut behind him.

Who am I? Where am I going? How did I get here? The questions swirl in his head. Who am I where am I going how did I get here who am I how did I get here where am I going who am I? These are questions he should know the answers to, words that should carry weight, carry meaning. He thinks of his knapsack, the stack of letters inside, probably destroyed from the rain. He raises his head to look around him and sees the bag, resting against the bale of hay across which his coat is draped. The sight of it makes him think of mining country, where he has come from, and he feels in his chest the burden of all that those letters contain. He has given an account of himself, there in those pages; he has already explained himself once. Having written the story, he thought that the memories would disappear from his mind.

He lays his head back and closes his eyes. He is feverish and uncomfortable, cold waves traveling up and down his skin. Images flood him and he squeezes his eyes tight against them: Madame

Denis in the doorway in her apron with a broom; Cricket, the three-legged bird, hopping on the windowsill; Alard laughing by a bird's nest at his feet; a pair of men in dark suits and top hats, looking down at him with stern expressions; Angeline, the outline of her dissolving into darkness; then blood, strewn across the field in front of the mine, bodies wriggling, severed limbs, Madame Denis with a dark red streak down her cheek.

He sleeps, and when he wakes, it is to the smell of coffee. On the bale beside him there is a tray: a porcelain mug, a roll, a bowl of some kind of stew. He is not sure of the last time he ate—was it yesterday that he started to walk? He sits up weakly and rests his back against the stack of hay behind him; the barn spins a bit and then settles. The coffee is perfect; he holds the mug in both his hands and breathes in its smell. The stew is cold but hearty, with large chunks of tomatoes and chewy meat. He devours it, using the bread to scoop out every last drop. When he is done, his stomach rumbles with confusion at the sudden work. He thinks he will probably be sick for eating this much this fast, but he doesn't slow down.

The bull in the stall across from him is quiet now; the sun still shines outside the dirty window, but there is no longer a rectangle across the floor. He feels like he has swallowed a whole bag of flour. He turns onto his side and caresses his belly.

When he next looks around, the whole barn is cast in a thin pink hue. Through the dirty window the sun is setting—a line of deep pink on the horizon. He looks around him with amazement: How the most ordinary things can be transformed by the whim of nature! The saddles and horseshoes that hang by the window have been softened and look like disembodied shapes, strange sculptures with no earthly purpose. He hears the beast breathing again behind the stall door.

What can he do to express his gratitude? He has nothing. In the pocket of his damp coat, which is draped on the bale that held the food, he finds a piece of paper still sodden with rain. He sits back on the hay bale and, lightly touching the paper with his pen so as not to tear it, he draws a quick sketch of the window, the saddles and the horseshoes surrounding it. It is an image, he thinks, of how man speaks to nature: how man has gone out to meet the world, how man has conspired to keep the world at bay. With quick, light strokes he sketches the outlines of what he sees, barely looking down at the page.

But when he finishes and inspects the drawing, he feels dismay that he has not captured it: Everything is flat to him, the window merely a square with six smaller squares within, the saddles and horseshoes simply abstract shapes with strange smudges of black. In his rendering there is no relation between the objects, as he wanted. They are not in conversation; they are only sharing space—window in center, horseshoes on right, saddle on left. He looks from the drawing to the wall before him and then back again: He has been faithful to what he sees; he has even tried to capture the waning light on the leather of the saddle, the angle of fading sun on the edge of the horseshoe. Why doesn't it please him?

He is embarrassed by the drawing's crudeness, but it is all he has to give. Perhaps the man will see something in it that he cannot see; he hopes that it might be enough for the man to remember him with something other than the effort he has cost him.

On the paper, beneath the sketch, he writes, *Thank you for your hospitality and generosity. It was more than I deserve. Vincent van Gogh.*

His name is Vincent Wilhem, but he is not the first. His brother, who had his name, was born dead on the same day that, one year later, the second Vincent was born alive.

His parents heralded the second Vincent's arrival as a miracle—or so they were sure to tell him every year on his birthday, though he was never quite sure that he believed them. He was Vincent Wilhem, that was all—not the same one who died, but then again, who could be sure? Perhaps he was the same; perhaps the Vincent Wilhem who died was the Vincent Wilhem who lived; perhaps there were never two of them. His birthday was a death day, a time to celebrate a life and death that were, he understood from the earliest age, in many ways the same.

It is built into the very foundation of him: a wonder, a sensation he can never shake, the vague but sometimes nearly positive sense that he is already dead. He is a ghost in a human's skin. There are days that it feels like only a part of him has died, while the rest of him went on to live; other days it feels like all of him has died, and then a different him was born. And some days it feels like there has only been death, death, and always death, with no life to follow.

Every Sunday until he was almost ten years old, he went to the cemetery to look at the grave with his name on it. The whole family—his parents, Theo, Anna, Elisabeth, Wil, and he—would put on their worn black clothes and make their way out the rectory and around the back in a mournful group to the cemetery, where, if it was warm enough for her to clip them from her garden, his mother would stop at the creaking iron gate and hand each of them a small cluster of flowers.

Every Sunday, he'd hear his mother crying at the grave of Vincent Wilhem, and he'd hold back the impulse to cry out to her, "Mama! I'm here!" His mother knelt by the foot of the grave, her skirts growing even darker by the knees, and she clasped her hands before her and closed her eyes, her shoulders shaking with sobs that never failed to come. The five children stood behind her, their father next to them but with his mind in a far-off place. Only once, Vincent had cried out to her, and his father had put a large hand firmly on his shoulder. "It is not advisable," his father said simply, "to disturb a mother's grief."

The tiny little gravestone spoke Vincent's name, and the words of Luke 18, "Suffer little children to come unto me, and forbid them not: for such is the kingdom of God." It was a quote that his father did not preach on but that they all knew by heart, a warning from a far-off place that had the power, at times, to make Vincent feel as if there were a hand tightening around his throat. He went over the page where the quote resided in his own copy of the Great Book so many times that he could picture the entire paragraph in his mind, but he was always perplexed by the meaning. Did Jesus really want the children dead when they came to Him? Vincent pictured a kingdom of tiny dead children, babies dressed in colorful nightdresses, tiny hands stuck in perfect tiny mouths, while groups of perfectly clean and proper older children in neckties and dresses lay together on clouds, all of them languishing under the golden throne of God, and he wondered if he should desire to join them. If this was the kingdom of God, a land of dead and frolicking children, what kind of kingdom was the one where his feet were presently standing, the low branches of the willow tree bending over his head?

Who was this Vincent Wilhem whom his mother cried for, and who hushed his father as he stood behind her, his large hand placed gently on her back and his head bowed? Vincent imagined himself as a dead baby, caressed by a silken bassinet in the Kingdom of God, bathed in the light of his parents' perfect and everlasting and unshakable love. Was his mother crying for what was dead, or for what was alive? Could there even be such a separation? He never knew.

He was always happy when they left for home, so close but so far that it seemed an apparition. When they finally turned from the grave, it was like a curtain was being drawn over something he truly did not want to see.

How could a person who never lived have so much power? Vincent wondered, lying on his back in bed at night after a scolding,

Theo sleeping soundly next to him under the checkered quilt. He imagined the look on his father's face when he shook his fist at him. There was a moment, he was sure, when his father ceased to see him—it was a clearing in his eyes, a sharpening—when his eyes would harden to a tiny pinpoint and he was no longer seeing him as he stood before him, but the ghost of him as he lay under the ground.

His father never said so; if he thought of Vincent's dead brother when he looked at him, he did not say. His mother, however, would frequently conjure the dead Vincent when she was upset with him, holding fast to his arm and reminding him of who the dead baby would have been: The first Vincent would have been obedient, and quiet, and ever-loving, and why not the second? How could he be so full of hate when the Vincent before him would have been so full of love? Always, then, she would repent. Almost as soon as the words had left her mouth, she would pull the living Vincent close, holding him fiercely, apologizing, insisting that she loved him and that he was special, so special, and that he was all that mattered to her. "You're mine, you're mine," she would say, and rock him back and forth. At times she held him so close that he was afraid she'd break a bone.

Did he provoke his parents so he could make them see him? It is possible. Often it seems to him that his whole life has been an attempt to find someone who can see him, his blood and veins and his beating heart, the recesses of his bowels and the aching of his groin, all of him so terribly alive, so terribly unseen.

It reached a point where he was sure that he hated his dead brother, Vincent. He walked by the cemetery every day and felt that little grave calling to him; he squeezed his eyes shut and looked the other way. He loathed that grave, that stone, that body lying there, that life that had cursed him before he could even speak. Such confusion at that grave on those gray Sundays, standing on that damp cemetery ground beneath that willow tree! He loved his brother; he hated him; he was not his brother; they were one and the same. Baby Vincent was alive, he was dead—no, it was the other way around—Vincent Wilhem was alive and blessed, the baby was blessed and dead. He pictured the baby, his tiny body tucked in a box somewhere below their feet, his miniature hands permanently and for all eternity crossed in a perfect prayer, perfectly pious in death.

It is nearly dark now, a band of shrinking light on the horizon. His thin coat is still damp, and he thinks it might make him warmer to take it off altogether. Instead, he pulls it tighter around him and blows into his hands. It wasn't advisable (he hears his father's voice say the word) to leave the farmer's barn just as it was getting dark. But he couldn't face the man's kindness again. Eventually he would have had to answer for himself. And what sort of answer could he give? He knows how he looks, a mirage appearing on the horizon in rags and with darkened face, a shuffling shape moving slowly, inadequately dressed, improbably thin, across a stark landscape. He knows how he looks, how he seems; it is what people have been telling him his whole life.

He walks on, beginning to feel hungry again. He shouldn't have eaten that stew; it is when he doesn't eat that he feels the least hunger.

His knapsack over his shoulder, he moves down the road, trying to hear the sound of his footsteps over the voices in his mind. *Who are you where are you going how did you get here. You are not the same any longer.*

1879

Dear Theo,

I am having trouble writing to you. My thoughts are loud but disorderly; I write through a cloud of sadness and fury. *You are not the same any longer*, I keep hearing your voice say, and then a thousand other words jump in. I approach the desk with my pen and paper again and again, tearing up start after start to this letter.

When we last saw each other—that is, before your recent August visit—it was soon before I left Brussels for the Borinage; I expect you remember how excited I was, after all that failed study in Amsterdam and useless training in Brussels, to finally be on my way to mining country. It was December 18, just nine months ago, when I finally arrived by train from the capital, the fare paid with the last money Father had given me when we parted the week before. For most of the ride, the view from my window was of a long procession of fields and peasant cottages, the sky over all of them gray and uniform. I sat back in my seat and let the scenery soothe me, trying to let my eyes lose focus. Remember I told you about this technique for seeing when we were boys in Zundert? It is a way to become aware of the grandness and the breadth of the scenery; when I relax my eyes this way, the landscape grows and I can see all corners of whatever is before me—I can pay attention to the great sweep of where I am rather than to the specific details. It calms me, to pull back this way, allowing me to feel as if I am not myself but simply a pair of eyes, free to see things as they really are.

I was having trouble remaining calm. For days before I left Brussels I barely slept, waking nearly every hour with a knot in my gut, the feeling that I was late for something. It was a feeling not unlike how I felt as a child on the days leading up to Christmas, but with a heavier weight to it, not pure anticipation, but anticipation tinged with fear. It was the trip I had been waiting for, it felt like for my whole life, and here I was finally on the train, the distance shrinking between me and mining country.

The train car was paneled with dark wood, the air thick with cigar smoke coming from a gentleman across the aisle. It had the feel of someone's living room, warm and close, and was somehow pleasant despite being packed with people facing forward, many of them nodding off or chatting with the person next to them. From where I sat I could see the peaks of hats over the seats in front of me, round shapes and summits of felt and feathers sticking up over the lines of the chair backs. The winter sun streamed in through the windows; a few people had propped their coats against the glass to keep out the glare, but where the rays streamed in, I could see the cigar smoke rising through the light in slow, twisting waves. I remembered afternoons in the front room at the parsonage, watching specks of dust float up and travel through the angles of the setting sun, trying to trace the lines they made to make shapes and pictures. It was hot on the train, though the window was cold to the touch. I had stripped down to my shirtsleeves.

I relaxed my eyes and saw the expanse of the country we were passing through. Two figures walked across a long field, one figure taller than the other, both of them in long black coats, tiny houses in the background on either side of them. I imagined that those two figures were the two of us, and then I thought of you treading the floors of the Goupil gallery in Paris, that place where I was no longer wanted. I saw you, your mustache freshly combed, your shoes polished and gleaming, smiling while you shook hands with a woman in a long dark dress, the familiar images surrounding you in gilded frames on the walls. It was a strange feeling, but in that moment I told myself we were both doing what we were meant to do.

The entry to mining country was marked by black pyramids of earth on the horizon and a layer of thick dark coal smoke that covered the light of the sky. The pyramids were perfectly shaped, clearly man-made, bringing to my mind the image of Egypt as we saw it in picture books as boys, yet even from a distance I could tell that these pyramids were less solid than stone. I turned to the man next to me, who had been silent since we pulled away from Brussels. "Black Egypt," I said. This was the phrase that came to mind.

The man turned his watery eyes to me. He was brawny, tough and leathery, wearing a thick coat that could have been made from burlap and which must have been uncomfortably hot.

He grunted in approval. "Got that right."

"What are the pyramids made of?" I asked him.

The man looked at me with surprise. "Coal slag," he said, and then: "I suppose you've not been here before."

I shook my head. I told him I was to be the new lay preacher in the Wasmes area, feeling a surge of excitement and doubt. I couldn't believe it, Theo, it seemed so surreal—after a year of failed study for the theological degree in Amsterdam and then sitting through those dreaded, useless evangelical training sessions in that school in Brussels, wondering desperately why I needed to know Greek in order to bring the Gospel to those who needed it most, there I was! At long last, on my way to a new land, equipped with nothing but my two hands and the book in my knapsack. I felt that I was on a path I had chosen, despite the maneuvering Father had to do to get me there; this might sound silly to you, but I was so much happier on that train than I ever had been traveling back to work at Goupil's.

The man, though, made a noise like a snort in response to my statement, the sound someone makes when they don't believe a word you've said, or when they want to laugh but don't want anyone to hear. I looked at him to discover what he meant.

"Forgive me," the man said. "I've lived in this place a long, long time."

I got off the train in Wasmes and watched it pull away, curve round the track, and disappear. As soon as it was gone, a boy in a dark cap, tall boots, and tweed trousers and jacket stepped out onto the track with a shovel and began to tamp down the dirt that the train had displaced. I was the only person to disembark, and when the train was gone, the boy and I were the only people in the station. I pulled my coat tight around me; it was colder than it had been in Brussels.

I asked the boy on the tracks how I should get to Petit Wasmes, and the boy pointed in the direction of the only slag pyramid that could be seen from there, great and towering and black. His breath came out of him in short white clouds. "Follow the coal," he said. I left him there with his shovel, wondering how many times a day the boy performed this labor, smoothing out the tracks for the next train to come through and deposit its one passenger. Noble, thankless work, to be sure.

I think I told you some about Wasmes, where the train let me off, when you were here, but I don't think you were listening. I will tell you again: Wasmes is made up of a few streets of redbrick buildings streaked with dirt, cobblestones, a church, a meeting house, a prison with crumbling bricks. It is the home of the mine administration, the foremen and managers, so close to the miners but a world away. The miners live in villages at the bottom of a long hill down from Wasmes, and they rarely make the climb up to the town. As I walked through Wasmes that first time, I noticed the strange vacancy of everything—only a few people crossed the streets and no one noticed me, the curtains were pulled in most windows, and flowers crumbled in hanging window boxes. The haze of coal smoke made it seem as if night were falling; the black was so thick, I felt I could take hold of it with my hand and pull free a piece. What light there was came through the thick black in slices and arrows, and I thought of Heaven, of all things that cannot be understood, hidden from mortals behind a cover of impenetrable smoke.

My knapsack over my shoulder, I made my way to the house of one Jean-Baptiste Denis. The regional evangelical committee, on which sat Pastor Pieterszen, whom I had gotten to know in Brussels, had secured me lodging in the Denis home—perhaps Father told you this? Jean-Baptiste Denis is a baker, and one of the most fortunate men in the congregation of Petit Wasmes. His house is the only brick building in town, and sits at the crest of the hill leading down into the mining village.

At the house, Madame Denis was waiting outside for me, in a scarf and knitted wool hat, dusting soot out of the door frame. When she saw me, she clapped her hands and exclaimed, "Monsieur Vincent! You are here!" I was stunned at her warmth, never having received such a greeting from our mother and father, or perhaps anyone else ever before. Madame Denis is a large woman with glowing red cheeks, and her brown dress under her apron was marked by a purple flowered print. I wanted to fall right into her arms, but I restrained myself, giving her a tip of my hat instead. "You must be Madame Denis."

She curtsied and replied, "So I must!" sweeping her arm across her body and smiling. "Welcome! We have been looking forward to your arrival. How were your travels? Did you come too terribly far?"

I assured her the trip was just fine but that I was relieved to have arrived. "Well, we're relieved you're here, too!" she declared, and with a gesture of her arm invited me into the house. "Come on in," she said. "Welcome to your new home!"

Inside the house the air was warm and thick with the smell of baking bread, a most welcome and delicious smell. Madame Denis removed her scarf and hat and hung them on a peg by the door; then she led me through the large kitchen-bakery, lined with wooden shelves packed with jars of all sizes, all touched with a fine film of flour and containing all number of ingredients. I glimpsed a stack of wooden mixing bowls piled high in the sink, a hook with a handful of different-colored aprons by the door, and a fire burning in the hearth on the other side of the room. Outside the kitchen, we went through a hallway and climbed a short set of stairs to a room that she declared was mine, a small space under the eaves with a drastically slanted ceiling. I entered the room so timidly, I was almost on my toes; I could not have imagined anything more suitable. It reminded me immediately of the room where our sisters used to sleep in the house in Zundert, their neatly made beds under the slanting ceiling, and I thought of the giggles we used to hear coming from there at night when we lay in our bed, do you remember? In the room at the Denis house that was to be mine, there were also two beds pushed into either corner of the room, which had no door, only the stairs leading back down to the kitchen. Small wooden tables sat next to each bed, and wooden chests at the base of each bed. Against the wall there was a handsome chest of drawers. The wallpaper that lined the walls was a floral pattern, but it was tasteful and not oppressive.

"I hope it's all right," said Madame Denis, behind me, watching me take in the room. "You will be sharing this room with our son Alard. That's his bed there"—she gestured to the bed in the far corner, neatly made. "He is eight, and he's a good boy. Very quiet and thoughtful, he's the wisest man in the house."

She smiled and winked at me. "Or perhaps he *was*, now that you are here." She added, "He will be no trouble to you, I am sure, none at all."

Alard's bed had a blue bedspread pulled across it, quilted in panels of differing shades—the bed that was to be mine had one in red of the same pattern. Everything was so neat and tidy, so perfectly presentable, I could suddenly feel the dust on my clothes from the long journey, and thought I would sully the bed if I were to lie on it. "Of course that is fine," I told her. "I look forward to meeting him."

"Yes," she said, "he is out playing now with some friends, I think—I have trouble keeping track of where they go." She leaned against the door frame, watching me put my suitcase down next to the bed—I wanted to put it on top but feared that the valise would made a mark on the spread. "Most of the boys his age," she began, and then seemed to hesitate. She looked at me, as if surprised—she had started her statement too soon and now wished she could take it back. "Well," she said, looking down, wiping her hands on her apron, as if that were to be her last word on the subject. Then she must have decided to continue. "Most of them have started to go down into the mines to work. Alard doesn't have to because his father is not a miner, but it means he has a lot more time to himself these days."

I was silent, watching her, wondering if she would say more. For a moment she seemed strained, unsure what to say next, and then she recovered. She smiled at me again. "But that's enough talk for now," she said. "I'm sure you must be tired from your journey. Why don't you settle in and have a rest before supper, which will be in just a couple of hours. The bathroom is just next door, and you should feel free to use anything you see. This is your home now."

She turned to go, and I felt a flash of panic to be in that room alone. Of course I should bathe, have a rest, be presentable for supper, but I was too restless. The thought of lying in that bed with the red quilt in my present frenzy of excitement was unthinkable. I needed to see what surrounded us, what kind of place I was standing inside.

I called Madame Denis back. I asked her if it might be all right for me go out and explore the landscape a bit, rather than rest. "I am eager to see this place," I explained. "I have been wanting to come here for so long."

She seemed surprised and a little puzzled but was gracious nonetheless. I left my suitcase next to the bed and followed Madame Denis back down the stairs and outside once more. A few steps from the house, she pointed out the way down to the village and the mines, a long path that wound down the hill. I thanked her and walked quickly down the path toward the mine. I could sense her looking after me for quite a while, but I did not turn back.

From the base of the hill the Denis house sat on, off to the west was a landscape of sunken roads, hills, meadows, and brief patches of woods, all of it practically overrun with cottages, crisscrossing over and against one another in winding lanes that seemed to have no order at all. There were blackthorn hedges and occasional gardens, gnarled and twisted trees, all of it covered with a layer of snow and over that, everywhere, the omnipresent scatterings of soot. Off to the eastern side of the hill was a vast field, a giant black pyramid and two smaller ones, and nestled among them, the machinery of the Marcasse mine. This was no painting, Theo; I had stepped into one of God's own masterpieces.

How can I describe it? It was a squat beast, an evil-looking thing. There were a few long buildings and two chimneys, and then, extending from the tops of two of the buildings, giant iron framelike structures like the skeletons of twisted church towers, exposing on the inside their wheels and ramps and thick cables and ropes. I had seen a picture of a Belgian mine in the same geography book that told me about the Borinage—remember I showed that to you in my fit of excitement? But seeing it with my own eyes was quite a different thing. The mine was terrifying, awesome. It was dark and powerful and loomed up out of the landscape like some magnificent mythical metal minotaur. Looking at the landscape, the trees dead and nearly dead, the ash heaps, the hills of discarded coal, the huts collapsing into one another, the thick smoke pouring from the chimneys and blocking the sun, I nearly fell to my knees. What was I doing in this place? The sound from the mine was a clanking and banging and a general roar. I was far, far from Zundert now, from home, from you, my brother. I watched the mine and it seemed to come to life; it turned and shifted, and a quick horror came over me: This was what I was to minister to, this beast was what I had come here for! But no—I was here for those poor souls who worked inside of it.

And where were the people? There were very few figures about, save for the few I saw moving around the mine buildings, pushing carts and pulling levers, their breath visible even from where I stood.

I had made it to the bottom of the hill when a bell rang three times, and soon after, men began to stream through the gate. Black men. Their clothes, their necks, their faces, their hair, all was black, too black even to draw an arm across a brow and leave a smudge. Only their eyes were white, and they squinted and held their hands up against the sun, so painful, I imagined, after hours underground with only the occasional dull lamp to see by. It was eerie, those triangles of white in an otherwise-uniform sea of moving blackness; the whites of their eyes looked like fresh and unnatural grubs, like they were not attached at all but could leap clear out of their sockets and land on my skin.

The bodies blended together as they moved by; it was like one giant and throbbing black creature was on the move, a creature with a voice the sound of a crowd, a creature that trailed a cloud of dust and breath.

There were children in the crowd, their clothes tattered and worn, some of them wearing hats. A few of the miners looked at me, the white eyes landed on me and lingered, but no one ventured to find out who I was. The image that they made as they passed through the gate was so striking that I felt my voice had been stolen away. The monster moved on, through the gate and over the lane to the other side, dividing and depositing its limbs on the paths and cottages. The village came to life, doors opening and closing, voices rising and exclaiming, dogs barking, and all the while the black monster moving across the lane and dissipating, breaking apart, discarding its unified form and becoming once again what it really was, more than a hundred humble souls going home.

Soon I became aware that a miner had stopped and was watching me while the rest of the crowd moved by. Our eyes met; I tried to make out something that would distinguish this one person from the rest. It was the strangest thing, Theo, to be looking at a person and be unable to see any distinguishing features, to be unable to see what an individual actually looked like! But slowly, as I gazed at the miner, I became aware with gradual amazement that it was in fact a woman—a girl, perhaps; I couldn't tell her age, though she was nearly as tall as I am. Something about the quality of her gaze marked her, the way her eyes were soft as they watched me, curious rather than confident, about the way that she blinked rapidly, and then about the sweep of hair that disappeared under her cap. She stood watching me for one more moment, our eyes locked, and then she turned without fanfare and moved toward the village. My suspicion was confirmed by the slight sway to her hips as she walked away from me.

—

Supper that first night was in the Denis kitchen at the thick
wooden table, the largest table to be found anywhere in the village. All three of the Denis boys were there, along with Jean-
Baptiste Denis, the baker, his wife, and two guests: Paul Fontaine
and his daughter Christine. Christine was engaged to the Denises' eldest son, Karl, and the Denises thought I should meet
her father, Paul, who was a foreman at the mine and lived in
Wasmes, though he grew up in Petit Wasmes and had worked
in the Marcasse mine for many years. He had a lung disease and
could no longer stand the work down in the mine. "But still,
Monsieur Vincent," Jean-Baptiste said in his booming voice, a
marvel of unself-consciousness, "despite his promotion, he is
still a good friend to the miner." He clapped Paul on the back,
and Paul blushed at his plate. "Which is a lot more than can be
said for many others who have been promoted," added Karl,
across the table.

"Yes," Jean-Baptiste went on, "more than once during a
strike Paul has been the only person with any influence on the
miners; they will listen to nobody, they will follow no one's advice but his, and he alone is obeyed in the critical moment. Don't
be shy, Paul," he said, with his hand still on Paul's shoulder; "it is
true. We have seen it happen."

Paul continued to blush while Jean-Baptiste spoke about
him. He was not a large man, Paul, but I found him commanding nonetheless, a confidence exuding in the way he moved and
in his ease. His eyes were circled with dark, the skin beneath
them sagging in ripples like the movement of mud; his cheekbones, however, were sharp and defined, chiseled as if out of
rock. His daughter was fair and quite beautiful, resembling Paul
only in her nose, which was shaped with the same slight curve.
She sat quietly next to Karl and, once the meal started, she ate
lightly while the rest of us shoveled it in. Her cheeks had a lovely

flush, in the warm kitchen, and I thought silently that Karl was a lucky man. Then I thought of the woman I had seen at the mine, and wondered what she looked like when she was not covered with coal dust. I kept seeing the image of her, standing before me with that curious gaze, even as I sat there in the warm kitchen.

"Will you say grace for us, Vincent?" Madame Denis asked me, and I did so happily. The meal was rabbit with rosemary and potatoes and asparagus, simple food prepared simply. When we raised our heads and began to eat, Madame Denis said, "I don't know, Paul, but if I don't have a good feeling about this Monsieur Vincent. I daresay he will bring something good to Petit Wasmes as an evangelist." She was smiling at me, and I smiled back at her with a grateful nod, but when I looked at Paul, he was shaking his head. He quickly looked up from cutting his meat, hoping I hadn't seen the gesture; when he saw that I had, he flushed.

"I am sorry, Monsieur Vincent," he said. "You will have to excuse my manners and my skepticism. It has been many years of the same thing here in this valley, and many kind souls like you have come to try to help us. I am just not sure anymore what there is to be done."

I wasn't sure how to address this statement. "Can you tell me more of what you mean?" I said. "I must know all I can about conditions here."

Paul shook his head again, chewing and swallowing his food, and I was sure I saw a change in his eyes, an assertion of sorrow that swept down the inside of them like a shade. "Conditions are not good, Monsieur," he said. "For me, okay, they are not bad, I always have food for my family and I no longer need to go down into the mine, which is a daily blessing. I became a foreman when I was twenty-nine, about fifteen years too late for my lungs, unfortunately. But I live in a brick house and we are never

cold. For the miners, it is a different story. They struggle for
everything. And though the belief in God is of course important, and can make a man keep on longer than another man who
does not believe, I am afraid you will find that often the word of
God cannot be heard in a place like this." He paused, and then
said again, "Forgive me."

Silenced, I chewed for a few moments, thinking. The food
was so tasty, it was distracting, the taste buds rejoicing while the
mind pondered in difficulty. I hadn't eaten anything all day. I had
been so excited to arrive—instead of food, I ate the sky, those
coal pyramids across the horizon, that woman miner standing at
the edge of the crowd. No one said anything, though Madame
Denis looked at Paul with a hint of distress that he would challenge the newcomer so soon.

I took in the room, the eight of us around that table, the
three Denis boys next to one another in gradually ascending
height, then Karl's fiancée with her flushed cheeks, a porcelain
doll at a table of bears. I saw the wooden frame of the kitchen,
the table laid with plates of food and pitchers of drink, the clock
on the wall looking at us like a sun on a landscape, Madame
Denis at the head with her apron still on, her wonderful girth
surpassed only by her husband's, at the table's other end. It was
an image of fellowship, of abundance and joy, but it was not an
answer to Paul's statement.

Finally, I spoke the phrase that was repeating in my mind.
"When I would comfort myself against sorrow, my heart is faint
in me."

"Isaiah?" asked Paul.

"Jeremiah eight eighteen."

Paul smiled mildly and nodded. "Yes," he said, "that is just
it." Soon after, he was racked by a fit of coughs, accompanied
by the gurgle of liquid deep in his chest, and had to excuse himself to go to the yard and spit numerous times into the hedge.

—

After supper, Paul took me down into the village. He wanted me to meet someone, he said, an exemplary miner whose name was Charles Decrucq.

In general, Paul explained as we made our way down the hill, no one told the miners when a new lay preacher was on his way, but they would not be surprised at my arrival and I should expect them to be skeptical. For years, evangelists had been popping up in their villages, ducking into their huts with eyes full of pity and speaking to them of the kingdom of Heaven and the nobility of their sufferings. But whoever came soon went, and because of that the general attitude in the village would be skepticism, not of the teachings that were offered so much as of my very presence, of the idea that I could be there to stay.

Could I be here to stay? I wondered quietly. The evangelism committee had given me a three-month trial period. Was it possible that I could succeed? I dared not even think of it, for what would happen if I did not? I had failed at everything else.

Yes, do you think I don't know it, Theo? Do you think I don't feel the weight of my failures like a monster on my back? I was desperate, Theo, desperate for this trial to work, not only because I didn't want to disappoint you and Father and everyone else all over again but also because this time I thought I might really have a chance. You knew how desperate I was, didn't you? And do you not think of that in your judgments of me now?

Charles Decrucq was a commanding man, not unlike, I thought, our own father. If fate had made our father a miner, he would have made a good one; I could easily imagine him there, with a different family, and many sons more thick-blooded than you and I. Always upright, never complaining or downhearted, never particularly striving or eager to move beyond the community radius: Our father has the qualities of an ideal mining man.

Paul told me that Charles had worked in the Marcasse mine for thirty-three years already, and he was only forty. I thought of the children I had seen that afternoon coming out of the mine, and then again of the woman stopped on the edge of the crowd. How old was she? We were making our way to the cottage, winding through the huts on what were barely paths, so close were they to the doors and windows of houses, hands and faces disappearing as I glanced at them, plain curtains swinging closed. Chickens scampered away from us, dusty gray feathers lingering after the frantic scurrying bodies; a goat tied to a post stared after us with a serious expression. A pair of mangy dogs cautiously approached, sniffing at our pants to see if we were carrying food. The sun was almost set, and the remaining light made everything seem sharper, the angles of the wood, the soft green-brown moss on the slanted roofs, the gnarled limbs of the blackthorn bushes, tree branches holding empty birds' nests tipped with snow. The landscape made me think of a print I had already put on the wall next to my bed in the Denis house: do you know Maris's *Washerwoman*? A woman bent over her washing in a crowded country lane, surrounded by chickens, a pig, a few ducks, and a young girl looking on.

I was overwhelmed by what I was seeing and could barely take in what Paul was saying: Decrucq was the man who could tell me everything I needed to know. His wife had worked in the mine with him for many years before they were married, hauling the coal away from the seam where Decrucq and his men were working. This was generally what the women did in the mines: haulage. She was twenty-seven now, and hadn't been down in the mine since their second child was born.

A few times Paul had to stop to cough and spit; the sound of Paul's coughing was like the sound of a large animal coming awake in a thick swamp. The cough bent him over, and I could see his back heaving through his canvas coat. I fought the instinct to put my hand on Paul's back as he coughed. He spit dark liquid from his lungs that landed on the ground like dollops of mud.

Finally Paul stopped before a house and knocked on the

door. A man answered, stripped to the waist, the top half of him clean and the bottom half still wearing his filthy mining pants. He was huge and looming, filling the whole doorway; there was a streak of dirt on his arm, but otherwise his skin looked well scrubbed, pink and fresh, though it was marked all over by scratches and scars. On his right side where his ribs should have lain flat, there was a jutting lump that I quickly drew my eyes from. When the man saw Paul, his face broke into a wide grin.

"Why look who it is!" he boomed, "Paul Fontaine! To what do we owe this honor?"

I blushed at being announced so completely to the whole neighborhood, but Paul grinned just as widely as Decrucq and clapped him on the shoulder. "Decrucq!" he bellowed. Volume, apparently, was a feature of this community. "It has been far too long."

They stepped into the house and Paul introduced me. Decrucq shook my hand. His grip was formidable and I could feel my bones roll against one another; I resisted the urge to massage my hand afterward. Inside the hut, it was warm and dim and smelled like mud and potatoes; it is a smell common to all the miners' homes, and though it overwhelmed me at first, I soon became used to it. It took a few moments for my eyes to adjust. Hannah Decrucq appeared from somewhere in the depths of the room and shook my hand, as well. She wore a faded dress and a night bonnet that had once been white but was now a light gray. She looked exhausted, her face sagging as if the skin were being pulled from below by a heavy hand, and I wondered if she were unwell. She was only two years older than I was but looked as if she had lived three more lifetimes.

We sat at the table by the stove, which was glowing pleasantly and heating the room. Hannah put the water on to make coffee. My eyes were clearing and I noted two beds in the back of the room, one of which was presumably full of all three sleeping children. Something moved beneath the bed—a snort and a shuffle and a flicker of shadow—but I thought it rude to point or stare. I learned later that it was the Decrucq's goat.

"I was just having my bath," Decrucq said. "Would you mind if I finish it up before we talk? If I wait too long the water will be cold, and there's no sense heating up a whole other tub just for my bottom half."

There was a half barrel near the stove that was filled with water. "Monsieur Vincent, I hope I will not offend?" Decrucq gestured to the barrel. "Of course not," I replied. I was surprised and refreshed by Decrucq's boldness. All flesh is insignificant, after all, and all of us equal in God's eyes; naked or clothed we stand the same. Nonetheless, I thought Uncle Jan would squirm in such a moment, and the thought almost made me smile.

Hannah Decrucq sat with us at the table while Charles stripped and squatted over the tub. The wind was picking up outside, and the sacking between the wooden planks of the hut strained and flapped. It was quite pleasant inside, the room warm and faintly lit, the children asleep in the corner, the sound of the water sloshing in the tub as Decrucq plunged his hands in with the soap. I felt myself relax, and a kind of peace came over me. I always loved being in the miners' homes—during the Bible meetings that I held weekly, or when I went to visit the sick or those in need of good words. In the dim light from where we sat, it almost looked like Decrucq still had on his pants, so strong was the contrast between his washed top half and his unwashed lower. "He will bathe in front of anyone," Hannah said with a smile and a shake of her head.

"Normally my Hannah does this part for me," Decrucq said, smiling, bending over his legs, and scrubbing vigorously. "She got spared the job tonight because we have company."

"Well, I think everyone's glad for that," said Paul, laughing.

Hannah brought us cups of steaming coffee, and by the time she sat back down with us Decrucq was done washing. He dried himself vigorously, scrubbing his body almost as hard with the towel as he had with the soap. He went to the back of the room and returned in a pair of dry trousers, carrying a candle, which he set on the table between us. He had a pronounced limp, his right leg dragging behind him, as if it were lazier, somehow, than the rest of him; when he sat down, by the light of the candle, I noticed a patch on the side of his head where the hair was stripped away and a rough scar protruded like a mountain range.

"Well, Monsieur Vincent, if you wish to learn about the Borinage, you've come to the right place," he declared. "Perhaps Paul has told you, but I am the man that the mines cannot kill."

I looked at Paul, who smiled and shrugged. "I thought it better that he hear it straight from you," he said to Decrucq.

"Ah," said Decrucq, "well, it's true. Long after all these other mining men are dead, I'll still be here. I'll die when I'm old and tired, from something simple, like a cold."

We were all silent.

"I saw you admiring my head, this here?" Decrucq angled his head toward me and pointed at the scar. In the flickering candlelight it looked savage and cracking, bulbous and yet somehow delicate, as if it were being eaten by insects from the inside. "I got this one when the pit cage dropped. We were going down one night—it was the night shift—thirty of us in the cage, and after a meter or two something just snapped and we went down. Thirty-one meters we fell. Everyone dead except me." He gestured to Paul. "Fontaine doesn't like to hear that story."

Paul shook his head, his face pained. "That was a horrible day," he said.

"Anyway, this here?" he gestured to the lump bulging from the skin on his side. "Firedamp explosion. Threw me against a coal car. Three men dead. Broke three ribs. Never had 'em set right after that. They're okay, though"—he patted his side lovingly—"don't give me too much trouble. My leg, though, that's another thing." He held his thigh, gripping it tightly, massaging it.

"Crushed it when the cell I was in collapsed around me a couple years back. Trapped for five days, could barely breathe. Two men dead. No one could believe it when they finally dug me out, that I was still alive. Right, Hannie?"

She shook her head at him and sipped her coffee. Clearly she didn't like him to tell these stories, though he derived such pleasure from them that he probably told them to whoever would listen.

"Anyway, never set this one right, either, and it complains at me every day. Won't keep me from going down, though. The company can't keep me out, no matter how hard they try!"

I glanced at Paul.

"Oh, don't worry, Monsieur Vincent, Paul has heard all of this many times. He works for the company, yes, but he knows how I feel, and he will not say so but he does not disagree." He smiled at Paul, who raised his eyebrows but said nothing. "It has reached the point now where I am sure they are *trying* to kill me. They give me the worst cells, the most dangerous parts of the mine belong to me. They don't like me because I speak out against them, but also because they can't understand how I refuse to die like everyone else."

My eyes must have been wide. Decrucq said, "I'm sorry, Monsieur Vincent, but if you are going to live here you need to know the truth. This is why you have come, after all, I am sure of it. It is because the people here are treated not as men but as animals and you are to bring us some peace."

It was exactly what I had hoped for, exactly what I had said to my teacher Mendes so often in Amsterdam! Long lessons with Mendes, the sun setting on our open books and pages, my frustration high and rising, he trying to get me to recite another Latin phrase, another and another, and me protesting, "But Mendes, why does one need to know these things just to bring peace?" To bring peace; yes, this was why I had come. My heart soared, but I responded with my most preacherly response. "I hope so," I said, "but if there is peace, I am sure it won't be because of me, but because of God."

Yes, I cringe at the statement now, just as you probably just did if you read it. Peace? PEACE? Did I really think I could bring anyone peace? Oh, Theo, it pains me to tell this story with honesty. I am trying simply to describe things as they were, but it is so much harder than it should be. Why is it so hard just to present things as they were, as they are?

Decrucq looked at me with a blank expression, as if he wasn't quite sure how to respond to that. He was probably thinking the same thing: Peace? "Yes," he said, "well. The point is, you want to know how things work here and I'm not going to tell you lies. Life is hard here, Monsieur Vincent, men and women work like slaves, our children go down into the mines at eight years old, most of us don't live past forty, there is typhoid and consumption and lung trouble from the age of fifteen, and at the end of the day's work there is barely enough money for food. We eat bread and cheese and coffee as if there were no other food on earth. We only ever eat meat because we keep rabbits in our huts and the company can't touch them!" He stopped and lowered his voice, presumably remembering his sleeping children. "A man can work in the mines his whole life and never see a raise," he said. "He is trapped underground for five days with no food or water and two dead bodies and then he is expected to go back to work like nothing happened, or else his family starves. Ask Fontaine if you think I exaggerate; do I speak the truth, Paul?"

"You do," said Paul quietly. "I wish it were not so."

"But why can't the company grant a raise?" I asked, feeling ignorant and foolish. "Don't the workers strike for more money or better conditions?"

"Oh, yes," said Decrucq. "Many, many, many times, but there is never any change."

At this, Hannah rose from the table and excused herself. I wondered briefly if it had been my question that annoyed her, but then I chastised myself for my vanity. "Hannie doesn't like all this talk," Decrucq said. "She has heard it all a million times and despairs of it ever doing any good."

Hannah went to the back of the room and sat down on the bed across from her children. Her back was hunched and she stared into the space in front of her.

Paul spoke. "Decrucq doesn't like me to say so, but I have to explain just a little of the other side of all of this. Many of the Belgian mines cost far more to operate than other mines, for here the coal is deeper and harder to reach. The coal is sold, however, at the same price from here as from any other place. This is why the workers are paid so little, and why there is so little change. The mine is on the verge of bankruptcy at all times."

"But still the owners live in fancy estates and have cooks prepare them delicacies for dinner! I have seen it with my own eyes, Fontaine; you can't deny that it is so!"

Paul shook his head. "I do not deny it. It is complicated. But they are not getting all that money from exploiting us, that's all I'm saying."

"I will believe it when one of them comes down here and spends a day in my shoes," Decrucq said. "Just once I'd like to see one of those fat owners in a mining cage."

Theo, I felt I was getting a sense, in that room, of how I was needed. While the men spoke of the company and its workers, I heard the story of suffering, and I wanted to help.

In the back of the room, Hannah lay down on the bed and let out a loud sigh, presumably aimed at the three of us, or perhaps just at her husband. She moved onto her side and pulled her knees to her chest. It seemed to me a gesture of defeat by a broken woman.

1880

May 12, 8:00 p.m.

He does not have a map, and now he realizes too late that he should have asked the farmer who took him in where he was. He's in France, that much he knows, but in which direction should he be going? He thinks that he should be able to ask someone where his brother lives, and have them point the way. He resolves to speak to the next person he sees on the road, accepting that he might walk for miles before he sees a single soul.

His stomach is rumbling again; he ducks behind a barn to relieve himself. In a pasture just beyond him there are two horses, one white and one black, their tails swishing casually as they nose at the grass. The white one stands close to the other, his muzzle nearly touching the dark one's flank. He looks as if he needs the dark one, somehow. The dark one takes a step, and soon after the white one follows. He puts his head to the grass, takes a bite, and then raises it up and seems to sniff at the dark one, making sure he's still there. There is a curious milkiness to the white one's eyes.

Standing, Vincent takes a few steps toward the horses, moving slowly so as not to startle them. The dark one snorts and shakes his head, stamping his hooves once, twice; he does not want Vincent to approach. Vincent holds up his hands in surrender and stops. The white horse raises its head, its nose angled to the sky. Its eyes are blank and vacant, save a vague quality of fear. There is no question: It cannot see.

He stands for a few more minutes, watching them. The dark horse, when he sees Vincent is no longer approaching, quiets again and slowly moves away into the pasture, the white one following close behind. Vincent sees them as if on a canvas, the white one's eyes made with dabs of white paint.

He used to feel that way about his brother, he thinks. He used to want to protect him, to give him sight, to lead him through every pasture and wood. But Theo no longer needs his eyes, and so to whom shall he give them? He wonders about the letters he is carrying in his knapsack; he should pull them out and look at them to make sure they were not ruined by the rain, but he cannot bring himself to do so. What if they are destroyed? All the letters he has written to Theo since his visit nine months ago, the whole story of his time in the Borinage, carried on his back. What would he do if he reached Theo's door and had nothing to give to him, no account of himself aside from his own stammering? He does not want to think of it, not now.

On the way back to the road, Vincent passes by the barn and glances at the cottage nearby: window shutters open, blue curtain blowing gently out of one window. From inside the house comes the sound of a child laughing. He walks on, thinking of the Denis house, Alard running inside with rosy cheeks and a drooping begonia flower in his hand; Alard helping his father bake, his face and clothes strewn with white powder, sprinkling flour on large pans and lifting loaves off wooden trays straight from the oven.

He thinks of his own father, of the trips he used to take with him to visit his parishioners in their homes, peasant cottages spread all over the Zundert countryside. The house where Vincent was born was not one of the thatched country cottages, but sat in the center of town, near the church where his father preached.

It was in those cottages, though, like the one he just passed, that he always felt most at home. He felt a comfort in the peasant houses that he did not feel in his own, and he always had to resist the urge to curl right up on their sanded floors in front of the hearth until his father's next return.

In the peasant cottages, the children were barefoot, and as he and his father crossed the first threshold Vincent would remove his shoes and socks. Outside in the yards, he stood with the peasant boys and girls by the chicken coops, watching the hens cluck over their eggs—a sea of moving brown feathers, a din of squawks, and in the nests a few round delicate peach ovals. The peasant boys showed him where the chickens were beheaded—a stain of red across a patch of sandy earth, a row of bodies hanging upside down on hooks, below them little buckets full of blood. In one yard, a chicken with no head chased him, running wildly after him; Vincent ran and then dropped to his knees in terror, the thing running wildly past him and then dropping to the mud. The peasant boys weren't his friends, not really—he stood and observed their games, and always he had to follow his father away from them when he called—but still he felt a kinship with them.

When he and his father ducked into the parishioners' cottages together, Vincent watched the men rise from their looms to greet his father; he was a good man, and they were glad to see him. Shepherds crossed their fields to shake his hand and share a moment with him, to ask his counsel; flocks of sheep surrounded them as the men talked. Vincent loved those moments, the sky holding the sun, his father tending to his flock as the sheep nudged quietly and not impatiently at the grass. The sheep trotted away from him when Vincent reached to touch them, their matted hair flinching and contracting in spasms if he managed to brush his fingertips along their necks.

He wanted to be like his father so much that it hurt like a

wound. He wanted to change himself to be like his father; he wanted the supernatural power to twist and fiddle with his insides until he could be a saint, until he could be the son that his father wished him to be. Inside the cottages, his father pulled from his pockets a gift of tobacco or a slim package of meat, sometimes a few coins, and without ceremony laid it down on the table or the mantel. He knew which families would be too prideful to accept his gifts, and for these he made sure to lay them down in moments when they were all otherwise occupied, tending to their fire or to their stove, where a bubbling pot of potatoes mumbled and hissed, or leaving them in places where they wouldn't be found until after he and Vincent had gone— even once slipping some money into a man's boot that sat inside the door. Vincent watched his father's face in those homes, taking in the group of peasant women sitting together on the floor, peeling potatoes with thick and blunted knives, the children so thin and needy, clambering at his pant legs because they knew the good pastor often traveled with treats in his pockets. He saw compassion and sorrow in his father's eyes.

The one thing Vincent never saw in him was anger. Though he may have shaken his fist on occasion at his eldest living son, he never shook his fist at God. He sat with the peasants, the weavers and shepherds and farmers, and he took their hands and listened to their troubles, and nodded and sighed and told them that it was God's will that some should suffer in this life. He told them that there was another world ahead of them where they would not suffer, and that they should take comfort in this while they struggled in this world. He sat with them and read a passage from the Bible, and then he told them that God had a reason for doing all that He did, and blessed them, and then he and Vincent ducked back out into the open air.

It often upset Vincent that his father could be so unflappable in the face of extreme distress. Once, when Vincent was eight or so, they visited a home where two people lay dying: an old woman, who had taken to her bed months before but was now near the end, her breathing short and shallow, her figure a skeleton surrounded by a nest of white hair; and a young boy, who had fallen from a horse he was riding with his father. The young boy's sister had been infirm from birth, one of her legs a few inches shorter than the other, and now the house seemed truly to be cursed. Vincent stood in the doorway and took in the scene, his father sitting with the parents of these children between the beds of the dying, holding their hands and praying with them, their heads all bowed to the floor, their bodies shrouded in shadow. In the corner of the cottage, two other children sat in near rags and played with a handful of wooden blocks, the sound of them against one another as they were stacked a sharp knocking that Vincent felt in his chest. A feeling of hopelessness overcame him; eventually he sneaked through the door to wait for his father in the yard, and had to recover his breath as if he had been running.

On the way home, Vincent tried to get his father to express his anger about the state of things in that hut, but all he would say was that it was God's will. This answer incensed Vincent. Why should it be God's will for good people to suffer? He considered the peasants his friends, his brethren, and he wanted his father to be furious that they were made to bear pain. His father was patient with Vincent's anger; he nodded his head and told him he was right to be upset. But Vincent could not understand. If he was right, why wasn't his father upset, too? Was it God's will that he, Vincent, should be angry and that his father should not? How could God's will explain agony and also joy? He wondered if that was just a phrase people used, or if it really had meaning, and then he felt guilty for the thought. It gave him a headache; he picked up rocks along the side of the road and threw them, hard, until his arm ached, so he could feel something else.

—

In front of a cottage, three boys and a girl sit in a circle, playing a game with a pile of pebbles. They are very intent, their voices low and murmuring, and only one of them looks up at Vincent as he approaches and passes by. The light is too dim to see them clearly, but he can see that they wear the usual uniforms of peasant children—the girl in a gray dress and her hair in a braid, the boys in short pants, all of them barefoot.

A week or so ago, the day before he left the Borinage, a trio of boys just like these, with ragged pants and dirty skin, threw rocks at him as he made his way down a winding path past them. Only one of the rocks hit him, on his right ankle, and raised a welt. He walked on, pretending not to notice that the boys were there. If it weren't for the prick on his ankle, he might not even have heard the words they yelled after him: *cracked* and *crazy* and *dog*. It wasn't the first time the Borinage children had thrown rocks at him, nor the first time, even before the Borinage, that peasant boys had bullied him. The irony is not lost on him: These were exactly the type of children that he would have wanted to play with as a boy, his father inside their huts, ministering to their parents: rough-edged, easily amused. They were just the kind of boys that he tried to teach at the school in Ramsgate, England, along the coast, and just the kind of boys he tried to teach at his makeshift school in the Borinage. What is it about him and boys like that?

When Vincent was a boy, he would watch them play, wondering at their stamina for such simple games—what fun was it to push a wheel around the school yard with a stick? After trying and failing too often to be like them, he found he much preferred long walks to school-yard games, no one commenting on his behavior or calling him odd, not the bird eggs he collected or the insects he brought home to push down onto pages with pins, labeling them in meticulous script. The Brabant countryside, unchanging and everlasting: the starlings all along a low tree branch, leaping from their perches and floating, circling in long, wide arches, exercising their wings and their throats as they swooped and squawked and squabbled; the white sandy path along the cornfields and gently sloping hillsides, his feet shuffling, a gentle breeze blowing against him; and the landscape, forever shifting, cottages appearing in the distance, crows drifting through fog, starkly black against a wet and heavy white, women in bonnets and dark skirts bent in the fields, unmoving, so that they, too, were as trees, growing up from the earth. The green of the potato plants, the amber of the wheat, the fluffy gray sheep moving across the distance, butterflies landing gently on the open and patient face of a flower: He never grew tired of the world he saw when he walked, it was never familiar to him no matter how many times he saw it. When he was alone, he would sit on a tree limb for hours, letting his eyes relax, listening to the noises around him, and feeling a sense of peace that he never felt in the world of men.

He thinks of Alard, his friend in mining country, another boy who was different, and the drawing that he had given to Vincent a month or so ago, a portrait of Smoke, the cat that lived in the now-empty salon, all fast lines and squiggles, the cat's eyes round and exaggerated amid sharp tufts of hair. Alard was a boy as he had been, not satisfied by the games of the other children. He thinks of Alard's little voice after he handed the picture to Vincent, and Vincent was holding it in his hands: "Do you like it, Monsieur Vincent? Is it good?"

Vincent's parents worried about his long absences from the parsonage, for he never alerted anyone to his departure and was often away for hours at a time, even at night. He especially loved to walk in storms, the sky and the flashing light enhancing the natural drama of the landscape. He almost always carried a fishnet on a pole and a jar for carrying home the specimens that he found.

One day he brought home a jar that was nearly full of crawling beetles, some he had found in the water of a canal and others in the mud on the edge; he had a notion that putting them all together in a confined space might bring out some interesting instincts among them, and he was interested to see if they would naturally separate. His sisters Elisabeth and Anna were waiting for him when he came home, and upon seeing the jar, they broke into squeals of distaste, calling him queer and saying he was horrible and insisting that he put the jar out at once. He did, leaving it just by the door of the house, not wanting to release the beetles for fear that he'd never find quite the same mix of them again. But when he came out to them first thing in the morning, they were all dead.

It was a horrific sight, that little jar filled with the carcasses of beetles that had been so energetic the day before. There seemed to be so much more space in the jar than there had been, the black shells lying carelessly about on top of one another, twisted legs jutting up and pointing left and right. Vincent held it in his hand and felt a revulsion that twisted his insides from his neck to his groin. It took all of his strength to carry the jar to the garden, twist the cap, and dump the beetles behind a flowering bush, to watch the way they tumbled out over the rim like pieces of weightless black licorice. The sound they made as they fell to the earth was almost the sound of a scouring brush lightly touching fabric. He spent the next few days inside, mourning those beetles and staring at his hands.

He felt a wonder toward learning, as a boy, despite his hatred for school. He remembered awe at the power of his hand, that he could take a delicate piece of lead and draw, and what he created was both an image and a word. What a miracle! When a word was written down, it became an image as well as a word; this was a revelation. The recognition of it allowed him to learn how to see words even when they were spoken, not only the shape of them but the pictures they called to mind. What was the world if not words and pictures?

But still, he had failed. His parents had removed him from the local school after a few too many scuffles in the school yard, and then for three years, his father had tried to teach him. "I will be unlike that man, that disciplinarian across the street," Vincent overheard his father saying to his mother one day in the kitchen. "If his own father cannot teach him, who can?" But schooling at home was no better—long afternoons in the front room at the parsonage, his father hovering over him, the smell of wood chips drifting off his clothes and enveloping Vincent, a reminder of his father's presence even when he couldn't be seen.

How could anyone stand it? How could he be blamed for slipping out of the parsonage when his father left for church, through the path in the garden hedge and out into the heath beyond? More and more he fled the house, sleeping for whole afternoons in patches of sun in empty fields, lying down next to fallen birds' nests and rising without knowing how long had passed, stumbling home, only to find his father had gone to bed, his fury at Vincent's delinquency present, for Vincent, in the silence that greeted him when he sneaked quietly in the front door. After three years of it, three years of his father's checking his homework when they had finished eating dinner and then sitting next to him at the same table in the morning, his father's constant presence next to him, judging him, shaking his head, saying, "Try again," try again, try again, neither of them could continue.

The last day was in the summer, and the front room, which was dim and close and normally cool even in the summer, was sweltering. Vincent wore a short-sleeved shirt and his father had taken off his jacket; Vincent was trying to focus on multiplication tables, but the numbers were dancing and forming patterns and pictures and he could not make them sit still. He was sweating.

Was it fear or was it the heat? "Which is it, Vincent?" asked his father. "What is the answer?"

How could he tell his father that the numbers would not lie still? Perhaps he should guess—perhaps a wrong number was better than telling his father the truth: that when he looked down at the page, he saw the numbers as a waterfall, the twos and threes falling over the sixes and fives.

He said a number. His father stood still for a moment, looking at the floor, and Vincent wondered whether it was possible that he had guessed correctly. But then his father erupted.

"NO!" he shouted, and then turned from Vincent to the mantelpiece, composing himself, his shoulders rising as he took a deep breath. "Vincent," he said slowly and softly without turning around—Vincent knew this tone was reserved for his most angry moments—"how do you ever expect to learn if you do not try?" He took a breath. "You are a smart boy; I know this. But you seem determined, just DETERMINED"—he paused again as his voice grew louder, forcing his tone down—"determined not to apply yourself. I do not know what we can do with you. I'm afraid I've done all I can."

He left the room then, abruptly, Vincent still sitting at the table with the waterfall of numbers and their checkerboard companions. He *was* trying to see them clearly; it was they that would not lie still.

And then came boarding school. His first night, he lay in the unfamiliar bed with its stiff starched sheets and pictured his family at home, all of them sleeping soundly, the sound of the clock in the main room ticking through the rest of the house. As he drifted off to sleep, he began to feel that he was still in his bed, and that Theo was there beside him, and that the ticking that he heard was in the room with them. All was quiet; all was familiar and safe and warm. But gradually he began to be aware of his body beneath the blanket next to Theo; it was not the body he knew, the gangly limbs, long and floppy and awkward, but something much smaller, much different from that, much more foreign and confining. He tried to move his arms and his legs, to feel his torso with his fingers, to roll over, but it was all wrong. He was cramped and tiny; there was no heft to him. He tried to stretch and felt fingers that were barely nubs. It came to him slowly and with horror: He was an infant. He was the baby Vincent.

He walks on, thinking of those children in that circle behind him, unfazed by his presence, just another man on a road. It will be dark soon, and he will need to find somewhere to sleep. What will those children turn into? Their parents, no doubt, the keepers of their family's land, the bearers of babies and future land keepers, and on and on into the future. Alard will become a baker; the miner boys will become miners. None of them will break from the flock; none of them will ask, most likely, what they are meant for, because the path for them is clear.

He thinks of Angeline, in his hut, her eyes pleading and sad; *Monsieur Vincent, will you tell me of other places?* Angeline, who wanted a different future for herself but did not find one.

He stops and gazes at a glowing field. His body is aching from the walking and the recent bout with fever in the farmer's barn after the storm, and as he stands, watching the last raindrops on the field catch the moonlight and glisten, he feels the chorus of aches in his body as music. He is looking over the field while a symphony plays in his ears. The music is melancholy and sad; then it is threatening, the pain in his legs rising at the sudden stasis. The field glints and shines; it seems to glimmer from within its very soil. He imagines a hole opening up in the center, blooming, growing, beckoning him to crawl inside.

Who is he without his brother? Who is a man without the skin he lives inside?

Then, his father's voice: Who is a man without a goal, a pursuit, a vocation?

Gradually he becomes aware of a cow, standing nearby, its nose in the grass and chewing. The cow does not notice him, or does not care. There is a haystack nearby where the cow is standing, and Vincent moves slowly over to it and sinks down. He wants to be near the beast for a moment, wants the simple animal to silence the voices in his head. He has always loved the sound of large animals chewing—the muffled crunching, the lap of the giant tongue, the snorting of the nostrils as big as his fists, the deep bass of the breathing into the grass. There is something joyous about it, something simple and joyous. It is the sound of a need being met, the sound of desire fulfilled, and yet it is more than that. It is the sound of patience, the sound of no rush, the sound of natural time, of no thought, of pure existence. It is the sound of the way things are.

He takes his stack of paper from his pocket and smoothes it against his knee. Watching the cow intently, listening to the sound of it chewing, he attempts to draw what he sees: the curve of the animal's back, the shape of its face, a distorted figure eight. He is frustrated that the drawing cannot contain the sound that he is hearing.

He draws the tail flung out from the body, wishing to capture its motion, the casual, content swing from side to side, an expression of the cow's satisfaction. The cow stands for its portrait without protest, only occasionally raising its eyes to take in the man crouching before it. What might an animal understand of a man's instinct to capture what he sees?

He remembers one night not too long ago in the Borinage, when he witnessed the birth of a calf in a stable. The expression on the mother's face was strained, her eyes threatening to burst from their sockets, her teeth bared. It was the middle of the night, and there was a girl there, a brown peasant face with a white nightcap. She had tears of compassion in her eyes for the poor cow when the animal went into labor and was having great difficulty. Vincent stood toward the back of the room, taking in the scene and imagining how it could be painted by Correggio: a black background, the cow illuminated from the center of the image as if from the inside, the moment of the calf's birth like the birth of an angel; or by Millet: an ominous sky, the calf birthed outside in a field, a peasant woman in an apron bending over to receive the animal; or by Israëls: the barn rendered in browns the same color as the cow, the peasant girl in the corner with red circles of blush on her cheeks barely visible except if one was to look closely. When the calf was born, wriggling on the stable floor in a casing of sticky liquid, the farmer turned to Vincent. His eyes questioned him: What was he doing there? What did he have to offer? Vincent stood forward and uttered a line from John 11:40, "Jesus said to her, Did I not tell you that if you believed you would see the glory of God?" but his words sounded hollow to his ears in the face of that calf wriggling on the ground. He saw the farmer's eyes roll over him, taking in his shabby clothes, his bare feet, and a familiar mixture of shame and defiance swept over him. He had been seeing that look more and more from the people of the Borinage. Yet in front of them was that newborn miracle, and surely this outweighed the judgments of men? He said nothing more, but took in the details of the image before him—the slick membrane that surrounded the calf, the way the mother immediately moved her body to lick the animal that had just come from inside of her, and always that little peasant girl in the corner, quietly watching.

He folds the sketch and reaches for his knapsack to put it away. With the bag open, he peers in at the stack of letters on the bottom. His heart speeds up at the prospect of touching them, remembering the possibility that they may no longer be readable. The labor of all these months of silence! He is nearly amazed that the stack is so small, holding as it does so many months of time. He reaches in and pulls the letters out; the stack is intact, still bound by the twine, and as he pages through he is relieved to see that the words look legible. He sits there, holding his voice in his hands, and watches the cow.

Something about the animal kingdom, he thinks; respite from the burden of choice, perhaps, or the capacity for wonder. He is grateful. The animal is fuel for him, the intact letters a message that he should continue on.

In the deep of night, his body exhausted, he lies down in a pile of discarded hay near a locked barn—not quite a bale, but enough of a pile that he tells himself there will be some warmth there.

He lies looking up at the sky. The sky is stunning, the stars spread across it in an ancient twinkling language, the moon exerting its bright dominion, giving permission to the smaller stars to shine. It occurs to him that he hasn't seen the sky like this in a good many months—in the Borinage, there is too thick a layer of soot between the ground and the sky for the firmament to reveal itself. Is this why it is so hard to dream in that land?

He watches the stars and a feeling of peace comes over him. His body aches, his muscles tense and tingling; he brings his mind to each part of him and wills it to quiet. Shoulders, neck, stomach, hands, thighs, toes: Piece by piece he calms himself, sinking farther into the hay. It's a technique he used to use when he was a boy, coming in after a long walk on the heath and being sent straight to bed, his body still walking and Theo already asleep. How do you calm a creature that will not be calmed? You hold it close and speak softly to it.

He thinks of Angeline, her body close to his, the curve of her neck where it met her shoulder just visible in the flickering lamplight. A sharp pain jabs in his chest. He tries not to think of her—it is not *productive*, he hears his father say—but the last portrait he made of her floats up behind his eyes: repeated nervous lines back and forth over one another in a frenzy of movement, revealing jaw, neck, head a bit too large for her shoulders, round shape of knee, her cheek half in shadow and somehow glowing pink even without an application of color. The image trembles in his mind just as the sight of her trembled in the light of the lantern, ghostlike and ephemeral, yet undeniable, alive. Where is the picture now? Reverend Pieterszen's house, propped up in his study in front of his easy chair, next to unfinished portraits of his wife. Somewhere in the world, Angeline looks out over a room—unwavering gaze, bemused expression. He hears her voice, soft and inquisitive: *Monsieur Vincent, is that you?*

He wills himself to stop thinking of her—*Stop!*—and closes his mind over the thought of her like the lid of a trunk. In her place comes Theo—another apparition he doesn't want to abide.

His brother's August visit nine months ago comes back to him in painful detail. He tries to will it away, but it returns. He had stood for hours waiting for Theo's train—he was so excited about his arrival that he had gotten there far too early. For hours, he leaned against the wall of the train station, watching the tracks. A cluster of people stood near, chatting and cooling themselves, waving their hands and their hats and their unfurled fans at their faces. Every few minutes one of the men stepped closer to the tracks and leaned out, peering down the line and watching for distant movement. The women's fans, constantly moving, fluttering like the wings of butterflies, were flapping patches of color—purple, blue, and pink—against the train station's landscape, grays and dusty browns as far as the eye could see. Vincent watched and imagined them taking flight, the women grasping after them as they took wing and flew away, and then the women floating up after them.

Despite the heat, he kept his hat pulled down low, not wanting to make eye contact. He chewed on his unlit pipe, then slipped it into his pocket to save it from his teeth; then, when the train still did not arrive, he took it out again to chew some more.

After what seemed an eternity, a train approached, a plume of white smoke unfurling and then dissipating in the air. The steady chug of the engine grew louder, the snake of the train curved around the track and grew larger, the people on the platform hushed in anticipation, the fans halted in midair, and then the train carrying Vincent's brother Theo rumbled into the station.

Vincent had not seen his brother in eight months, though after all that had happened in mining country, it felt a lot longer than that. Years had passed in the last eight months, centuries. But there he was, Theo, stepping down from the train with his valise, looking trim and professional in a slick black suit and tie, wearing his top hat despite the heat, and instead of elation, as Vincent had always felt when glimpsing his brother, he felt trepidation. A sort of dread swept over him as he watched Theo disembark. Who was that slim young man stepping down the metal stairs in dapper polished shoes? Theo had always been thin and sickly, pasty white even in the height of summer, often bedridden with illnesses caught at school that spared most everyone else. This man, however, seemed too healthy, his dark suit fitting perfectly across his narrow shoulders. He wore his brother's face— Vincent could see a version of that face on a young boy, his mouth smeared with the juice of plums, grinning up at him with crooked teeth—but the clothes of a man he did not know.

Vincent peered at his brother from the far end of the platform and felt tempted to hide. Theo had not yet seen him; he could still duck through the station door and avoid whatever message Theo might be bringing. But then he caught himself in his fear and chastised himself: Theo was here! His brother, despite all, in the flesh. He ran to him, ducking around the other reuniting passengers, and called his name.

Theo turned and saw Vincent, and his face broke into the smile that Vincent remembered, wide and goofy; Vincent's fear flew from him. Theo took off his hat and waited for his brother to reach him. They shook hands and embraced, and Vincent clasped his brother's thin frame and inhaled the familiar scent of him— a little sweet and a little musty, like a basket of raspberries shut in a cellar.

Theo told him right away that he didn't have much time. Pulling back from their embrace, he said, "I'm on my way to Paris; I have sent my luggage on ahead. They are expecting me there for work tomorrow morning, so I must catch the evening train. I'm sorry that only leaves us the afternoon."

Vincent, who had hoped Theo would at least spend the night, tried to hide his disappointment. The first words out of his brother's mouth were to put a limit on their time. "Of course!" he said, trying to accompany his voice with a smile. "We'll make the most of it."

Back in Vincent's room in Cuesmes—in the house of Monsieur Frank, an evangelist, and his wife, Grace—Theo asked Vincent about the pile of sketches on the table by the bed; Vincent showed them to him one by one, kneeling by the chair where Theo sat smoking his pipe, explaining each in turn. "That's a mining man," he said of a drawing of an old man wearing a burlap sack and smoking a pipe; "they often wear sacking as clothing for an extra layer of warmth." "And that's my friend Alard," he said of a sketch of a boy throwing a ball; "we used to share a room in the Denis house."

Theo was quiet; interested but reserved, asking questions but saying nearly nothing in response. Vincent chattered on, filling the silence, but all the while wondering whether something was wrong with Theo, or if perhaps this was just the way he was now. In the last year or so, Theo had become a success in the art-dealing world; perhaps along with his professional success had come a refining of personality, so all his rough edges had been permanently smoothed. In the past, their visits had been filled with gaiety and laughter; today, Theo was like a man with a terrible piece of news to unload who dared not speak it loud.

On their way back to Mons, a walk of over an hour, they went by the disused mine La Sorcière: buildings crumpled and leaning, wooden beams jutting here and there, birds flying in and out of windows. "Theo," Vincent asked as they moved toward the mine, "is anything wrong? I've been talking ever since you got here, and you have said hardly anything. Is everything all right in your life?"

Theo, his pipe still lit, shook his head. They stood looking out over the abandoned mine. He took his pipe in his hand and held it, a twisting line of smoke rising from it. "No," he said, "nothing is wrong. My life is good; I have everything I could ask for. I feel very lucky."

"Well, good!" said Vincent. "Of course I am happy to hear it." He looked at his brother's face. Theo was smoking his pipe again, looking at a turned-over mine cart in the field next to them, his forehead furrowed. "But you do seem gloomy. I'm not sure I've made you laugh once since you arrived."

Theo smiled. He met Vincent's eyes. "I'm sorry," he said. "Perhaps I'm just tired."

They kept walking, Vincent in front, and he pointed his arm out toward the mine and started to tell Theo about it, how the rumors held that there were people living down in the shafts, coming up for air only in the dead of night, when no one would find them. He stopped, realizing that Theo was no longer next to him, and turned around. Theo was standing a few paces back.

"I've had letters from Ma and Pa," Theo said. "They are very worried about you."

Vincent stared at him, silent for a moment, taking this in. "Is that why you have come, then?" he asked. "They've sent you to help me see the light?"

Theo shook his head. "No," he said, "I came because I wanted to see you for myself, and to see this place you have been living in." He took a step closer. "But now that I do, I think that maybe our parents are right to be worried."

Vincent, stunned, speechless, turned and started to walk away from his brother. A thread was broken. Inside his head a dark cloud rolled in, turning all of his thoughts to black. His brother had come here on bad faith.

"Vincent," Theo called after him, still standing where he had been, "don't run from me. I'm still your brother." He started to walk after Vincent. "But come," he called, "really, what is your plan? You have not told me what your plan is; all afternoon we've been talking but you haven't said. What will you do next? You can't stay here forever, living off Ma and Pa, you must know that."

The sun was sending blinding arrows of light off the quiet tracks where the mining carts had once moved. Vincent stopped walking but did not turn back.

"It has been over a month since your dismissal," said Theo, his voice quieter now, "isn't that right? And what have you been doing since then?" He paused, but Vincent didn't answer or move. "I come to visit you and you don't say a word of what has happened; all you do is show me this place as if it is glorious. But Vincent, it is not glorious! It is a sad place, Vincent, and you no longer have a job to do here. Why do you remain? What is there here for you?"

Vincent turned back to Theo. He could feel the blood in his face, the warmth on his cheeks familiar from whenever he exercised strenuously, particularly in the sun. He struggled to get the words out, pushing them from deep in his throat. "What would you have me do?"

They stood face-to-face by the fence that led into the mine.

The grass was overgrown and reached to their calves. "There are a million things to do!" Theo said, throwing out his hands. "So you won't be a preacher; so you'll try something else! It doesn't have to mean everything. I know a man who is a successful carpenter, I'm sure he'd take you on as his apprentice. You could learn the trade of a bookkeeper, a lithographer, a baker. How about a painter? How about a businessman?"

"A businessman?" Vincent was aghast; he couldn't begin to attempt to argue with this. Theo smiled then, but it was a cold smile, the smile of a stranger who politely steps over a dog he does not like. "Well, perhaps not a businessman. But I'm just trying to say that you have choices. You're only twenty-six; you're young; you can still do nearly anything. But what do you gain by idling around? What do you gain by staying here, with nothing to do? You're not seeing things straight, Vincent. This is not your home. You're only making yourself miserable, staying here, when there is nothing here for you, as well as making our parents worry."

Again, their parents. Again, the burden he was for others. Vincent felt a strange sensation, his skin beginning to feel cold while the inside of him grew hotter. He steadied himself on the fence, feeling the enormous urge to run, or to crouch his body down so small, he might disappear.

"Vincent," Theo said, his voice grown quieter again. "I know it has been a long road that brought you here. I remember the year you spent studying for that evangelical degree in Amsterdam, I remember the training school in Brussels after that, and I know that all you've wanted for a long time is to bring the word of God to the poor. I can't imagine how it must feel now that it is all over. But how can I understand if you don't tell me about it?" He paused. "Come," he said again, "don't you want improvement in your life? Don't you want more for yourself than this?"

Theo was quiet for a long moment, looking wistfully out over the mine, as if he were looking out over a calm sea. Finally he spoke again. "I remember when we walked together to that mill at Rijswijk. So many years ago now, it feels like a lifetime. But we agreed on so many things then, remember? We wanted the same things for our lives; we felt the same passions and excitements. We promised each other we would look after each other, we would help each other along the way." Theo paused, and sighed. "I felt so close to you then. Now"—he turned to Vincent and met his eyes, the two brothers face-to-face—"well, I fear you've changed so much that you're just not the same any longer."

All the way back to Mons after this, Vincent did not say a word. He was walking with a stranger who wore the suit of his brother's skin. His face was flushed with anger; he wanted to run and to weep, but he made himself accompany his brother to his train. "I'm sorry, Vincent," Theo said on the way back. "I know what I've said can't have been easy to hear. I only thought that perhaps it might do you some good to hear some of this from me, to put an end to some of your idling. And you must know I only want happiness for you."

He told Vincent he should go to Etten, where their parents lived, and take some advantage of the love and kindness that waited for him there. He shook his hand, covering it with both of his, and then he turned from Vincent and disappeared onto the train to Paris.

1879

Dear Theo,

You say I am not the same any longer. The same as who? You have known me at all the stages of my life. What can a man become if he must stay the same?

It is an outrageous claim. Do you think you are the same as you have always been? When you sat here in my room in Cuesmes, you crossed your right leg over your left and flapped your foot up and down impatiently; I've never seen you do that before. When you spoke, which was rare that day, you gestured widely with your pipe in your hand, wider than you ever used to. "I saw the Paris salon last month," you said, "Breton's latest is a masterpiece." On the word *masterpiece*, your arm swept way out across from your body, as if you were unveiling a horizon.

When I showed you my drawings, kneeling next to you in the lamplight, I watched your face; when it was at rest, it was a frown. When we were boys, your face was open and wide; I could take your hand and lead you away and you would follow me with curiosity, never fear. How many times did you hear me say that word, *masterpiece*, before you began to use it? Back then, your eyes were large and open fields, but now I see only narrow lanes.

That walk to the Rijswijk mill in The Hague, yes, you were

right to think of it. That was the first time you came to visit me anywhere, the first time we had ever visited together for more than a day away from home—it was the first time I had a job, my first job at the gallery, that stormy fall of 1872. I remember my room at the Rooses' house, the rain against the window, the wind howling against the glass and down the chimney, rattling the grates in the fireplace, and you wrapped in one of my blankets, your tousle of brown hair against my pillow. I was so excited to have you there; when I walked home from Goupil's gallery knowing that you would be waiting for me, I felt a swell of happiness in my chest. We walked the city together when I wasn't working, ducking into cafés to escape the rain, and I bought you cups of hot tea so you would not catch cold. You were still in school then, only fifteen, but nearly a man; back in my room, that thick red carpet under our bare feet while the world wailed outside, our shirts drying over the back of my wooden desk chair, our bodies warm underneath our two blankets, we sat up late into the night talking of all things.

I can see you, leaning back against the pillow on the bed, listening to me tell you about Goupil's and the prints in the gallery, your eyes ravenous for details. "I can't wait to get started," you said, referring to your own art career. "I am dying to get started. I wish I could trade places with you, or that Uncle would let me start right now and Pa would let me quit school." When I described the prints to you, your mouth hung open as if I were describing succulent cuts of meat, and sometimes you even brought out your notebook and jotted notes.

The day before you left The Hague, we went for a walk when it was just beginning to rain, and we were far away from town on a country road when it started to pour. We kept going, not knowing what else to do, ducking under tree branches for shelter, the leaves making an umbrella riddled with holes. Up ahead, there was the Rijswijk mill, a roof and warmth beckoning.

Your hair was stuck to your forehead underneath your hat, the water dripping off the brim in streams. Then the sun came out and there was a rainbow in the distance and steam rose up off our wet clothes. We stopped in the road to admire the rainbow and noticed each other's steam, and your face was full of glee, and you pointed at my jacket and said, "Look at you!" and giggled, and I pointed back at you and said, "And look at you!" and we laughed together, and I heard the sound of our voices and I knew that they were different from the way they used to be. Something in the world was different all of a sudden. The two of us were together again on a country road, and for a few minutes the passing of time was a marvel and a friend.

I remember you standing in the sunshine of the Rijswijk road with steam rising off of your clothes, grinning at me; I had a vision of the boy who slept next to me all those years becoming a man, which meant that I was, too, impossible as it seemed, for there we were together. Life was beginning, it was the beginning of life, and I saw the body of my brother before me as I never quite had before, as if it were a limb that had been cut from my own body and placed before me so that I could see it clearly. I saw that you were my greatest friend and strongest ally, and that you would be there for my whole life, no matter what curves it took. I saw my love for you as if it were as visible as the mill beyond us, the sails jutting into the clearing sky.

We walked along the canal to the old mill. The meadows were partly flooded, so that there was an effect of tonal green and silver against the rough black and grey and green of the tree trunks standing alongside them; the silhouette of the little village with its pointed spire stood against the clear sky while in the background there was a gate and a dungheap on which a flock of crows sat pecking. We spoke about books and about art, about the prints that I was working with in the gallery, about the way an artist could succeed at portraying a feeling in an image, could paint the very landscape where we stood and translate not just the beauty of it but the exact joy that we felt then, approaching that mill, the sun sparkling on the water of the canal, the sails of the mill slowly turning. We spoke of Israëls, of Maris and Mauve, whom I had gotten to meet a few times already and admired a great deal, and of Millet, whose pictures seemed to me to express an honesty I had rarely seen.

Perhaps I preached more than I listened, but nonetheless I was amazed at the two of us, walking together and talking as men, agreeing on everything. The future was a bright and winding path, and we were on it together. And somewhere along the way we made a promise to each other, do you remember? We pledged to always be there for each other, to support each other, and to be each other's companions on the road of life just as we were on that road to the mill. Do you remember this, Theo?

We stopped when we reached the mill, our clothes damp and heavy. A man was standing in the doorway, leaning against the frame and gazing out at the landscape, smoking his pipe, watching the water soak into the land. The raindrops were lingering on every blade of grass, perfect spheres, invisibly dissolving. The man took us inside and we sat at his table and drank cups of milk and grinned at each other, the milk staining our lips, the mustaches we could just barely grow. We clinked our cups together and toasted our new pledge, our new brotherhood.

You stayed only a few days in The Hague, and when you went home, I missed you, arriving back at the Rooses' in another thunderstorm and hearing no one say my name. I thought of you walking the six kilometers to school from our parents' new house, your clothes drenched, your feet soaked, your hat pressed down around your face. There was no shelter along that long road; how would you last in that weather? I worried for you, though of course you never needed me to. Though my room was warm as ever, I sat under my blanket and felt wet and cold. The first letter I ever wrote you was during one of those frequent storms. I had the feeling, after that visit, you were more than another one of our parents' sons, more than the boy from my childhood; you were my brother.

Oh, but when I think of that day, it is as if I am remembering something that has passed and will not come again. Is it because of all that has happened since then, because a man cannot be as he was, because the future must not be as visible as it was that day—it is against the natural way—or is it because you are gone? Theo, who is not dead, and yet whom I feel I no longer know. Theo! I need you now; I need that brother grinning under that rained-on hat, not the brother who told me how I had changed, not the brother who shook his head at me. I don't know how to reach you, boy; it has never been so hard. Without you I am more than alone.

Theo, my boy, my brother, my friend! I am not who I was? But who now are you?

•

Dear Theo,

I want to tell you about my first sermons in the Borinage. For my very first religious meeting, I spoke about the man born blind. I did my best.

We met on Friday night in the large shed set aside for this purpose, about halfway down the hill toward the labyrinth of cottages. It was a nice-enough room, with windows in the back and a view of the hills beyond, though I was never comfortable speaking in such a way, standing before the miners with my back to the wall, speaking at them as if I were a man more learned than they. I know this is why the clergymen thought me unsuitable for the life of the cloth, but I tell you that if it were up to me, we would all sit together, like Quakers or savages, no differences between men and women, perhaps even cross-legged on the floor.

I was nervous before speaking, for I wanted to start on the

right note, showing the miners something of who I was, and I couldn't help but hope I might be different from the evangelists who had come before me. I paced the room for nearly two hours, waiting for people to arrive. Just after sundown, groups of miners started to trickle in, huddled into their coats and hats, for it was cold that night, women with their scarves draped around their heads and carrying babies underneath their shawls. Children hid behind their parents, their faces flushed red, as if their mothers had given their cheeks an extra scrubbing before herding them out into the cold. I greeted most of the villagers at the door, introduced myself and shook their hands, my heart pounding in my throat, swells of feeling—joy and relief to be there, at long last, greeting the people, and they nodded at me before sliding onto the benches that lined the room. Decrucq and his wife and boys arrived, and he gave me a wink and a clap on the shoulder that was nearly enough to knock me down. Then I stood before them, with only one lamp to light the room and the Bible that I held in my hand.

I knew my voice was quiet, but I seemed incapable of making it louder, and it was all I could do to raise my eyes from the book every once in a while as I spoke.

I told them the story of the man born blind. "As he went along, he saw a man blind from birth. His disciples asked him, 'Rabbi, who sinned, this man or his parents, that he was born blind?' 'Neither this man nor his parents sinned,' said Jesus, 'but this happened so that the works of God might be displayed in him. As long as it is day, we must do the works of Him who sent me. Night is coming, when no one can work. While I am in the world, I am the light of the world.' After saying this, he spit on the ground, made some mud with the saliva, and put it on the man's eyes. 'Go,' he told him, 'wash in the Pool of Siloam.' So the man went and washed, and came home seeing."

"The man born blind," I told the miners, my voice rising

despite myself, "is a stand-in for all of us, for until we open our eyes to see Jesus we are all spiritually blind, and what we see before us is as nothing." I raised my head to look at the congregation, and in the dim light the miners were but shadows shuffling in the near dark. Nonetheless, I could feel their attention, and I knew at least some of them were listening. "Jesus," I continued, "uses the mud of the ground and His own saliva to perform the miracle and heal the blind man, and in so doing He is *creating* sight, rather than restoring it; it is not unlike how God created Adam from the dust of the earth. So when we believe in Jesus, we are allowing an act of creation to take place in us, and we should steel ourselves for the change; for after we begin to see, just as in the story, our closest associates may no longer recognize us. It is frightening, and it is an act of trust and obedience, but the payoff is great, for with the gift of sight comes the ability to see the kingdom of God here on earth, and to understand that all of our suffering is part of a larger plan."

It was not lost on me, Theo, the irony of the choice of this story, though it didn't occur to me until I was already speaking. To tell a story about blindness to a room full of people who spend their lives in darkness! Perhaps it was foolish; perhaps it was the perfect story to tell. I couldn't decide, but as I spoke I became increasingly distracted by the sense that something was wrong. The room was too big! The room was too bright! The room was too cold, too warm! I was looking out at a group of blind people, people who squinted when the light grew too bright, and telling them about a miracle of sight. These people, who had no experience with miracles, and would no doubt never be witness to one.

After I finished the sermon and bid the miners good night, thanking them for coming, many of them came to say hello to me, all of them calling me "Monsieur Vincent," a detail that brought me pleasure, for it made me feel I belonged, and that my sermon had not been too terrible. Many of them invited me to their homes, and told me of family members who were sick and might like to visit with me. I assured all of them that I would come to see them, and that I hoped I could be of some service. I loved them instantly. They had a characteristic simplicity and good nature that reminded me of the Brabant people we grew up with, and their requests and invitations seemed to me expressions of their characters, welcoming and accepting, rather than of some aspect of need.

Each week for those first few months I held a Bible class. I don't like the word *class*, for I certainly never thought of myself as a teacher—in fact, I felt I more often learned than taught—but I suppose that is what it should be called. These meetings were held most often in the home of Else and Hubert Aerts, for they were faithful Christians and Else a bit of a gossip. She liked to feel in control, as though there was nothing that went unnoticed in her village and everything important that happened took place under her nose. Occasionally I doubted, at first, the veracity of her faith, wondering if she didn't just want to host us because she liked to witness the occasional poor soul who came to her home seeking guidance from God; every time I felt this, however, she would make a gesture of such generosity to the strangers in her meager cottage that I had to make a concerted effort to repent for my uncharitable thoughts. Her husband, Hubert, worked the night shift at the mine, and so most often he was asleep upstairs when we were there, his snores audible whenever we paused for reflection.

The main room in the Aertses' hut was dark, as are the rooms in most of the miners' homes. The hut was modestly decorated, with a round wooden table and a set of chairs, a long cupboard at the back of the room by the large iron kitchen stove, and two worn armchairs set before the fireplace. The Aertses' three children had long since married and moved into cottages of their own, so their modest home seemed excessively spacious, which was the reason Else always gave when she was thanked for hosting. There were two oil lamps in opposite corners, and despite the coffee Else served to us, the room still always smelled of sour mud. The miners are used to this smell and do not notice it; it is a smell that pervades every dwelling, a smell of earth and bodies and the absence of sun. I am trying to think of a smell you will know that I can compare to it—do you remember the smell in the basement of the parsonage in Zundert where we played some days when it was too cold to go outside? The miners' huts smell something like that, if that old basement had been overlaid by a thick, fresh layer of mud.

I felt it was most appropriate to speak of God to the miners in rooms like that, dark and musty despite their warmth, for these were not people who were accustomed to sunlight. It suited me much better than the larger room I gave my sermons in. I found God more accessible in the gloom of the miners' cottages, and I felt that the miners did, too. In the Borinage, God does not exist in the twittering of birds, in the bloom of a flower. God is in the gloom, in the must, and in the space that we created for Him when we begin to listen, to each other, and for Him.

One evening, perhaps on our fourth gathering, there were only four people there, aside from Else, and Hubert snoring upstairs. One of them was Georges, who always came. He was an old man, over seventy I think, and spent his life down in the mine, beginning work at the age of seven. He said he came to God in his last year in the pit, when he knew he was to begin life aboveground. In the underground world the only questions were practical ones—when to timber the face to keep the wall from collapsing, when the flame that served as the firedamp warning was burning too intensely, when a piece of coal was sufficiently pried loose. There were no questions down there of where the next piece of bread would come from; there were no questions even of when it was time to stop for lunch, for the men just waited for the bell. It was only when he knew the time was approaching when he'd have to return to the surface that the questions began to come back, he said, and in the questions, there was God. Imagine that, Theo! Only when one comes out of Hell do thoughts turn to Heaven! I wonder what father would think of this, but it sure makes sense to me.

Also with us was a robust woman, Clara Gilmart, and her husband Jan, who had come off his shift at the mine just a few hours before and had gone to the pub on his way home, though he told Clara that very morning that he would not. Clara punished him by bringing him to see me, and I could smell the drink from across the table. Jan could barely hold up his head from the combination of fatigue and drink, but his wife, when she saw it droop, lifted it from his chin with no gentle tap of the underside of her hand. "Pastor Vincent," she said to me when she came in the room, dragging her husband by the collar of his coat, "How am I supposed to feed the family if this man drinks away his children's food?"

The final person in the room was a young woman of seventeen called Angeline Dubois. She sat quietly, with her hands clasped in her lap and her head turned down, yet I felt immediately as if I knew her from somewhere, though I couldn't place where. Very occasionally she would let her eyes lift to watch me, but whenever I turned toward her she looked down again. There was something so sweet and picturesque about her, so demure and civilized, a quality not easily found in the Borinage, and I was curious about her immediately. It was only after I had opened my book and begun to speak that I realized why she was familiar: Theo, she was the girl whom I had seen on my very first day, watching me from edge of the crowd of miners! She was the one I had wondered about since then, that strange vision of interest and boldness, that genderless creature all in black! It was she, I was sure of it, and the shock of it nearly left me speechless.

I had to clear my throat and pretend I had something caught in there in order to cover my surprise.

Else told me after the others had left that Angeline had been, until a few months before, engaged to a man who died in an explosion in the Agrappe mine. This man had been a Christian, and though Angeline had resisted religion before his death, she was attending now in an attempt to continue on the way he would have wanted her to. She worked in the mine, hauling the tubs of coal away from the miners and through the narrow passageways to where horses and boys pulled them to the shaft; it was expected that after she was married she would be able to stop working in order to raise their children. Now that her man was dead, Else said, she would no doubt have to work at the mine indefinitely, for the burden on her family of another mouth to feed was now without an end in sight.

Once I had sufficiently recovered, I pointed the group toward Acts 16:9, and we read together: "And a vision appeared to Paul in the night; There stood a man of Macedonia, and prayed him, saying, Come over into Macedonia, and help us." The inspiration to read this passage had come to me the night before, while I was reading my Bible by candlelight in my bed at the Denises', Alard asleep in the bed across from me. I saw my suitcase at the end of my bed, next to my worn knapsack, and I wondered about the suitcase that the man from Macedonia would carry; then I looked over at Alard and saw him, even as he lay in his bed in his very own home, as a traveler, too. What would his suitcase look like? That bed was his suitcase—he was lying inside of it; he was traveling right now through the world of dreams. Every one of us were travelers, that was it: you, Theo, with your valise and dapper suit, me with my torn socks, and all these miners in their dark huts with their barrels of water for washing.

"The man from Macedonia was a man just like all of us," I said to the group, "a laborer, a man who suffered and who had

a family to feed and who was tired from bending his back all day
long in his field. He came to Paul looking for knowledge of God,
looking for the Gospel, looking with desperation for God's word
to feed him and make him full." I pointed out that the man from
Macedonia had used the word *us* when he asked for help, for the
help he wanted was not just for himself but for all of his brethren, for all of the people like him whose lives were hard, and
that included the people in the room with me at that moment;
that included all of the people in the village, in the Borinage, in the
world. I thought of you then; I thought of Mother and Father
and Anna and Lies, of my old friend Harry Gladwell, whose sister
had recently died; we all needed help, all of us in so many ways.
Can you agree with me that much, brother?

But who was listening? Georges was awake, but his eyes were
unfocused and fixed on a spot somewhere behind me, a look I
had seen many times on faces in church; Clara was focused on
Jan, whose head was drooping and who had started to ardently
shake off her attempts to keep him awake; Else was watching
me, but she was sipping her coffee so lovingly that I was sure my
words were merely drifting through her head, unaccompanied
by any thought. Angeline, however, lifted her head at that moment
and caught my eye. She seemed surprised to find me looking at
her, and dropped her head quickly, but it was enough to convince
me that I should continue on.

"Jesus Christ," I said, "was the great man of sorrows who
knew our troubles, for He worked in a humble carpenter's shop
for thirty years in order to fulfill God's will. He was called the
son of a carpenter, though He was in fact the Son of God, and
this distinction is all we need to understand how we can learn
from Him." I paused, looking around the table to see if I could
catch any eyes, and taking the opportunity to sip my coffee. I
hated the sound of my voice, as I always did in these situations;
I fought against the sense that my words did no justice to the

notions I was trying to stir, and the voices in my head that wanted to silence me. "God wills," I continued with effort, "that in imitation of Christ man should live humbly and not reach for the sky, but should adapt himself to the earth below, learning from the Gospel to be meek and simple of heart. We have no splendor or glamour in our lives, just like the Macedonian man had none, but we all have immortal souls, and this is all it takes to belong in the kingdom of God."

I encouraged them to speak, to ask questions, though I felt unsure I would give the right answer. The truth is, I felt nervous and full of doubt every time I gave a class like that, as I admit I also did in every sermon I gave, mostly in the moments where my voice trailed away and I was left with a group of silent people who looked back at me with eyes darkened from years underground. What were they trained to see in the dark? These were not average people, understand; they could see in the dark, as I could not. Theo, do you suppose that eyes that live in the dark can see souls, or the shape of souls? What did they see when they looked at me sitting there—could they see the shape of my soul?

Angeline, finally, after a few minutes of silence, raised her head to ask what had happened to the Macedonian man. It was a question I hadn't anticipated, but perhaps should have, for it was practical, as these people most often are. "What happened to him?" she asked, her voice very quiet at first. "The Macedonian man? Did he get help?"

It was the first time she had asked a question. I wanted to have an answer, for I understood the need to find out how a story ended, frequently having stayed up late into the night to finish a book. But the Bible is often not this kind of a book. "Well," I told her, "we know that Paul and the other disciples did indeed go to Macedonia, and we can only assume that the man found in their teachings the word of God that he was seeking. Most important, however, was not the outcome of the search, but the search itself."

In many ways, I said, searching was the most important aspect of finding. Reaching for the Gospel may be the most important part of the Gospel there is.

As I said this, meeting her questioning eyes across the table, I felt the deep tendrils of doubt sweep through me, as seaweed moves from a strong current at the bottom of the sea.

•

October 22
Cuesmes, the Borinage

Dear Theo,

I want to tell you more about Alard, whose room I shared at the Denis house, and who remains my greatest friend in mining country. He is nine years old. He is the first boy I shared a room with since I shared one with you. You saw a drawing of him when you were here, but I'm not sure you will remember that, or if my sketch did him any justice.

Alard is thin and quiet, with sunken eyes and a head of dark and tousled hair. He is always listening, standing in the back of rooms or in doorways, and he is never afraid to ask questions when he doesn't understand. The other day, we walked in the nearby woods and looked at birds' nests in the trees, even came across one nestled in the ground. "What happens to the birds in the winter?" he asked me, genuinely concerned. I explained that the birds often left their nests for the winter, moving off to warmer climates, and would come back again when it was safe for them. He seemed satisfied with that, but he asked again, "What happens to their nests?" I told him they would remain, but he needed my assurance that we would come back to the woods in the winter to find them there.

He is a special boy, thoughtful for his age. He impressed me from the first day as a boy destined to grow to be just like his father, prosperous and smart, with his hands ever kneading fresh quantities of delicious dough. In my first few weeks in the Denis house, I was often up late studying my Bible, reading a book, or sketching an image of the miners that would not leave my mind. Alard, who knew how to read, sat up in his bed and read his Bible, too, though most often when I looked over at him I saw his head drooping, the book propped on his knees and his chin to his chest. The sight always warmed me, for it was the vision of a boy who so dearly wanted to be a man, a human spirit trapped in time.

There are boys who want to grow up faster and boys who don't want to ever be men; in the Borinage, the boys don't usually get the chance to learn the difference. I am grateful to Alard for reminding me of what it is to be a boy; he is a boy much like I was, struggling with adult questions long before it is required of him. Many nights before I moved from the Denis house, I turned Alard's lamp down and coaxed his knees straight, taking the book from him and easing him back onto his pillow. Most nights Alard was too asleep even to mutter a response, but occasionally he whispered a good night that made a knot come into my throat. Theo, not since the two of us shared that bed in the room with the flag in the window have I felt that kind of fellowship with anyone.

One day at the Denis house, I watched from an upstairs window as Alard and his brother Nathen played a game in the front yard. Nathen is four years older than Alard, and while I watched them I saw you and me. They were playing an imagination game, lining up rocks on the grass and moving them around, taking branches from a nearby tree to place in the path of the stones. I couldn't hear them from where I was, but felt as if I could.

I was telling you to move the branch just so, and you were doing what you were told, but I could see on your face that you saw something I didn't see. I told you to put four rocks on top of the branch—the front line of the advancing army—and you did so. I watched your face; what did you see?

"They're swimmers," you said.

"Swimmers?"

"Swimmers. See? This is the front line; they're about to jump off the dock and into the water. It's a competition! They're nervous."

And so they were. I saw them clearly then, the swimmers, wearing trunks and with their arms up, preparing to dive. "They're swimmers!" I said.

You grinned. You lifted the rocks up one by one and dropped them off the branch and onto the grass. I moved them through the water and you cheered for the one in blue, who beat the others by a healthy margin. You lined up the next group of swimmers for the next race. Your face was radiant, and the lake stretched out before us.

Nathen laughed at something Alard said; I saw him throw back his head and fall to the grass, his mouth open with glee. The look on Alard's face was pure surprise for a moment—he was amazed that he amused his brother enough for such a response—and then pure joy. They were two brothers, laughing.

I thought of you while I watched the two boys, thought of you embarked on a career at Goupil's selling art, just as I once did; you now treading the same floors and galleries, but getting commendations, raises, and promotions rather than scoldings, rebukes, and transfers from one place to another.

Do you remember when Mother used to paint those canvases in the garden in the back of the parsonage, canvas after canvas of blooming flowers, never anything else? So many afternoons the group of us would sit back there with her, sitting or playing quietly lest we disturb her. And when her mood turned dark, as it inevitably did, and she set aside her painting and went inside, she closed her bedroom door behind her and we could all hear her cries through the wood. None of us knew what to do, not even Father, to comfort her, except for you. Knocking gently, you let yourself in and after a few minutes the crying always ceased. It was the same if you were ever upset—you were the one she thought worthy of comforting. She never once held me the way she did you.

I punished you more than you deserved for this, for being my brother, for being younger and more at ease, for being the one with father's name, rather than the name of Uncle Cent and of that baby in the cemetery out back. I made you sleep on the floor, when I was angry and feeling spiteful; I made you do things that I wouldn't dare to do: sneak coins from Pa's coat pockets, steal milk from farmers' pails, or just-sheared wool from local barns. And you did these things for me, bringing me your loot like a dog bringing his master a bone, and I turned on you, showing the proof to our parents, standing before you like an accuser, like a man who knew righteousness. And though both of us were punished, you never turned on me as I did on you.

I can easily conjure up the strange pleasure that came from punishing you: peering down at you from the bed while you slept on the floor, feeling a curious mixture of guilt and pride and rage.

I repent for all of this, now. I think of it and I don't understand it. I wish to tell you I am sorry for it, but then I think of what you said to me when you came to visit, that all I've been doing in the Borinage is "idling," and I fear I would do it all over again.

And do you remember this? One day when we were boys, maybe eleven and seven, we were playing by a canal somewhere near home. I had stolen Pa's pocketknife and showed you how to whittle small branches torn off elm trees into little spears; we were using the spears to fish in the canal. Lying on our stomachs on the bank, leaning out as far as we could over the water, peering into the darkness to see a fish swim by. I thought I saw one—a shadow turned in the water, something dark turned darker, and I thrust my spear as fast as I could into the depths. Nothing. The spear floated back to the surface and I had to reach quickly to stop it from drifting away. It happened like that over and over again: nothing, nothing, nothing, the fish effortlessly slipping away.

I looked up at you, whom I had forgotten in my concentration. You had your face in the water, your spear poised above your head. Why hadn't I thought of that? All of a sudden your spear went down, you were lightning fast, and you sat up with a fish. Your face and arm dripping, you grinned at me and held it up. It was a little fish, not as big as your forearm. "I did it!" you squealed.

Anger and jealousy flooded me; the sight of your grinning face was a taunt. You were always better than I was, always. I reached for the fish and yanked it off of the spear and threw it; it cleared the canal and landed on the other side, where it flopped helplessly. You watched it in horror, and looked at me with confusion. "Why did you do that?" you wailed, your voice quickly turning to tears. The fish flopped and jumped. You got up and ran along the canal, trying to find a way across to help it. "Why did you do that, Vincent?" I could hear you crying, your voice high-pitched and desperate as you ran. I sat on the bank and watched the fish slowly suffocate.

•

October 28
Petit Wasmes, the Borinage

Dear Theo,

A month into my stay in the Borinage, in mid-January, a letter arrived at the Denis house; the committee had granted me a temporary salary and a six-month appointment, to begin on February first. If, after six months' time, they were happy with my work, they would make the appointment permanent.

When I told Madame Denis, who watched me with a grin of anticipation while I read the letter, she cooed and sat me at the table to eat a piece of bread spread with homemade apple jam. I forced myself to eat it, not wanting to disappoint her, but the happiness about being able to finally support myself, after three years of relying on Father for everything, and the eagerness to get to work made the food dry up in my mouth.

Soon after the letter came, I set out with enthusiasm to start a school for the children of Petit Wasmes. I had learned from Alard that for the children of the town there was little schooling save what their parents might teach them, and that only in rare exceptions did this mean learning to read. I decided I wanted to give the children a sense of school, maybe a better sense than I had ever had.

Paul told me he thought he might know just the place to hold the school; we walked together through winding paths past the main part of the village to the outskirts of where the houses began. Nestled in a thicket of pine trees there was a large wooden building, overrun on all sides by thorny bushes and dried-up ferns. Strange to think of this now! I am writing to you now from inside this same building, which has grown to be a home of sorts to me. "It used to be a dance hall," said Paul as we approached that day. "Many years back, there was a group of miners who loved to play music, and all the people from the village came on Friday nights for dancing." He stopped on the path to the front door and gazed at the building. "They called it the Salon de Bébé. There was a lot of carousing and carrying on," he said, "a few fistfights and someone's broken arm before the management shut the place down." He smiled vaguely and then shook his head. "Things did get out of hand, but generally the village was a happier place back then. I heard that a few of those musicians sold their instruments during a strike a few years ago."

We went in. The door swung open easily, sweeping over a mat of pine needles and revealing a cavernous empty room. A couple of mice scampered out of sight with a panicked squeak and then it was quiet. Our footsteps echoed over the floorboards. The room was designed as a simple barn, with thick rafters overhead but no loft. Two windows along each wall let in the winter sun, but the windows were dirty and the light in the room was muted and dim. There was a low wooden bench and a stove on the far end, a number of chairs lined up along the sides, and a general musty smell. On the floor in one corner were a few discarded bottles. "I'm sure the young people come here to be alone," Paul said.

I moved slowly into the room, my footsteps echoing. "It's like the whale," I said out loud as I stared with awe up at the rafters. Paul looked at me with a puzzled expression. "The whale," I repeated. "The whale that swallows Jonah. It's like we're inside the giant fish."

Paul uttered a noise of surprise and looked around him, apparently trying to envision this. He smiled at me. "Does that mean you like it?"

"Oh, yes. It's perfect. It brings to mind Delaroche's *Good Friday*, an image I used to keep on my wall wherever I went." Do you know that picture, Theo? They have prints of it at Goupil's. A group of people huddle in a dark room, all of them turned toward the window, where bright light pours through. The women are bowed, praying, and the men are bracing themselves for what they see out the window—the whole picture is composed for that window, really, where the light comes in, though it is not large and it exists at the far left of the frame. In the salon, light poured similarly through the dusty windows, though the inside of the room was dark. I said to Paul, "It is like we are in the manger where Jesus was born. It will be the perfect place to teach the children."

Paul, still smiling gently at me, nodded. "Well, good. To me it is just a barn, but I am happy that you see all those things here. We'll have to get it cleaned up a bit, but before too long it will be ready to use."

"Oh," I said, "I think it is ready just as it is."

As we left the salon, Paul asked me what my schooling was like when I was a boy. Walking behind him, I was so struck by the question that I had to brace myself against the salon's door frame before I could answer. Thoughts of Zundert are never far away, but to be asked a direct question about my boyhood invited me to bring my melancholy into the open. I didn't want Paul to know how much of a failure I had been.

"I went to the school across the square from the parsonage where we lived," I said finally, walking next to Paul toward the village cottages. "And then I was schooled at home for a few years before going off to boarding school. My mother believed that a man's education was a stamp of his class. Both of my parents were very serious about all of us children succeeding in school."

But I didn't succeed, not ever, did I? Not like you did. I skipped school, got into fistfights with the other boys, and was beaten more than once by the schoolmaster, sent home across the Markt, to mother's disapproving face. I sat diligently next to Father for lessons for three years before he gave up, sending me away to the Provily school a few towns away. Was that the first time Father gave up on me? Certainly it was not the last. Oh, what must it be like to give up again and again on someone you love? What is that, Theo, that giving up? It seems to me the opposite of faith, which otherwise Father has so much of. Now that you, too, have given up on me, perhaps you can tell me what it is, how it feels, where it comes from.

It was raining the day Mother and Father drove me to the Provily school. I can still see the bare trees with the rain falling among them, making the bark shine and gleam, the carriage growing smaller as it raced away, seemingly never to return, driving on ever faster through the meadows until it could no more be seen. You and the others were still at home, and I imagined you all sitting around the table together with my empty chair, filling my absence up with your joy to be free of me, the moody, unpredictable one, the sullen one with the disposition of a grumpy old man. I watched the carriage drive away from me and I knew that my worst fears were true. My family had gotten rid of me.

Paul and I walked together back to the Denis house, where he left me. Mostly, we walked in an agreeable silence. I told him the committee had granted me six months, and he nodded and smiled at me. "I am happy to hear that," he said.

The salon was ready for the boys' school in just a day. I swept the cobwebs and pine needles out with a broom I borrowed from Hannah Decrucq, and put a number of my favorite prints up on the walls: Weissenbruch's *Mill by the Trekvaart*—a man on his horse stands next to a dog on a path overlooking a river, in the distance an old windmill, all dwarfed by a patient sky; Breton's *The Feast of Saint John*, which I got to see at the exhibition in Paris in 1875—a group of barefoot peasant women dancing, holding one another's arms in a joyful circle around a glowing fire; Millet's *Fields in Winter*—a wide snow-covered field with an abandoned plow and harrow in the foreground. I wiped the windows with an old coal sack and stepped back, pleased with my work. Paul had found me a few old schoolbooks and picture books somewhere in Wasmes and had brought them to the salon; I lined them up on the windowsill as if it were a shelf. They are still here now, collecting dust.

It was cold, though—even after the boys arrived. No one

was older than seven except for Alard, for he was the only one excused from work in the mine. The boys huddled in their coats and leaned over the books with their hands tucked into their armpits, their breath coming out in white clouds. Alard must have mentioned the cold to his mother, for a few days later, at noon, a near crowd of women appeared outside the salon, most of them carrying the ubiquitous burlap mining sacks. A few of the women pushed wheelbarrows and small wagons. Madame Denis handed me a sack. Alard was with her, and he smiled at me shyly. In the back of the group I noticed Angeline Dubois, who nodded her head at me. She and I had grown a bit more familiar, as she had continued to attend my Bible classes, asking me questions that I could not always answer. One day we had spoken to each other for quite a while outside the Aertses' hut, and her persistence in asking me questions about a Bible passage made me wonder why it was she seemed to not want to go home. I was happy to see her that day at the school.

"Come on with us, Monsieur Vincent," said Madame Denis. "It is time you learned how it is we find our coal."

The women took me up on one of the nearby slag heaps to collect coal. Each family is typically given eight hectoliters of coal each month, and particularly in cold months this is an inadequate amount, so the women either buy more from the company or go scrambling for more over the heaps. Madame Denis told me this as we made our way to the heap we were to scavenge, Alard walking next to us, scrambling to keep up. Most families were too proud and too poor to buy more of the coal that they spent their days and sweat excavating from the earth, so most often the women and children took to the slag mountains to scavenge for themselves. But this was no simple thing, Theo, lest you get the wrong notion: Not only did the company police often patrol the heaps—"even the refuse is company property, after all," Madame Denis said with a tone of real frustration—sometimes confiscating the women's sacks and

breaking their wheelbarrows and wagons, but also the mountains of slag could shift underfoot, and every once in a while a
woman was swallowed by the quicksand of shifting slag. They
timed their visits to the pyramids carefully, aiming for the first
number of hours of a shift at the mine, for it wasn't until after
the coal had been excavated and sifted through the breakers, the
good stuff separated from the bad, that the cars were ready to
move to the slag heaps.

We approached a small mountain that looked more like a
ravine or the bank of a small creek, though of course there was
no water running through it. Madame Denis said this one had
been recently begun, but that it was always good to pick coal on
the banks that were most recently in use, for these were the least
picked over. There was a roughly built scaffold along the side of
it, the planks of wood hastily nailed together, a rickety way for
the company to lug the coal cars up to the top to dump them.
Atop the mound was a thin dusting of snow, like an icing of sugar.
I thought again of black Egypt, feeling that we were about to
tread on holy ground.

I glanced around at the little group as we came close, the
women all dressed in long, thick skirts and aprons, the bottoms
of their skirts darkened from the mud and soot they walked
through—stains they could never quite clean away. Some of them
had their heads covered with cotton scarves and bonnets, and
many of them smiled if they met my eyes. Else Aert, my gossipy
Bible group hostess, was there, as was Clara Gilmart, Hannah
Decrucq, and a number of other women I knew. There were
a few little girls who were dressed just like their mothers, and I
recognized two of the boys from my school, Pierre and John, in
their little black caps, their earnest faces looking to the mound
of discarded coal with determination. Angeline Dubois blinked
and looked away, shy of me in a way that flattered me and made
me uncomfortable all at once.

We took to the mountain. I pictured how we must look from

above, tiny figures scrambling up a dark, shifting mound, dwarfed by the blackness, using our hands to try to gain some traction to get higher, though it seemed that every time I looked up I had gained no ground. We were a group of ants crawling up the side of an anthill. Some women began sifting and picking as soon as their feet touched the bank, but Madame Denis called to me, "Monsieur Vincent! It is always best to try to pick near the top!" so I clambered up after her and Alard, who was already near the ridge. There was immediately soot in my eyes, and when I looked down at my hands I could not see them, for they were the same color as the ground.

Something strange was happening to me, Theo. I had the momentary feeling that I had disappeared. I could feel my muscles moving, but it seemed that my limbs had plunged into the body of some unknown creature and had been absorbed. I was moving over the surface of something that had no surface, which meant that I was inside of it, climbing up its body from underneath its skin.

Through my soot-covered eyes I looked up and saw Alard, and the sight brought me back to myself. Alard's hat had flaps that covered his ears. "Monsieur Vincent," he called, "you are looking for the pieces that look like this!" He held up a piece of coal, proud of himself for finding one so fast. His face was swept with soot as with a thick paintbrush, his hat just as dark. Madame Denis was standing near him, looking pleased. I tried to stand, and took a scoop of the mound up to my face to inspect it. A handful of dark matter sat in my palm, and it all looked the same to me. I let a couple rocks fall, for I was sure they were not what I wanted. Already I could feel cuts on my skin from trying to keep my balance as I scrambled up the hill.

"There," I heard a voice next to me say, and I turned to find Angeline. I was relieved to see her, as if she could pass me a map to all the treasure hidden in the mountain. She was pointing at my palm. "You've got a piece."

I blinked at her and used my arm to try to wipe the soot from my eyes. It did only a little good. The image of her was darkened around the edges. "I do?"

"Yes," she said. "Here, show me."

I lifted my palm to her, and she pulled out a piece of the rubble. She held it between her thumb and forefinger, up by her face, and smiled at me. "Coal!"

We picked through the coal for over an hour and I barely had a third of my bag filled. Most of the women had bags so full, they could barely carry them. My hands were scraped and bleeding, my face chapped by the soot and wind, but I was exhilarated by the work, which made my body feel vibrant and alive. What were we doing but ministering to the earth? We picked our way back down the mountain and Madame Denis clapped me on the back and raised her voice to the other women. "Has any other evangelist climbed the heap with us? Monsieur Vincent is different; he is one of us!" A few of the women laughed, and I could see derision in a few of the faces I had encountered less often. I shook my head and raised my voice—"It takes a lot more than a trip up a slag heap to make a miner"—and I could feel my cheeks blushing underneath the soot that covered my skin. Inside of me I was on fire, Theo; I had found a way to belong to these people, to this place, and it was by digging my hands deep into the coal. Angeline came down the mountain next to me, and I could feel her presence by my side as pricks of cold ice all the way down my skin.

It was the first time I had done any physical work in the Borinage, and in the euphoria of the exercise and the vision before me, I felt sure I saw something new: Physicality was the way the people of the Borinage expressed their version of God. It was in their muscles and their bent-over backs; it was in their breasts given to an infant, in their broken ribs healed wrong. What a beautiful scene; the peasant women moving in dark skirts and white bonnets over the black mountain were like Millet's images of women sowing, yet they were excavating a heap of the earth's insides. Remembering Millet, I was invigorated, struck by the melding of art and life. How strange, to be moving in your life and at the same time feel you are an image, perfectly realized, seen by yourself from the outside!

I was exalted; even remembering it I can feel the charge, a coil of fire that comes up from inside of me and lights me all the way up. I felt powerful and clear, as if I understood everything all at once: the coal, the darkness, the filth, the warmth of the people and the blood on our hands, the way the earth communicated with our bodies to bring us understanding, the way we were born from that coal and then returned to it, and the way that God provided us with the ability to see. Just by looking around us we could learn what it was to be alive; we could be fully present; we could fully communicate. No words were necessary, only this place! Only these hands and these faces streaked with black!

When we had all descended the mountain and walked back to the path, I took Alard, Pierre, and John with me back to the salon for our afternoon lesson. The other boys came soon after. By the time they arrived, I had forgotten about the coal dust on my face, and only one of the boys mentioned it when he saw me, a particularly precocious boy named Harry. "Monsieur Vincent," he said, "you look like a real miner now!"

"Welcome, boys," I greeted them, feeling a new charge of confidence. "Alard, Pierre, John, and I have just been up one of the slag mountains collecting coal. This is something you have all done before, I am sure, with your mothers or sisters or aunts."

There was general nodding and smiles from the boys, who were no doubt thinking how different I looked with my face smeared black. Carel, a boy who sat at the back and always wore his cap indoors—an eccentricity I did not mind—spoke up. "Monsieur Vincent, you should be careful doing that. My next-door neighbor went collecting one day and the slag heap swallowed her. She never came back. Now my mother won't let me go with her anymore."

It amazed me that these boys could be forbidden to go up the slag heap but were allowed to go down in the mines and haul coal. I asked the boys if the slag heaps scared them, and though they vehemently said no, there were a couple of boys who said nothing, and I took that to mean yes. Though they were tough children, they were children nonetheless, and I thought they were not old enough yet to be deliberately dishonest.

"It's all right to be scared of things," I said, trying to coax them. "All of us, even the toughest of us, are scared of certain things. Being scared can help us to protect ourselves, and to tell good from evil. Tell me some things that you *are* afraid of, if those slag heaps don't scare you." There was silence. The boys looked at one another and then at me. I could see I would have to go first. "Okay," I said, "well, I'll tell you some things that I'm afraid of. Sometimes I wake up in the dark and for a little while I'm frightened of the shapes in my room. I think I see the chair moving like an animal before I realize it's a chair. Sometimes I'm afraid of running chickens"—at this the boys laughed—"really I am! And when I was a boy, I was often afraid of my father when he was angry . . . and sometimes I still am."

After that, Pierre volunteered that he was afraid of fire, for once he had touched the stove without knowing it was hot and had burned his hand so terribly, he still had scars (he held out his hand for the other boys to see). Alard said he was afraid of dogs; he had seen one rip the head off a chicken by shaking it in its jaws. A usually quiet boy named Hugo said that he was afraid of losing his father in the mine; at this, a few of the boys lowered their heads and nodded. Hugo was the boy whom I had once caught with his foot raised over a caterpillar in the dew-laden grass. "Why do you want to kill that little creature?" I had asked him, taking his arm. "God created it, and it lives!" There are

many caterpillars in the Borinage, and whenever I see one slink-
ing along I pick it up and place it on a tree so as to preserve its
strange beauty.

Carel, then, raised his hand and said, "Monsieur Vincent?
My father says I am to be afraid of God."

The stove was warm from the coal I had picked from the
heap, but the boys had their coats on nonetheless. The lamp was
burning in the corner, and the boys' little legs were swinging
from the benches they sat on, their feet not yet touching the
floor. I was still on fire from the slag heap, my skin tingling with
a strange sensation, and I tried to calm myself, knowing that I
could scare the children in my present state. I knew Carel's father, Mark, was a believer, but one who seemed twisted in his
faith, so that his relationship with Christ was more similar to
that of a slave and a master. He had been to quite a few of my
religious meetings and I had often spoken to him down by the
mine as he came out of the gate after a shift—a hard man, with
dark eyebrows thick as grubs. When Carel was near him, Mark
almost always had a hand on his son, a thick paw on his shoulder both protective and threatening.

The boys were confused, but I knew I could not help them. I
have had too many of my own troubles on this very topic, as
you know; I tried to warn myself to tread lightly. But I could not,
Theo, not as I was in that moment, my hands still bleeding and
black. "Well," I began, "we see there are many different types of
fear. Carel, your father is not wrong. Certainly fearing God is an
important part of listening to Him and obeying His commandments. We obey and fear our own fathers, so all the more should
we obey and fear our Father in Heaven." I held out my hands in
front of them. "Look at my hands!" I said. "Do they not scare
you? God made them, and God turned them black and bloody.
God brought me up on that heap today so that I could be closer
to Him, so that I could be closer to all of you. Now here I am,

and the darkness has marked me, and perhaps we should all be afraid." I was looking at my hands as I said this, and then remembered to raise my eyes, and I saw that the boys' eyes were wide and frightened—not by my hands, of course, yes, Theo, I understand this, but by my outburst.

Reaching for my Bible, trying to recover, feeling a confused urge to calm myself and at the same time to rage further, to blow off the front of that furnace fed by the coal I had retrieved and to show them all the visions I had seen, I read to them from Hebrews 12:9, "Furthermore we have had fathers of our flesh which corrected us, and we gave them reverence: shall we not much rather be in subjection unto the Father of spirits, and live?" I couldn't help myself, Theo, I continued: "Live, boys! That is what God wants us to do! But we cannot do that without getting our hands dirty, without becoming covered with black. We cannot continue through our lives pure and white and untouched; we must dive into the earth and, through its dust, find the way to reach one another."

Looking up from the book, I saw a cluster of boys in woolen pants looking back at me with fear and awe and confusion. In each one of them I saw myself. I was one of those boys, just as I was standing in front of them. I saw you, too, Theo, sitting in the front row, looking at me with that confused expression you sometimes wear.

Later that evening the miners poured into the salon. Else and Hubert Aert; Carel's father, Mark; Decrucq and his next-door neighbors the Adelgondes. As they came through the door I greeted them, feeling pleased that I recognized so many faces. Even Paul Fontaine was there—he stoked the fire so well that with all the bodies, it was warm enough in the room for shirt-sleeves. I spoke about the parable of the mustard seed, where the tiniest kernel of faith was enough to grow a whole tree, a whole universe, a whole kingdom. I felt confident, as if the Spirit were really speaking through me, perhaps for the first time, and all the souls in the room were lifted up and were as one.

When I got home to the Denises' and looked in the mirror above the washbasin, I was staggered by what I saw: A miner's face looked back at me. For a moment I did not remember the slag heap, but thought that by some miracle I had been transformed; I had come so close to the flock that evening that even my appearance had changed, and belonging had been granted to me. Then I remembered, but was no less pleased, for in the image of myself with my face turned black I saw a vision of myself as being of the place, and it was a vision of acceptance.

I turned back to the room I shared with Alard, who was already asleep, and saw it as if for the first time: the bed with its warm quilt of feathers, the vase of flowers on the bedside table, the white chest of drawers decorated with a delicate rendering of an apple orchard. It was lovely and simple, but nonetheless it was not a miner's cottage; it was removed, its construction and its decoration and its placement and even its smell, always so pleasant and sweet, removed.

I could not stay at the Denises' any longer; I knew it suddenly and with certainty. I climbed into bed without washing my face. I did not plan to ever wash it again.

The next morning, I left the Denis house and moved to a hut I had noticed near the salon, abandoned some time ago but not yet falling into the earth. Mrs. Denis was worried when I left; when she saw me with my suitcase, she was surprised, her eyebrows turned in. She questioned me. Where was I going? Where would I sleep? Was there a bed in the hut, was there food? Was I unhappy at their home? Had they not done everything to provide for me? I answered that her home was beautiful, her home was a sanctuary, but from time to time one should do as the good God and go and live among one's own. The words coming out of my mouth sounded feeble and forced. I could hear the way they must sound to her and knew they were not as I meant them. She looked at me as if to say, You, like them? Like us? Her face was confused, her mouth tight. She was concerned; she did not understand. She pleaded with me to have a bath and wipe the soot off of my face, at least, before I left. I refused her.

•

November 10
Petit Wasmes, the Borinage

Dear Theo,

When did you get to be older than I? When we were boys, you would do everything that I did—I stepped first in the snow and you followed. But somewhere along the way you must have grown older, or grown past, for there you were telling me in front of the Sorcière mine that you are worried for me. Isn't it my job to worry for *you*?

It has been three months since your visit, and here I am in an empty room, writing to you. But which version of you am I writing to? Is it the boy whom I shared a bed with, or the man in his top hat and dapper suit? I remember you, sick in that bed in Zundert, the curtains drawn and Ma insisting that I tiptoe quietly into the room so I would not disturb you. Am I disturbing you now, Theo, am I disturbing you?

I remember wandering over the heath with you one morning when we were boys. We came across the skeleton of a bird. Do you remember this? It lay in the tall grass by the edge of the lane, as if it had been moved off the path in order to decompose undisturbed. Most of the flesh was gone, save for a piece of the belly, the part of any creature that always looks the most revealing, as if it is the seat of an animal's personality, as a man's plump stomach can tell you much about what his life is like.

The bird's wings lay beneath it, long bones tucked in close, and we could still see the rounded crown of the head, though the flesh was gone and there was no longer a face. The skeleton was perfectly intact: tiny ribs like bridges emerging from the remaining cover at its belly; an incredible immaculate spine, bleached all white from the sun, knobs fitting together like perfect minuscule fists linked in a chain. Little pieces of white fluff clung to where the face had once been.

We crouched by the skeleton for quite a time, taking in its details and contours, windows into the processes of death. For a while we were both silenced by it, the story that it told, one of creation and destruction, one of artistry, of perfection, of time and decay, and of what lay beneath the surfaces that we saw. Then I said I wanted to take it home with us. You erupted at this idea; you were horrified and frightened. How could I want to do such a thing? You grew tearful at the prospect that I would remove the bird; your eyes grew large and wet and you wailed at me, your neck and face flushing red.

I was taken aback by your protest. I had assumed that we were both seeing the same thing, while we crouched there peering at the skeleton, but your cries made me realize otherwise. What I had seen was an object—one that contained mysteries of the universe, certainly, but an object nonetheless. What you had seen was a bird. A creature once alive, now dead, that deserved to return to the earth in peace.

Your vision in that moment inspired me. I had been so focused on the object before us that the rest of the world had gone fuzzy and fallen away; it is a focus of vision that I still have, and that is dangerous, for when I come back to myself after looking so closely my brain is so tired that if that sort of work is repeated often I become totally distracted and incapable of a whole lot of ordinary things. You, with your forceful cries, brought me back to the earth, the two of us kneeling in the mud by the side of a lane, that little skeleton but a tiny detail in an otherwise enormous world. My little brother was so much wiser and more sensitive than I, I saw then, with such an eye that even at your age you could already recognize that some mysteries were meant to remain so.

I have not yet mailed any of the letters I have written you since your visit. I begin to wonder if I will ever send them, if there will ever be any further contact between us again.

•

Dear Theo,

I remember a night in Amsterdam, toward the end of my time there, when my failure at study was near. I let myself out of the house after everyone was asleep and I walked all night, across the city and back, meandering through lanes and lots and parks and over bridges, resting on the steps of houses that held sleeping families, boys and girls tucked in tightly, mothers and fathers with their arms around each other in sleep. How does a man know if he has chosen the right path?

I was yearning to see things; my mind was crammed with the images that I encountered every day but had to ignore for the words in books. I walked and gathered images to my mind as if they were salves for wounds. There are moments when the common everyday things make an extraordinary impression and have a deep significance and a different aspect. As I walked that night, I passed a big dark wine cellar and warehouse, with the doors standing open; for a moment I had an awful vision—men with lights were running back and forth in the dark vault, and I felt suddenly sure that those men were not men at all, but creatures inside my own brain. I was looking not into a warehouse but at a window into my own mind, and the men were the workmen in the yard outside Uncle Jan's, that long line of black figures. It was a sight that often comforted me, although in that moment it filled me with dread: Those men were a symbol of what I could not change. They were arriving for work in my body and mind; I could not turn them away. Then one of them brushed past me, and his shoe touched my ankle. "Excuse me," he said gruffly, and I could tell from the way he looked back at me that he was wondering if I were mad.

I pushed on to the canal. There was nearly a full moon, and the light threw a glow on the gray evening clouds, against which the masts of the ships and the row of old houses and trees stood out; everything was reflected in the water, and the sky cast a strange light on the black earth, on the green grass with daisies and buttercups, and on the bushes of white and purple lilacs, and on the elderberry bushes of gardens in the yards.

What I am trying to say is that I will go on. If we are tired, isn't it because we have already walked a long way? And if it is true that man has his battle to fight on earth, aren't the feeling of weariness and the burning of the head signs of our struggle?

Lift up your eyes, cast yourself like a net into the sea of the world. Lift up the hands that hang down and put them to work, use them to render what you see.

My head is sometimes heavy, and often it burns and my thoughts are confused.

PART II

1880

He wakes at first light. He seems not to have moved all night: His arms are still crossed where they were when he fell asleep, stiff like branches. When he moves, his bones creak; they have fallen into one another, entangled.

How far along is he? He imagines he is nearly halfway to Paris. His body groans; it is complaining, despite the night's sleep, it does not want to embark on another long journey. His feet in particular are unhappy. The soles of his boots are beginning to wear thin, and with a few more hours of walking he feels sure his feet will be touching ground.

He walks on and on, past farm after farm; shepherds look at him with curiosity. He stops frequently to give his feet a rest; he sketches elements of the countryside, all brown farmland or the almost coffee-colored marly soil, with whitish spots where the marl appears. He thinks of Theo, his top hat, his mustache, and feels a strange twinge of fear. *You are not the same any longer.* It is not true. Angeline appears before him in her miner's uniform, her eyes twinkling, but when he reaches out his arm her face contorts into an expression of desperate fear. Where is he going? What will it solve to see his brother, to give him his story, when Theo has never asked for it? *Monsieur Vincent, is that you?* He tries to quiet his mind with sketching, to focus on the lines of the drawing rather than on the questions about where he is going, and what he will say when he gets there, but always at a certain point he hears his father's voice: *What is this for, Vincent? What is this idling?*—and then he looks at what he is drawing and sees it, makeshift and amateurish, expressing nothing. Often then he tears the drawing into strips and tosses them into his knapsack; if there is wind, he lets the pieces be carried off of his palms. Every time he tears up a drawing he feels a twinge of pain, which he tells himself he deserves.

In the afternoon he stops in a village to find out where he is. In a pub he sits and eats a few potatoes and sips some black coffee.

The woman who serves him is plump and kind, and agrees to give him the food for free. He imagines that it is her kindness that makes her cheeks so round and pink. She is the first woman he has seen outside the darkness of the Borinage; he cannot help the desire to see her body without its clothes, the desire to have her kindness lavished on his aching limbs.

She tells him her name is Bertha and he is in a village called Busigny. When she comes to collect his dish and sees him inspecting his boots, where the thin rubber over the soles is giving way, she asks him suspiciously, "How far do you have to go?"

He does not tell her, for fear she will think he's mad. "About fifty kilometers," he says, which is not half the distance before him.

She calls over the bartender, James, to take a look at Vincent's shoes. He, too, is plump, though in a hulking way; his girth stretches across a frame of enormous shoulders, and a U-shaped mustache reaches down past his chin. He is Bertha's husband, Vincent gathers, as she puts her hand to his shoulder as he bends down. "I'm fine," Vincent tells them both. "I'll be fine." He smiles at the way they make a fuss over him. "I've been through worse," he says. Suddenly he feels drugged. The sudden food in his stomach, the rush from the coffee, the caring attention of these two people; he represses the urge to laugh. He wonders how he would look with a mustache like that, but when he tries to imagine it he sees Theo's face instead, his brother standing before the train to Paris; then a mustached man with his stomach torn open and spilling its contents onto the muddied earth, his hands perched on top and fluttering like butterflies.

Bertha tells James that Vincent is planning to go on another fifty kilometers in these shoes. James shakes his head and sits back on his haunches like a surprised squirrel. "You cannot!"

Of course he can. He knows he can't explain to them about the rhythm, the way that the walking undoes the pain in his feet—is the only cure for it, actually, until he has a real chance to rest. He can't explain the way that he needs it, the walking, right now, to clear certain images from his mind. He simply nods. "I can."

Bertha says, "Well, there must be a way we can make these boots stronger." She looks to her husband when she says it, which makes Vincent smile, for clearly he is the executor of her ideas.

Vincent asks them if they have any cardboard. This is an easy way to fortify his soles, one that he has employed on a number of walking trips before. The two of them act as if he is a genius for coming up with it. James goes into the back while Bertha helps Vincent off with his shoes; he is embarrassed for her to see the filthy socks he wears beneath the leather, bloody in spots and torn. She clucks over him as if he is her child, holding his feet gently and with such care that he feels his face flush.

He remembers Madame Denis feeding him soup one spoonful at a time during one of his bouts with fever. He looked up through his delirious daze and saw her hovering over him, a kind apparition in a brown dress. Had she come to his hut? He didn't remember her arrival, and wondered momentarily if he were back in her home again in the room under the eaves, but he was too tired to work it out. "Eat," she was saying, "eat," as she moved the spoon slowly toward his mouth, the liquid in it quivering quietly and threatening to drip but never doing so. "Eat, dear." He can still hear her saying it, her voice the very sound of kindness itself. "You must eat."

He and James and Bertha tear the cardboard into the right-size strips and slip them into his boots. James goes up to their bedroom above the bar and comes back with a clean pair of his own socks, which he insists that Vincent take, despite his nearly tearful refusal. Vincent is ashamed at the kindness of these two people; he shakes his head no and pushes their hands away, but they remain. Why does he deserve such kindness? He does not deserve it. He puts the socks on, and then puts his own socks over the new ones, and then slips his feet back into the boots. He needs to leave; he is determined to do so, before he breaks down and burdens these good people with far more than they deserve.

It is with great sadness that he takes leave of them. He wishes them both the best of luck, and thanks them deeply for their generosity, handing them a drawing of a haystack and a few crows in a field. He watches them take it, Bertha exclaiming over it with too much gusto, handing it over to James as if it were the drawing of a young child they needed to encourage.

He makes himself turn his back and leave. How do we resolve it, the constant coming and going of people from our lives? Often it seems a burden to him, the touching of one life and another, and the inevitable loss that accompanies every crossing. He thinks of Theo, his body next to Vincent's in the dark of their bedroom at Zundert, then his face grinning, a mustache of milk, by the mill at Rijswijk; he sees Angeline, standing before him covered in coal dust. Life seems a series of meetings and then leavings, of givings and receivings and then losings. You clasp a person to you, you inhale the scent of him, you feel the bend in his back beneath your palm, and then you must let go, and what has just touched you cannot be brought back.

A light drizzle is falling; his hat catches the rain before the drops hit his face. He begins a letter to Theo in his head, repeating the words until he has them exact, though he does not write them down.

Dear Theo, I am a bird, you are a man. Dear Theo, I have changed into a bird, you were right, I am not the same. When I see you next, I will have shed my feathers; I will have turned into a man.

Dear Theo, molting is a powerful experience, and I hope not to have to go through it again.

His body draws to a stop before a majestic wheat field. He does not notice that he has lost movement, he is so arrested by what he sees. The stalks of wheat duck and bow, dance and lower their heads and bring them back up again, shake themselves, bow and wave again. There is a smooth wind blowing, and he can hear the faint whistle as the draft drifts through the wheat, a whoosh of sound that somehow seems to unify the movement it provokes. He has, of course, seen many wheat fields before, but in that moment he feels as if he is seeing one for the first time. The wheat stalks are somehow separate and all one; one bows, then another, then another. Does each of them know that there are so many others doing the same? Do they sense their neighbors, bowing to the same wind, or does each plant feel that its plight is its alone? The effect of the field is of a rocky sea—not one wave breaking, but a whole sea rolling this way and that. Over everything, the sun casts its warmth, so that as the wheat falls and grows in the wind, the waves look alternately gold, silver, and a color that is some amalgam of both.

It is the unity of it that overwhelms him. The way sun, wheat, and wind are in such harmony, each contributing equally to a symphony of movement, color, and sound that is one simple image. On one side of the field, a patch is missing. As he watches the field, allowing his gaze to grow wider and wider, taking in the sky with its quickly moving clouds and the trees at the far edge of the field, he sees two crows swoop in and land on the patch of field where the ground is exposed. The scene is so different from anything he has seen in the Borinage, so wild with color and movement and vibrancy, he stands before it in awe. Everything shimmers, glittering with life and peace; his body is erased as he stands there, his self folded into what he sees.

There is always more life. No matter how you feel, no matter how you reach it, if you stand and look at a scene for long enough, you will always find more and more life. The baby Vincent hovers over the crows. He is dead; they are alive. This is it, Vincent thinks, this is life; this is my life.

He trudges through a town, the streets suddenly populated, women wearing pointy shoes and frilly hats and men in bowlers and jackets. Everyone is so busy; where are they all going? The day is warmer than yesterday was, and he stops at a pub and greedily drinks three glasses of water. When he is finished, he puts the glass on the bar and then sits there for a minute, watching the condensation fall off the sides. There is music, strangely, in the slow dance of the water drops; he realizes as he concentrates on them that he is hearing each of them as they slowly move. Each drop of water sounds a note.

In front of the pub, a woman who he is sure is a prostitute asks him for a match and holds out her pipe. She is wearing a worn velvet bodice and full, flowing skirts, torn in a few spots; her hair is done in some kind of black lace tied tight. What kind of woman smokes a pipe? She is not pretty, but coarse and manly, her face pockmarked in a strange pattern. She has a dark bruise across her right cheek, so that the pocket below her eye is yellowing and drooping low. He likes her instantly, but he tells her he doesn't have a light. She curtsies to him, the pipe in her mouth, and smiles, showing him the grip of her teeth, which are all nearly brown, a few of them missing. She calls him "Sugar" and tells him her name is Marie-Ann. She invites him upstairs.

Angeline, he thinks. Marie-Ann, Angeline. He peers at Marie-Ann and wills her to be Angeline; she is Angeline, wearing another woman's skin as a costume. Perhaps this is where she went; she ran away to here, to this woman's life. He tries to see into Marie-Ann's eyes and find Angeline there, and nearly reaches out to touch her face, to pull the skin and see if it will come free.

"Sugar?" Marie-Ann asks.

He sways before her. He shakes his head and moves on.

In London in 1873, when he was twenty, his first full year at Goupil's, he lived in the home of Eugénie Loyer, and secretly loved her. For nearly a year, he let the love of Eugénie fill him up. His longing was his constant companion; it was the heat in his heart all day long, from the first light of the sun until long after dark. His longing was London, his longing made the whole landscape bright and precious; so this was what was meant when poets wrote of love! London was an exalted place; all of life was out in the streets: There were stilt walkers and dwarfs, dancers and musicians with flutes and guitars, men singing ballads, women crooning love songs, people on horseback, people selling coffee, apples, sandwiches, children selling flowers and newspapers. There were fish on wooden carts, peppermint water in little cups, books and prints by the hundreds in stalls, chimney sweeps and dustmen calling out their services with their dirty hands to their mouths. London was a microcosm of the world; it was lit up and glowing and incredible. And at his home with Eugénie and her mother, the gardens were in bloom, the lilacs and hawthorn and laburnums in every garden and the chestnut trees along the lanes.

In love, he understood everything. He knew the souls of the trees and the songs of the birds and the movement of every body inside every building, the growth of every flower in every garden. Men held out their hands to shake in greeting and he felt the tenderness of their palms; it was as if every person he met in those days had their beating hearts in the bones of their hands. Nothing could be wrong, he understood, for the state of the earth was one of love. *Love, love,* he had heard the word used so many times, in church and in poetry and in books and on the streets, but only then did he understand.

He thought he and Eugénie understood each other, that their love need not be spoken to be true. One day at work in the showing room at Goupil's, he was seized by the notion that he would give a print to Eugénie; with the right print, he wouldn't need to explain his feelings, for she would see the expression in the work, and it would be better than any words he could ever muster.

For days he went to work as if he were a hunter, inspecting every print he saw to see if it might be the one for her. This one was too pastoral, this one too romantic, this one too black, too sentimental, too contrary, too religious, too rushed. Then, one afternoon, just as he had almost fully turned on himself and given up the project for good, his eye fell on just the right print. It was a pastoral scene, but not too tender and sentimental; not *imagined*, he felt, so much as captured. The image was of a mother and her daughter in a field of wheat. The two females were not touching; they each bent toward the ground. Their backs were to the artist. The little girl was crouching, her arms stretched out in front of her, and her mother bent next to her, her legs straight, skirts lost in the wheat. Though they were both occupied, they seemed to communicate deeply with each other, and this was what made him stop and hold the print up and lose himself in it as if it were a lake. Somehow, the artist managed to convey a sense of security in the two women, a sense of the feeling between them, the mother trusting the little one to do her work, the little one learning from the example of her mother, the bond between the two of them as clear and crucial as the growth of that field, as much a part of the earth as the soil under their feet. It took his breath away, that little print, which had been buried in a stack of other images, none of them even the slightest bit comparable to this work, only about the size of his two palms pressed together. He gazed at it for a long time, until someone moved in the other room and the floor creaked and he came back to where he was standing, in the back room at Goupil's, in London, holding the print in his hand.

He paid for it with nearly the whole of his week's salary, and that evening after he left work, the walk home to the Loyers' was more beautiful than it had been any night before. On the Westminster Bridge, there was an Italian iceman named Sal, a man he often interacted with on walks home from work, because he stationed his cart on the bridge toward the end of the afternoon and stayed there until evening. Vincent had a great fondness for Sal, though later when his mind was twisted with heartache he found different elements in him—stinginess, fear. In those happy days, though, he saw he was a hardworking man, a man who had his sights set on the future and yet one who was able to enjoy the present. He was a foreigner, as Vincent was, his English stilted and curved, and yet he had a comfort about him, a confidence. He stood inside of his life, he knew that his choices were right, and what his purpose was.

There was often a crowd of children clustered by his cart when Vincent approached, their faces streaked with the dirt of a day spent in the streets, their caps worn and dusty. Sal had his long and frayed cloth draped over his shoulder, streaked with the colors of his flavors where he'd wiped his hands: strawberry pink, raspberry purple, lemon yellow. "Ciao, Vincent!" he'd call over the heads of the urchins, who would all turn to look. Sal loved his celebrity, the way the children looked up at him from their spots in front of the cart with eyes full of wonder. He would pull the ice from beneath the cloths he kept over the wooden bucket and slip it into the paper cones, concealing it all as best he could on his side of the cart while he poured on the sugar water, so that he could then present it over the top of the cart to the children as if it were magic.

That day, Vincent pulled the print from his satchel and showed it to Sal. They had often stood together on that bridge as the sun waned, exclaiming together (as best they could with the language between them) over the colors that nature displayed, the beauty of the bridge, which was man-made and yet so pure that it seemed to wholly belong to the earth. Sal told Vincent the Westminster bridge was his favorite place to sell ices, even though it was a fair distance from Saffron Hill, where he lived, and though he had to push his cart all the way home after sunset and often got back far later than his colleagues, which sometimes meant that he got the worst spot for leaving his barrow overnight in the barrow yard.

He looked at Vincent's print, with the two women bent in the field; Vincent held it up to him because he was afraid he might get the sticky sugar on it if he were to take it in his hands. Sal peered over at it and Vincent could see that he was really looking. Was he curious to know where Vincent found value? Vincent didn't think Sal knew much about art, but this was just why he wanted to share the print with him; it was why he loved that print, really, because he felt in it something that would translate to anyone, not just to someone who had learned how to read the language.

And it seemed like Sal understood. He nodded and looked at Vincent's face, and he said, "*Bella.*" And then he told Vincent about his mother, who worked in a vineyard in Italy and who always had grape stains on her clothes. And he smiled, pointing to his own stained hands, and said he knew something about the way love and work was passed on.

That evening, Vincent unveiled the print in the sitting room after dinner, and Eugénie and her mother cooed over it just as he imagined they would. It was an image of the two of them, looking at an image of the two of them, art and life reflected back at each other. Watching the two of them looking at that print, Vincent was deeply moved. He helped Eugénie to hang it on the wall next to the fireplace—Eugénie holding her finger in the right place while he leaned over with the tool to hammer in the nail. He placed the nail where her finger was and for a mere fraction of a second their hands touched, and a fire blazed in him.

Eugénie had often asked where it was Vincent walked on his long afternoons of rambling, and he had told her about some of the places he liked to visit: Rotten Row in Hyde Park, where hundreds of ladies and gentlemen rode on horseback, all the parts of town where there were beautiful parks with a wealth of flowers such as he had never seen anywhere else. One Sunday in May, a few weeks after he gave her the Goupil's print, she asked to go with him on a walk to Covent Garden. On their way, they walked through Lambeth, and Vincent told Eugénie about a couple he had met who worked in Covent Garden, the wife as a flower woman and the husband as a horse keeper, his hours daily from four in the morning to eight at night. They had come to London from the country, hoping for higher wages, and lived in Lambeth, but they had been turned out of their last home because of the most recent flooding of the Thames, when the rising water had flowed right into their room and climbed up their walls, and in one terrible night they had lost everything they had, including their infant child, who had caught an illness that night while they sat up with her above the water and had not lasted for a week beyond. The walls in their new home were stained with water, and there was mold in all the corners, but it was clean and they were settled again.

Vincent caught himself telling all this to Eugénie and felt

foolish, for what girl wants to hear about the trials of the poor? These were stories that interested him, and he found them beautiful, but he knew enough to understand they were not the images of seduction, and that Eugénie was a delicate girl who surely wanted to think more about the growth of flowers than the deaths of babies from floods. He shut his mouth and tried to keep quiet, to walk in silence next to her, but he could not keep himself from chattering. She pointed to a robin and he behaved as if he knew everything there was to know about robins, their mating habits and their nocturnal rhythms, the number of feathers they had on each of their wings.

By the time they reached the Westminster Bridge, Vincent felt wretched and wanted to turn around. But there was Sal. "Ciao, Vincent!" he called, as he always did, and they made their way toward him. Inside, Vincent was grumbling, his mind turned dark. He needed to tell Eugénie how he felt. What good were all the words he had to offer, if he couldn't say "I love you"?

Sal cleared all of the children away to make way for Eugénie to approach his cart, swinging his arms and ushering the urchins back. He made a real production of making her ice, hiding it beneath his cloth, and then presenting it to her with flourish, using his hands as if he were unveiling a magic trick, and she clapped and reached for it with joy. He looked at Vincent and declared Eugénie "*bella*," and winked, and Vincent felt a fraud. For all those months he felt that all was understood between Eugénie and him, and yet suddenly he felt it exposed for what it was, which was something imagined, something unreal, and therefore sinful. He was suddenly jealous of Sal, of the way Eugénie reached for what he had to offer her, of the easy way that he declared her beautiful. He felt a bolt of hot anger. He imagined himself with long, battering-ram arms; he wanted to sweep them across the bridge and push all of those children, and that cart, and Sal, too, clear off and into the river. He saw the group of them in the water, their hands thrashing above the surface, grasping for something to hold on to, their mouths like the mouths of goldfish, starved for air. He clenched his fists and commanded himself to remain still.

They kept on for a ways beyond the bridge, Eugénie eating her ice, but inside him was a great tumult and he knew he could not keep on for long. He tried to stop the tide in him; he could feel the rush in his gut and his groin; a tingling had begun under his skin. They walked next to each other and he closed his eyes. He savored those last few moments of walking as if they were steps taken on a gangplank over a cold ocean.

They came to a stop before an Italian street band; a boy played a harp, another a fiddle, and a man with a bushy beard the guitar, a pipe hanging from his mouth and slowly emitting smoke, the occasional puffs he took causing it to bounce up and down. The music they made was dissonant and interesting, it sounded like no tune Vincent had heard before, and it gave him a deep surge of confidence. He grabbed Eugénie's arm. "Eugénie," he half whispered and half rasped, his throat closing on him, "I love you."

She turned to him and blinked, surprised. She looked down at his hand on her arm. "What?" she said, though of course she had heard him.

He pushed on. "I love you," he said again, leaning toward her. "I have always loved you."

She wriggled her arm from his grip and her face fell into shadow. She shook her head as if she were trying to shake off an insect. "Vincent," she whispered, embarrassed, and her next word was said with force: "No."

She moved away from the musicians and he followed, his heart leaping, his blood like drums inside his ears. She walked quickly, her face flushed, her eyebrows turned into each other and the piece of flesh between them raised in little hills. She was still shaking her head; she had learned something she had not wanted to know.

"I am engaged, Vincent," she said, hustling now toward home. "I am going to be married. Don't you know that? Didn't you know that, Vincent?" Her voice had a mix of accusation, of anger, of frustration, and of pleading.

He had not known. His name was George, she told him, and he had been the lodger before Vincent; he had slept in Vincent's room, in his bed. He had looked out Vincent's window; he had looked up at his same ceiling; he had looked in Vincent's mirror and seen his own face.

Vincent went to his room that night reeling and sick, shamed and angry. He didn't want to stay there, but where could he go? He already had a trip home planned; he was to leave at the end of June, and it was agreed that after that he would not come back to the Loyers' home. The family that had been his were now strangers; they were crumpled puppets. They turned from him when he came into the room. He had once again become a ghost. He stumbled through his days as if shades had been pulled down before his eyes; the city turned sinister and frightening, filled with spirits and wickedness, a city of broken hearts and dirty corners, old and twisted bony fingers that reached for your money and clasped onto your soul. He faltered at work, the women in long silken dresses asking after paintings that meant nothing were intolerable, and he scowled at them and retreated to the cover of the dark back room for entire days.

It was one long night that June that he found the woman called Anna and gave to her what he had been imagining for so many months would be shared with Eugénie. He had passed Anna's house many times and had looked in with curiosity, but he had never gone inside. The first floor was a pub, as was the case in most of those houses, and there was frequently music, the beat spilling out to the sidewalk, men and women dancing and twirling, skirts swishing and boots stomping, loud laughter rolling and voices catching and competing with the melody.

He went inside timidly, and the smell of the place came over him as if he had entered the bulb of a pipe: it was smoke and drink and bodies, sour and sweet, leather and whiskey and breath and perfume wafting from skin. He sat at the bar and ordered a drink. He was feeling wretched, and something about the atmosphere in that place calmed him. There was an equality to it; no one cared who you had been before you came through the door, if you'd ever done anything you were proud of or anything you wished you could take back, only that you could hold your drink and enjoy a tune. It was invisibility of a different sort, not brought on by who you were, by something you had done, or by anyone else that had come before you; invisibility, rather, that was fellowship, invisibility that was welcome, belonging, invisibility that was granted to all.

Around his second drink, she sat down next to him. She was perhaps ten years older than he, and told him her name was Anna, his sister's and his mother's name, a fact that gave him pause. But this woman was so unlike his sister and his mother that he quickly left this fact behind, a ripple in a lake that gently and gradually went calm again.

She was rather tall and strongly built—she did not have a lady's hands, but the hands of one who works—but she was not coarse or common, and had something very womanly about her. Dark curls that barely hung together and dark charcoal under her eyes, one of which was diverted always to the right, as if it were keeping watch. She reminded him of some curious figure by Chardin or Frère, or perhaps Jan Steen. She had had many cares, one could see that, and life had been hard for her; she was not distinguished, nothing extraordinary, nothing unusual. He thought of a quote from Michelet: "Every woman at every age, if she loves and is a good woman, can give a man, not the infinite of the moment, but the moment of the infinite."

She took him up the staircase to her room, where there was a wooden four-poster bed with one side covered by a faded pink curtain, presumably to block the light coming from the window beyond, where the hanging curtain was thin and torn. There was a worn couch that appeared to have once been brown velvet but was now patched and bald in places, and a washbasin on a stand by the base of the bed with a stack of cloths next to it. Other than that, the room was bare. The wallpaper peeled and cracked like sunburned skin; his senses were so alive, he was sure that he could hear the fragments crumbling, disintegrating, and floating away.

It was a journey between darkness and light, the hours he spent with Anna. She was a warm woman, and she took her time with him. He was angry and heartbroken at the same time that he was awestruck by what he saw before him, by what was given him to touch: a woman's body, available, every inch of flesh revealed. He was lucky and grateful and in love with Anna that night. He wanted to treat her with great loving care; he wanted to give back to her the compassion he saw when she looked at him, when she bent to kiss his face, when she laid her palms on his skin. And at the same time he wanted to crush her. She was a woman, as Eugénie was, and who was to say that compassion wasn't the same as pity? He felt out of control and rabid; he could not rein himself in. There was no distinction between inside and out; his organs were touchable; she closed her hand around him and he felt his lungs, his liver, his heart, his intestines respond.

He seethed. She was beautiful, she was ugly; she was not Eugénie, she was Eugénie; he would flay her, he would puncture her perfect goose bumps, she did not love him. Love was hatred, love was love. He couldn't see; he was blind; he saw the world in a collarbone. Her breasts were his mother's, they were hers, they were flopping and used, the site of so many men's hands, so much love and violence, and then they were tender and sweet golden apples, Eugénie's breasts, which he took into his mouth with tenderness that brought tears. He felt sure that when he brought his head to her chest he could leave it there; he would lift his neck and his head would remain, buried and burrowing, disappearing into her skin.

When it was over, he came back to himself, intact and broken. He felt shame, but he also felt no small measure of joy, and the combination of these was confusing. He lay in Anna's bed, and her leg was draped over his, and the weight of it was so pleasing and he felt such excitement over what they had done that he wanted to do it again, and he was sure that if he touched her in the right way, it would be as simple as that. This was new to him, and he allowed himself for one brief moment to let it make him feel like a man, with a woman at hand who would respond to his touch, who was waiting for him to touch her. He thought perhaps he should love Anna, perhaps he did love Anna, perhaps he was supposed to love Anna all along.

Then she got up to wash, standing at the basin by the bed, and the spell was broken. Anna was not the woman he loved, he did not know her, and yet he could still taste her flesh in his mouth. She was washing the evidence of him from her body. Her face was expressionless as she squeezed the washcloth over her knee; the water ran down in beautiful crystal trails, erasing him. He was a thing that could be washed off with water. An invisible, creeping thing, sinful, unclean; a thing to be scrubbed and sloughed and purged; eliminated; purified; exorcised; punished; sterilized; burned.

The road is quiet once again, the houses spread far from one another, crows alighting in groups from the side of the road. Once again it is nearly dark. He shifts the weight of the knapsack he carries over his shoulder and thinks of Theo in his freshly polished shoes. What is he doing now? Vincent imagines Theo at the Goupil's office in Paris, with a customer, a woman with a bustle and a feather in her hair. He is nodding and smiling at her, that thin, polite smile he gives when he doesn't agree, the same smile he gave to him, Vincent, that day by the Sorcière mine. Or perhaps he is in the back room, his top hat resting next to him on the table as he eats his lunch, hard-boiled eggs and green beans, a perfect cut of turkey breast, and a steaming cup of coffee.

His stomach growls at the thought of food. When was the last time he ate?

Dear Theo, he thinks, I am not the same any longer! Don't you see?

Dear Theo, what is the point of being a man if you must stay the same?

Dear Theo, I do not wish to be a man who stays the same.

In front of him on the road there is a man walking next to a horse drawing a wagon loaded with tools and miscellaneous things. The horse is old and thin and moves at a glacial pace; Vincent is quickly alongside them. He can see the horse's ribs, which protrude left and right from his sides as he slowly clops along.

"Good day," Vincent says to the man next to the horse as he comes up alongside them.

"Good day," the man says in response. He is wearing a wide-brimmed hat and a coat that looks warmer than Vincent's. He looks twice at Vincent, once fast and then once with a lingering gaze. Vincent is not sure which aspect of him could be so interesting.

The man tells Vincent that he sells the items in his cart to the farmers in the area. "Whatever they might need, I have," he says with a smile. Vincent notices he is missing two of his teeth. "I like to say I make people happy all day long." He asks Vincent if he needs anything, or if he has a knife that he needs sharpened, as he does that, too. They are stopped now, and the horse sends a spray of urine into the dirt of the road.

"I have nothing," Vincent says, "and so I need nothing." He

says it quietly, wishing it to be a statement of fact and not a dismissal. He wants to ask the man if he has any food or water, but he guesses by the horse's ribs that they are both as hard off as he is. To his surprise, then, the man produces two apples from a bag at the front of the cart and offers one to Vincent, giving the other to the horse, who takes it greedily. "You hungry?" he asks Vincent. "I was just about to stop anyway."

They sit at the side of the road and share the apple, passing it back and forth between them. They hardly speak. Vincent listens to the sound of the horse chewing and of the crunch of the apple as he and the man bite into it.

"So where are you off to, then?" asks the man after a long while.

Vincent swallows, and fights the familiar resistance to answering any questions. "Paris," he says, "to see my brother." He passes back the apple.

"Ah," says the man. "Paris. Too big and busy for me." He takes another bite.

They chew in silence for a few minutes, and then Vincent finds himself speaking. "I'm coming from the Borinage," he hears himself say, and is surprised. "In Belgium. I was a lay preacher there for almost a year."

The man hands the apple back to him; there is only the core left now. Vincent bites off the bottom.

"Ah," the man says, "and so what do you do now?"

Vincent chews, and hands back the rest of the core. He shakes his head and then nods. "That's the question everyone wants an answer to," he says.

He can see the man is waiting patiently for more, but he has nothing else to say. He looks out over the field and is quiet. Next to him he can sense the man coming to understand that their conversation is over. Vincent does not look at him because he knows he will see the familiar look of confusion, disappointment, and then resignation, the stages he always to seems make a man's face pass through.

"Well," the man says, "I guess we should be moving on, then." He stands and wipes his hands on the sides of his pants.

They walk on alongside each other for a few miles, nearly silent, the horse clopping, occasional clinking sounds coming from the cart, before the man, who has told Vincent his name is George, turns off onto the road into a farm. He holds his hand out to shake Vincent's in order to say good-bye. "Wait," says Vincent. He reaches into his pocket and pulls out his sketches. "I'd like to repay you for your kindness."

"What's this?" asks George.

"They're just little sketches that I've done along the road." He riffles through them, unsure of which one to give away. He chooses the sketch of the cow chewing, and looks up at George as he passes it over.

"So this is what you do, then," says George, grinning at him. He takes the sketch, looks at it, and nods. Vincent can read nothing on his face of what he thinks of the picture.

"Thank you, Vincent," George says, "I will keep this," and holds out his hand.

They shake hands and Vincent watches him and his horse amble away, feeling strangely bereft of them, not wanting to continue on alone.

He meditates afterward on his encounter with George. What kind of pride is it that has him put his hand in his pocket and bring out those sketches, when he knows they are not adequate payment for the kindness he receives? A day or so ago he gave a different sketch to a farmer's wife in exchange for a few slices of bread and a cup of coffee; he remembers her face as she looked at the drawing: unimpressed, confused. James and Bertha, too, accepted the drawing as if it were the work of a child. Still, he hears George's voice: *So this is what you do.*

Two months ago, in March, he had made a different trek, walking to Courrières, a town not too far over the French border, to try to see the painter Jules Breton. He thinks of it now, remembering the longing in it, how desperately he felt he might gain something from the encounter with the artist.

In 1875, when Vincent was working with Harry Gladwell at Goupil's in Paris, he saw Breton at a salon opening with his wife and two daughters. He was a commanding presence, a hulking man with long hair combed back from his forehead and a thick beard of black and white, ragged as a mountain range. That year his painting at the salon was *The Feast of Saint John*, peasant girls dancing on a summer evening around the St John's bonfire, in the background the village with its church and the moon above it. From across the room, Vincent stared at Breton, trying to match the man with the work. It was as impossible as looking under a man's skin while he passed by. He tugged on Harry's sleeve, pointing out the artist, trying to impart to Harry why he was important, but he could tell that Harry barely cared. Later, back in their room while Harry slept, Vincent wrote in his notebook: *Even if we could see inside a man, glimpse his blood and his brain, we would not see what we were looking for. There is a reason why feeling is invisible; it is why art is necessary.*

How would Breton paint the miner's life? A dark palette, with single brushes of light—the glow of a lamp lighting the sweat on a man's body; the canvas taken up with rock, only a sliver where a man lies. A canvas covered with strokes of black, a single corner of glowing yellow and a man's face, illuminated in the lamplight but black as the night. For months in the Borinage, Vincent had meditated on what such a painting would look like. He spoke to Alard of it one day in February in the salon, telling him about Breton, "a living being of the artist species," and describing the difficulty of representing the miners, who worked in the dark.

"How would an artist do it?" he said, his eyes glowing. He had made Alard and himself cups of tea on the coal stove in the front of the room, the cups on loan from the Denis house. Alard sat on the floor with his cup in his hands, Smoke, the cat, purring on his lap. "I have thought about it a lot. The experience of being down in the mine is unmatched, and I have never seen an image that comes close to it. Can you imagine? A painting that could capture the way the cage drops, the way you fall through the earth with the speed of a train? I wonder what Breton would do if he were to try it."

Smoke watched Vincent through a quarter slit of his eye. Vincent told himself to stop, to change the subject, to engage the boy more generously, and yet he could not make his mouth remain closed.

"How do you paint a subject with so little light? How do you represent what is unrepresentable? All that darkness down there, those bodies toiling in the lamplight, it is so beautiful and awful, it deserves to be painted, but I wonder if it is impossible. It would be like—well, can you make a painting of despair? Can you make a painting of grief? Can you make a painting of God?"

Alard put his teacup down and picked up one of the pieces of coal that was in front of him, pulling a piece of paper toward him. "Let's try it!" he said, and quickly went to work, covering his paper with dark strokes of coal, leaving only one streak white down the middle of the page. When he was done, he held it up to Vincent, who was still pacing. "Here you go!" he said with glee. Vincent took the paper and looked at it, then turned to the boy. "Alard," he exclaimed, "you're a genius!" Alard blushed with pride.

A month later, in March, desperate to see and speak with Breton, he trekked to Breton's house in a too-thin jacket. The first night, he slept in a thin haystack while a steady drip of freezing rain fell on him all night, and then turned back before reaching Breton's house, with no money and a terrible foolish feeling.

He walks on past the bend in the road where George turned off, and thinks that perhaps it is up to him to make the painting of the miners that he dreamed about. *So this is what you do.* Could it be? He dreams of how such a tribute might come to be, and what such a thing might look like. He walks with his eyes closed, concentrating, thinking of the descent into the mine, the cage falling fast, Angeline's elbow a stone in his side; he sees lamplight cast onto wet stone, glints of white on a mottled surface, and a dot of light at the top of the tunnel like a single star on a canvas of black. He sees cells with men working, like the caves of a honeycomb, lit one next to the other in dancing shadows and warm lantern glow; a man's body, stripped to the waist, lit from the side where a lamp is hanging, body gleaming with sweat and streaked with black, behind him a canary in a cage.

He can see the images in his head—arresting, beautiful, convulsive images of human toil luminous in darkness—but he knows his hands could never execute his vision, and so the idea deflates and crumples. He sees a man's back, a landscape of burning flesh, skin rippling and blistered, then flakes of skin floating in a pan of water. A man's eye stares up from a face without skin; the shape of Angeline disintegrates, again and again, into obscurity.

Dear Theo, I cannot do it; I can see it but I cannot make it. Dear Father, you were right: I am good for nothing. He walks on, the baby Vincent next to him, chanting, *This is your life, this is your life, this is your life.*

1879

Dear Theo,

I know it would not make sense to most that a man could give up a warm bed in a house that always smelled like fresh bread to sleep in the dust and cold of a hovel in the depths of a February winter, but this is what I did.

In the hut, I laid a few coal sacks end to end in front of the hearth and filled them with straw. I didn't have much coal, and I didn't want to take any away from the miners and their children, so I lay close to the fire and reached out to stoke it every few hours with a poker that I found when I arrived. I lay listening to the fire crackle and pop, watching the shadows that were cast onto the walls opposite the flame. In them I saw scenes of consolation, a peasant with a scythe, a landscape like Van der Maaten's *Funeral in a Cornfield*, which I had sent to Father to hang in his study, black figures making their way into the tall stalks. I thought of Zundert, the family gathered in the back room at Christmas, the candle lights dancing all around the room, Father's voice reading us stories from the family history. It was better, I thought, to have a space that I could call my own.

I curled up before the small fire, silhouettes of light and darkness moving before me. The spider's web in the corner grew, silently.

•

Dear Theo,

In late February, ten months ago, Father came to the Borinage to visit. Madame Denis sent him a letter, reporting with concern that I had moved from her house to an abandoned mining hut; he came at once. One afternoon I looked up from my bed of straw and there in the doorway stood Pa in his long dark coat. Can you imagine? I thought for a long moment that I must be hallucinating, but then the vision spoke: "Vincent, what is this?"

I sat up, blinking into the light. "Father?"

"Of course. Did you think I would not come when I heard about this decision of yours?" He came into the hut and stood near my pallet, looking around. "And do you think this is a home fit for a man of God?"

Getting to my feet, I felt my cheeks flushing with shame, though as I stood next to Father, I was not sure why. Father looked me over in the dim light, leaned his head close, and sniffed at me. "When was the last time you washed, boy?" he asked, his face twisted in disgust.

I kept my eyes on the ground. Do you remember how he always made us show him our hands before supper? That was how I felt, like I was waiting for him to pronounce them clean enough for me to eat. I ignored this last comment and said quietly instead, "If this is a home fit for miners, why not for a man of God? Are they not the people of God?"

Father looked at me sternly. "There is not even any place clean enough to sit," he said.

We went for a walk in the snow to see the coal brought up from a mine called the Three Mounds. While we walked, Father spoke. "We have spoken of this before, Vincent," he said. "Degrading yourself is not the way to reach God. Surely it is not the way to get what you are after in this case, which is a permanent position. How do you expect to serve if you starve yourself, or are too tired to rise to preach?"

I didn't know how to express myself to him; you know I have never quite been able to. I scrambled to think of ways to explain myself that he might understand. "But Father," I said, "how can I be a friend to the poor if I do not suffer like them? How can I minister to this flock if I know nothing of what life is like for them?"

"Did you ever consider that your job is other than to be their friend?" Father responded. He reminded me of the days when I used to go with him to visit the Zundert countrymen, how the friendship between them and him was different from one born of collective circumstance. "If God had wanted you to be a miner," he said, "He would have made you one!"

It was God's will, said Father, that I be who I was, and that I help the miners in the way that I knew how, and was sent there to do, by teaching them the Word, and by being with them in Christ. That was all God wanted from me. "Each of us has his own trials," he said. "Each of us has his own sufferings to face. Yours are different from those of these miners, but that does not mean you cannot understand them as men and women who are on this earth the same as you are, and, the same as you, are in need of fellowship, and the path to Heaven."

I was confused, of course, because this was precisely what I thought I was doing—understanding the miners as best I could. If my way was different from his, did that make me any less capable or pious? But I couldn't speak with him about this, Theo; we simply didn't have the same language, and I didn't want to argue.

He asked me how I was keeping up with the preaching, whether I was holding regular services where the miners would have a chance to learn and pray. I assured him, yes, though I admit to you that I had begun to think of the preaching as less important than the other kinds of fellowship I could offer.

Despite the scolding, I was glad to have Father with me. I pointed out to him the way the blackthorn bushes burned like black flames against the white snow, and how our footprints left white craters that were traced with black, imprints of our humanity on the otherwise pure expanse of nature. When we reached the mine, we stood by the place where the carts were brought up from the earth and went up the ramp to the breaker. I told Father what I knew about how the operation worked. Father was pleased, and remarked at how the carts of coal were signs that there was life underground; he said, "Think of all the activity, all the work that is being done beneath our feet!" He looked at the ground with reverence, as if it were glass and he could see through it. I was happy to see him so moved.

On the way back, I agreed to return to the Denises', and we gathered my things from the hut and climbed the hill. I washed in the Denis tub and donned my suit, which I hadn't worn since my first days in the Borinage. When I came into the kitchen wearing it, my face scrubbed clean, Father was sitting at the table in his shirtsleeves, Madame Denis standing nearby, wearing her apron. Both of them looked at me with relief and joy. "There's my boy," said Father, and I felt my heart swell with a confusing mixture of pride and rebellious anger. Why should he love me more when I wore a suit?

I took Father to visit the Decrucqs, and on the way there we passed Angeline. She was coming from the slag heap; her face was swept with black and she carried a filthy sack stuffed with coal. I saw her eyes dart over me, taking in my suit and my cleaned-up appearance, and I felt caught, embarrassed, as if I had betrayed her, though of course I had not.

We stopped to say hello next to a house that had been partially consumed by the earth. It had been built over land that had been weakened significantly by the mining underground, and at some point the ground had shifted and the kitchen had been swallowed. This was apparently not too uncommon an occurrence, for when I asked about it, I was met by nonchalance. What did a person expect, if he lived in mining country? The family that lived in the collapsed house lost most of their furniture, but they managed to salvage their stove before it went too deep, with the help of a few of their neighbors and a long length of thick rope.

I introduced Father and Angeline, and they briefly spoke, and I explained to Father that the slag heap was where the villagers gathered their coal. Angeline told Father she worked in the mine but that still she had to climb the heap to gather coal to heat her hut. Father expressed surprise at her mining—I do not know if he thought no women worked in the mine, or if he just didn't expect those women to look like Angeline. "It is hard," she said, looking down at her hands clutching the bag. "My family has many mouths to feed."

"Is there no other way?" Father asked, and I could see his mind trying to come up with one. "There is no other way," she said stoically. She nodded to us and went on, and I could tell Father was moved, because he said nothing the rest of the way to the Decrucqs'. I wondered at his silence: What was he puzzling over? It seemed possible that Angeline had taught him something in that brief encounter, something that I had been trying to say but could not. Her presence, her circumstance had silenced him. What could he say back to her? Nothing—there was nothing to say. It made me feel vindicated, I admit it, Theo, and I admired Angeline all the more.

In the Decrucq house, they were just sending the boys to bed. Charles was placing the hot bricks in the bedclothes at the foot of the bed before the boys climbed in. This is a frequent technique in the miners' houses; they heat the bricks in the oven and then wrap them in towels or cotton cloths or even, when there is nothing else, sacking, and transfer them to the beds to keep them warm after they have tamped out the fire. Usually it is just one or two bricks, but in the dead of winter a family uses as many as four to a bed. "When you wake up in the morning," Decrucq said, tucking in the boys' thin blanket, "the bricks are often still warm."

I was happy to see Decrucq and Pa talking, Decrucq telling him all the same stories about his accidents and scars, and Pa leaning back in his chair and nodding, holding his warm cup of coffee, as I had so often seen him do in the cottages of so many other peasants in what seemed such a long-ago and familiar time.

That night I sat up with Pa in the Denis kitchen with its sweet smell, and we spoke of many things. Father said, "That man Decrucq strikes me as a very solid person," and then he recalled a parishioner of his back in Zundert, a man who looked a lot like Decrucq but with fewer physical scars. Father was leaving in the morning, and I suddenly felt as if I were mourning for him, though he sat right there before me; I had such a melancholy feeling, I thought for sure I was going to weep. I remembered when he came to visit me in Amsterdam at Uncle Jan's, and after having taken him to the station, after having watched the train until it disappeared and the smoke was no longer visible, I returned home; Father's chair was still near the table with the books and copybooks we had examined that day, and though I knew that we would see each other again soon, I cried like a child. This is not a side of me that I like to show to Father, or really to anyone, even to you, Theo, but there are times when I cannot hold it back.

There, in the Denis kitchen, across from Father, I had that same feeling. He was saying, "She was a fortunate woman, Mrs. Beelin, with two beautiful children," speaking of another parishioner, and I was fighting against time. I watched him and slowly I couldn't hear his words at all, I could only see him, his lips moving and his familiar face expressing his thoughts, and it was as if he were drifting away from me even as he sat there unmoving. I felt time coming at me like an enormous ocean wave. I thought myself too weak to face it. I wanted to grab hold of Pa's body and cling; I wanted to reach and hang and grip and clamber and hug, for fear of being swept away.

If only it were true that a man, holding tightly enough to another man or woman, to his mother or his father or his lover or his friend, could stop the moving of time. If only! If only there were a way to shield ourselves, to stop it from pulling us down and away and along. If only our bodies were strong enough to keep us tethered to the shore.

•

December 10

Dear Theo,

No doubt you remember my friend Harry Gladwell, whom I lived and worked with in Paris—the one who took over my position when I left Goupil's? He must be your colleague now; I admit this is strange to think about.

Harry and I used to stay up late in our tiny apartment and read together passages from the Bible; he was new to it, and I was just coming into my fervor for it then, having recently left London and becoming increasingly dissatisfied with the art-dealing life. I remember I dragged Harry to countless sermons on our off-hours, walked him to churches all over the city to listen to different preachers and sit in different halls of worship. He said he was interested, and humored me well, but often I could see he was tired, his hair falling in his face and his feet dragging, and had only come with me so I wouldn't be alone. I suppose I did a lot of that with you, too, didn't I, when we were young—though then I dragged you to birds' nests rather than to churches.

I was thinking of Gladwell today, remembering a trip I took to London to see our sister Anna—must have been three years ago now—and how I stopped off along the way to see Harry's parents. I was in Ramsgate, England, at the time, working at that boys' school on the coast, and every day at dusk I would walk along the ocean. It never ceased to be amazing, watching how the day waned, the waves growing luminous in the slowly dimming light, the seagulls flying lower and seeming to hush out of respect for the ritual of the coming night. I would take off my shoes and walk barefoot in the sand, enjoying the sensation of the grains against my feet. Occasionally I saw a seal emerge from a wave, its dark, massive head turning to calmly observe me before going under again, and I thought of how at ease the creature was in the ocean, which was such an inhospitable place for me. Some evenings I walked so far away from the school that I missed supper and was late putting the boys to bed, arriving back long after dark, making my way back by the light of the swinging beam of the lighthouse.

Those walks were a great balm to the confusion that roiled in me then; they encouraged me, with their joyful solemnity, to continue on despite my fears. I walked for hours and hours, back and forth over that beach, when I was preparing my very first sermon, which I gave at the little church near the school.

I remember all of that so well, and it is so strange to think of it now. I paced the floor the whole night before I gave that first sermon, wanting so much for it to go over well, hoping I was not keeping the boys, who slept in the room with me, awake with my feverish movement. The next day, after the sermon was done, there was a charge in me, the feeling that my whole body was lit from the inside, that I had a power inside my fingertips that was magical and true. I thought it was because I had spoken the word of God; I thought it was because I was on the right path, because I had identified what I was meant for and was moving toward it. Now I know that was not true. So what was the source of that powerful feeling, and how can I make it come back again?

A few days after that first sermon, that energy unabated, I walked from Ramsgate to London to see Anna, who was teaching in Welwyn, just past the outskirts of London. It was a journey of about a day, if I walked fast, and slept a few hours somewhere along the way.

I arrived at Gladwell's parents' house in the evening, where I was to stay the night. His parents settled me in Harry's bedroom, which had a familiar sensation even without my friend there.

"Vincent," Gladwell's mother asked me over supper, "are you happy in your new position?"

The room was warm and smelled of yams and a sharp spice I couldn't identify. Gladwell's sister was there, her hair tied back in a braid; she did not look at me, but kept her eyes on her plate while she cut her meat. Gladwell's father chewed his beef while he waited for me to answer.

"Oh yes," I said. "The boys are such fun, they don't give me much trouble, and the other teachers at the school look out for me because they know that I'm new."

"So is teaching what you want to do, then?" asked Mr. Gladwell, still chewing, then taking a sip of wine. He looked at me with purity—he was not judging me, he was only genuinely curious to know who I was.

"Well, right now I'm just an assistant teacher," I said. "I'd say my job is more to be with the boys than it is to really teach them. We read together at night, we play games together and go for walks. I don't really prepare any of their lessons."

Mr. Gladwell nodded. I hadn't answered his question, we both knew.

"I'm not sure if I want to be a teacher, Mr. Gladwell," I said, and put down my fork. I knew I could trust them. "Really, I'm not sure what I want to be. Actually, I have written some letters to ministers here in London to try to see if I might get a position in the Church."

Their eyebrows went up, and even Gladwell's sister looked up at me, a quick glance. "Oh!" said Mrs. Gladwell. "Well, that sounds promising! Harry told us all about how you helped him learn his Bible while you two were living together."

"Yes," I said, picking up my fork again and smiling as I remembered my nights with Harry, bent over the Bible in the candlelight, Harry's eyelids drooping with fatigue. "I think I might be better suited for work in the Church than in a school like Mr. Stokes's. They have been good to me there, but I can't help feeling like I might be able to be of more help elsewhere."

There was a pause. Mrs. Gladwell looked at me for a moment, smiling, then shook her head as if to get rid of a thought and turned back to her plate. I looked to Mr. Gladwell, who gazed across the table at her and said, smiling, "Mrs. Gladwell?"

She looked up, still smiling. "Oh," she said, "it's just that for a minute there I felt I could see why you and Harry are such good friends." She paused, as if wondering whether to go on. Her husband and I were watching her with curiosity. She continued. "You both carry the weight of the world on your shoulders, that's all," she said. "Here you are, what, twenty-three?" I nodded. "Twenty-three, and you are frustrated with your job because you are not helping enough people."

She and Mr. Gladwell laughed. I was puzzled, though I smiled politely.

After supper I helped Mrs. Gladwell clean the dishes and put them away, and then retreated to Harry's room to be alone. When I said good night to Gladwell's parents, Mr. Gladwell kissed me on my forehead. "Dear boy," he said, "don't forget, you don't need to have it all figured out. It is foolish to even try."

I think now of that visit with Gladwell's parents, and I see new wisdom in the way that they dealt with me. It occurs to me that though they were kinder, they may have been saying much the same thing as you were when you came to visit me.

Just two months after that visit, their daughter, Harry's sister, died. She fell off her horse while riding on Blackheath. I went as soon as I heard, and when I got there, they had all just come back from the funeral; it was a real house of mourning. I had feelings of embarrassment and shame at seeing that deep grief, I'm not sure why. That evening I talked with Harry for a long time about all kinds of things, about the kingdom of God and about his Bible, and we walked up and down on the station platform waiting for my train, talking. We knew each other so well, his work was my work, the people he knew at Goupil's I knew, too, his life was my life. I felt that it was given to me to see so deeply into their family affairs because I loved them, not so much because I knew the particulars of those affairs but because I felt the tone and feeling of their being and life.

I see now that I knew nothing about death then, nothing at all. I wish I could say so to Harry.

•

December 13

Dear Theo,

It was Paul Fontaine who took me down into the mine for the first time. It was a few mornings after Father left, in early March; I had been in the Borinage for almost three months. "If you do not go," Paul told me, "you will not know this place at all." Of course he was right; I had no idea how much so. I thought that climbing the coal mountain was a turning point, but I should have known—it was not the ascending but the descending that was essential. It shames me now that it took me so long to go underground.

We met outside the Denises' at quarter past three in the morning. The world was total darkness; even the birds were quiet. My boots crunched over a thin layer of frost. Paul strode confidently down the path toward the mine, as sure-footed as if it were daylight. I followed close behind him. As we neared the gate we could see bodies begin to materialize out of the dark, miners shuffling forward to work, half-asleep. No one spoke.

I followed Paul into one of the buildings. Inside, it was dim and disorienting, passageways leading off this way and that, the echoing clang of noises I didn't recognize, shadows flickering onto stairways and into unknown rooms. "This is the boiler house," Paul said gruffly, and briefly paused for me to peer in. The heat was intense; sweat leapt to my forehead and hands. Inside the room I saw six boilers, and clouds of white steam hissing from what I assumed to be safety valves, steel pistols on their sides, the steam shooting out of the boilers like silos that had sprung leaks, violent and then easing into clouds as it billowed up. There was a man standing in the midst of the boilers, feeding one of them with shovels of coal, the door to the boiler standing open and exposing its guts, the coal burning red inside. I wondered how it was possible that he was not burned from the heat in that room.

We continued on to the locker room, where we found miners busily removing their clogs and thick wool stockings and locking them into the small cupboards that lined the walls. The cupboards were roughly built, and some of them hung from the wall, padlocks broken and rusted, the cupboard doors drooping from their hinges. Some of them had been patched with newer pieces of wood and twisted nails.

In the center of the room there was a glowing stove, packed to the brim with coal, sputtering and hissing. I thought it seemed angry, this fluttering creature. This was no tame hearth, Theo, nothing like what we had in our living room in the winter; it was a monster, gurgling flames and guzzling the precious coal. The miners were not afraid of it; they clustered around it on wooden benches, closer and closer, and if a spark flew onto them, they waved an arm as if to shoo an insect. There was a general lively din in the room as the miners warmed themselves and got ready to descend into the earth; they teased one another and flirted with the girls and laughed and shouted and stood with their backs to the fire and took deep breaths, storing up the heat in their bones. It was a form of worship—I could see that right away, and had no doubt that our father would agree with me.

I saw Hubert Aert, whose wife hosted my weekly Bible classes, sitting in the group; Mark Florine was there as well, the father of Carel, who came to my makeshift school. When the miners saw me and Paul coming into the room, a general call went up. "Fontaine!" someone hollered. "Come for your annual tour?" "Look sharp," bellowed someone else, "Fontaine's here for inspection, and he's brought Pastor Vincent for extra judgment!"

"All right, settle down," Paul said, smiling. "Don't mind us."

I saw Decrucq sitting by the furnace. He was in his element, holding court; it was as if all the other miners were his minions. "Monsieur Vincent," he said, grinning, "have you come to see how we earn our fifty centimes a day?"

"That's right," I said. I looked around the room and was surprised, suddenly, to spot Angeline among the miners. Seeing her in her miner's pants, thick jacket, and tight cap pulled over her hair, my eyes nearly swept right over her; she blended into the group, along with all the others. She was a miner, that was all: sexless, her story eliminated. Was this a comfort to her or a burden? She smiled at me—shyly, I thought.

I followed Paul through the door on the opposite side of the room and then up a staircase. "We're going to the pithead now," Paul called over his shoulder. I could not see him, it was so dark, and I was grateful for the banister along the stairs to hold to tightly as we climbed. "I want to see how things are going there, and then we'll go on to the lamp room to get lamps before we go down." We were moving along what seemed to be a gangway, for it trembled and bounced underfoot; I was too blind to know how far it extended on either side of me, and held my arms out before me lest I run into a structure or another man. We could have been in an enormous room or on a tiny plank of wood, I could not be sure. There were noises all around us, deep groans from places near and far, men's voices bellowing, and coming slowly closer, the sound of a high-pitched bell and a thunderous knocking like one massive rock falling on another. In front of us were faint flickering lights, and we headed toward them.

And then suddenly we were there. It was a frightening and exhilarating sight; I had never stood in a place so strange and foreign, so fast, so loud, so filled up with elements I did not understand. I became only a vessel for seeing; the world—machines, action, noise—was too present for thought. The gaping shaft was in front of me; there were reflectors that cast the lantern light toward the mouth of it, though the feeble beams were swallowed quickly and completely by the darkness, a black so total that it hurt my eyes. Before the light disappeared, along the sides of the shaft I could see the wooden guides, along which the cages slid, taking the human cargo to its destination. Where the guides met the mouth of the shaft there was a network of beams and bolts and levers, a maze of gleaming parts, every piece of which was no doubt crucial to the safety of hundreds of people at all times of day. The lantern light danced over it all in flickering shadows. As my eyes got used to the light, I could make out the entire framework over my head, the giant cables lifting out of the shaft and rising to the pulleys and into the headgear, the whole thing supported by a huge tower of iron that rose up and up, seemingly forever, for I could not see the top. Considering the enormity of the thing, it was a miracle it was as quiet as it was. The gears merely purred, while the only screeching came from inside the shaft, where the cages were moving.

There were men on one side of the pit, gathered around one of the pulleys, and Paul went over to speak with them. "Vincent," he called back, "don't go anywhere."

Theo, I couldn't have moved! I felt frozen, paralyzed, as if I, too, were made of metal. I was nearly blind from the darkness and the dancing shadows, nearly deaf from the noise; there was so much to take in that I could take in nothing at all. It was cold, too; there seemed to be drafts blowing from all directions. I could see the lamp room in the far distance, glowing like a beacon. Shadows from the lanterns flitted over the walls, large and small, red and nearly purple, and the walls that they lit were glistening and wet. I peered through the darkness at the miners passing me, wondering if one of them was Angeline, imagining that the glow of particular lights were held by her hand.

Set back a ways from the mouth of the pit was the engine, with the enormous drums on which the steel cables were wound that raised and lowered the cages. The drums alone were probably five meters across, and when the cages were moving, they turned so fast that you could no longer see them. A man stood at the engine and watched a display. I moved a few steps closer to where I could better see what the man looked at, which seemed to be a sort of diagram of the pit. Lead weights moved up and down vertical slots, presumably telling him where the cages were. This guess was confirmed as one of the weights reached the top of its slot and a cage rumbled up into the mouth of the shaft.

The cage was a sort of basket with two levels, and each level held thirty squatting people and two tubs, often filled with timber. If the tubs were empty, men climbed in them to conserve space, fitting even more people in the cage. I wondered how much weight the whole thing could hold before it would snap, but I did not ask.

I stood back and watched as the cage came to a stop and the men disembarked, first the bottom level, then the top. The wall of the cage was reinforced wire netting about waist-high, with a chain drawn across one side to give a way out. When they came up, the men were silent, presumably exhausted and ready for sleep, their white eyes staring passively out of the cage as it rose into the shaft. Those eyes, Theo! They reminded me of the eyes I had seen on my very first day in the Borinage, the same passive gaze, the same stark whiteness, so awfully contrasted against the black masks of coal on all those human faces, and then as now, I had the same fear: that they might somehow jump from their sockets on spider legs and land on my skin. Most of the eyes weren't even looking at me, and yet they somehow moved toward me, became unattached from the bodies they lived in and floated away. A cage full of white eyes in the dark! Can you see it?

The men shuffled by me and disappeared into the darkness. In their place, a new crop of bodies arrived and filed into the now-empty cage, the men rowdier, their faces clean. One of the men hooked the chain closed, and a man by the shaft yelled something into his megaphone that I could not understand and pulled on a rope four times, which made four loud hammer sounds, signaling to men at the bottom that a cage was on its way. Then the cage made a little jolt and was instantly gone, dropped out of sight as a bucket into a well.

Suddenly, Paul was standing next to me; I hadn't seen him approach. "Trust me," Paul said, "it looks bad, but it's a lot better than the ladder."

"The ladder?"

"The only other way out of the mine is the ladder," he said, looking at where the cage had been. "There's an escape shaft, smaller than this one. The ladder is built onto the side of it all the way up, seven hundred meters. If something happens to the cages, men have to climb up on their own. I was down there once when there was an accident." He stopped, presumably wondering how much he should tell me, about to go down in the mine for the first time. "Well, let's just say the cage is a breeze by comparison. Men die who can't make it up the ladder; they let go and fall right off, and sometimes they take other people with them."

Another cage ascended, leaping into place like a giant bird landing, and another group of ghostlike people looked out at us with indifference. "Come," Paul said, "let's go get our lamps."

In the lamp room, hundreds of lamps sat on racks one above another, each labeled with a number. A man sat at a desk and watched as each miner examined the lamp with his number, which had been cleaned and inspected the night before, and when he was satisfied with its condition, he closed it himself. Then the man at the desk wrote the time in a big ledger. "If a man doesn't return his lamp," Paul explained, "that's how we know who is missing." On the way out of the room, another man checked to make sure each lamp had been lit and properly closed; a lamp not closed properly could ignite the firedamp.

Paul handed me a leather cap to wear for extra protection; against what, I didn't want to think. Then it was time to descend. We were back at the pithead, the machinery whirling and swooping and the men yelling into their megaphones and the whistles and hammer blows signaling the movement of the cage, and then we were piling inside. "Keep your hands and feet and nose inside the cage." Paul nudged me, and I thought I could just barely make out his smile. "I wouldn't want you to lose them." People climbed into the cage after us and squeezed in; I moved back as far as I could, but Paul's warning had frightened me, and it was especially awkward trying to hold on to my lamp. It was just as the four hammers and whistles were sounding that I realized that Angeline was next to me. "I am afraid, too," she whispered. "Every time I go down."

"I feel more curious . . . deathly curious . . . than afraid," I said, and I felt goose bumps stand up on my skin. But, Theo, I was nothing at all except afraid; my fear was my body and my body was my fear.

I want to take you down there with me somehow; I wish my words could pick you up and drag you down. When the cages were all loaded, there was a jerk and then the bottom dropped out and we fell. There was suddenly no bottom or top. My stomach leapt into my throat, my hands were my feet, my head was my gut, and I had no legs at all. We were tumbling, tumbling; Angeline's elbow was in my side, and the place where she touched me was the only part of my body that I could feel; the rest of me had disappeared. Next to me was the wall of the shaft, there was maybe an inch between the cage and the rock, and I could see the slickness of water glinting on the stone as we hurtled by. I felt freezing-cold water on my face and did not know where it came from.

Then suddenly we jerked to a halt.

"Are we there?" I asked of no one, of everyone, and the whole cage laughed at me. This was only the fourth level, Paul explained, speaking into my ear. The mine had five, but the three upper ones had been exhausted and abandoned; they were no longer worked because there was no more coal. On the side of the shaft, water was flowing, there were tiny little streams running down the stone, and the sound of water falling on water could be heard. For one brief moment I felt a strange sense of peace, gazing at the wall of stone where the water was trickling down, my eyes just barely able to pick out a glint here and a sparkle there, Angeline's elbow quietly touching my side, warm against me, just a tiny little elbow, the very part you see the whores in The Hague polishing sometimes with a lemon—such a small little piece of a body, but so comforting, and there was comfort for me, too, in the sound of the cageful of miners breathing and adjusting, waiting for the next plunge; and then the bottom dropped out again and we fell. And where were you when I was going down there? I wonder what you were doing in that exact second, whether you had any premonition of how far beneath the earth your brother was. Because I think I would have known, Theo, I would have known. I would be walking in bright sunshine and feel a strange weight in my belly, something sinking lower and lower, as if I had eaten a stone. And that would be you, my brother, down in the earth, much deeper than any grave, down in the earth and going deeper.

When we stopped again, we were at the bottom—seven hundred meters down. "Here we are," said Paul. He must have seen how stunned I was, because he said, "I have been coming down here for thirty years and I still don't like that drop. You get used to it, but you always feel some measure of horror when the cage falls." Angeline took her elbow away at last and said, "I hate it, too."

Looking upward from the bottom of the pit, the daylight was about the size of a star in the sky. I stood for a minute looking up at it as the cage jerked and lurched upward once more, and then the star was extinguished.

"Come on, Vincent," said Paul, standing nearby, "stick with me. It will be very easy to get lost, and we don't want that."

The miners from our cage were splitting off into groups and disappearing down the passage. I lost Angeline until we started to follow one of the groups, and it was with happiness that I saw she was in front of us; it was only a slight swing to her hips that identified her. I knew none of the men with her, save for one, Louls Hartmann, a strong, silent creature who towered over Angeline and seemed entirely too large for that underworld.

It was a big passage, with narrow railroad tracks running through it, and only occasional timber shoring up the walls. We tramped along it quietly, no one speaking, each person carrying his little lamp, lit now, and casting only a very faint light, barely enough to illuminate a body's width in front of him. As we moved along, I thought I heard the sound of shuffling and the deep exhalations of animals, but it was a sound I associated with open fields, horses and cows nosing at their feed and chewing, and I assumed I must be mistaken. How would an animal live down there?

But after a few more yards we passed what could only be called a stable. It was carved into the rock off to the left side; about seven old horses stood between iron rails and in front of troughs of feed. Our lamps barely lit them as we passed by, but it was enough to see them standing there in the darkness, calmly chewing. Paul materialized next to me. "They pull the carts of coal to the *accrochage*," he said, "the room where they are pulled to the surface. You'll see one go by soon, I'm sure."

"But how do they live down here?" I asked. "Don't they need light?"

"A lot of them eventually go blind," Paul said. "They don't need to see to do what they do, they learn to follow the driver's voice. Sometimes they lose the pigment in their skin, too." We walked on past the stable, keeping up with the little group of miners. Paul continued, as if trying to reassure me: "It's not a harder life for them down here than it is on the surface. A lot of the boys adopt them and feed them treats. I think on the whole they're quite happy; they often live to a ripe old age. Sometimes they'll take a horse up who is getting too old to work, and he behaves strangely on the surface; we think it is because he wishes to be back in the mine."

I found it hard to believe that any animal could be happy living in darkness its whole life, but I didn't argue. I imagined the death of a horse in a mine, the eventual raising of it to the surface just so that it could again be put in the earth to decompose. Could the body of a horse fit in the cage we had just ridden down there? There was something so unnatural about a horse underground. But then, why a horse more than a man? Nothing belongs down there but worms and dirt, stone and dissolving bones. I tried to think of it, Theo, I tried to picture Mother and Father down there, mother in her apron, Father wearing his tall hat; I tried to picture you and Anna and the cat that used to visit us when we were children, Roo; I tried to picture even the images that I had pinned to the wall next to my bed. Could they be hung down here? No, it was unnatural. Only the worms and the dead belonged; all the rest of us were someplace we shouldn't be.

Paul was coughing as we walked, and I heard him spit his mouthful of phlegm into the darkness. Breathing the air down here could not be good for him. I was stumbling and stubbing my toes against every rock and uneven place, but the miners stepped nimbly, even the giant Hartmann; it was as if they had the placement of every stone memorized, their feet moving seamlessly over them. Off the road we were on there were galleries opening up on each side, and cold wind blew from them as off a mountainside. We lost half the group in front of us to a gallery on the left, but we kept on after the other half. Angeline was still before us—I had memorized the vague shape of her in the dark—but then as I watched, the outline of her seemed to dissolve before me as sugar into hot water. Did she turn off into one of the passageways? I felt frantic wondering where she had disappeared to, and squinted into the darkness, trying to find her again, but she was gone. We had to keep moving; it was ridiculous for me to worry about her. Oh, Theo, how it pains me to write that now! I am haunted by that image of her, just visible and then out of sight.

I heard a rumbling in the distance that sounded like the beginnings of thunder, growing quickly louder. "Move off the track, Vincent," Paul called to me. "A cart is coming through!" The rumble grew louder and louder, and then with a whoosh of warm air a white horse materialized, pulling a series of coal tubs and a boy, maybe a teenager, who sat on the front of the first tub. They were close to me—there wasn't much room between the rail and the wall—and I could hear the horse's breathing and smell the sweetness of his musk. Then they passed fast into the darkness, and the rumbling grew less and less, until it was gone, leaving only the hair standing up on my arms, and the thrill of something so large passing by so fast.

We turned down a passageway to the right, which quickly began to grow narrower. The walls were more frequently shored up with timber, and the ceiling was lower and lower, so very soon we were walking stooped and slumped. Again I was amazed at the miners' confidence in the terrain; they knew where to duck and dodge, where to lift a foot. I felt my chest constricting, and tried to quell the certainty that we were walking to our doom. A couple of times I bumped my head; I was going slowly enough that I didn't hurt myself, but still I was grateful for the cap Paul had given me.

Now we were in territory where the men were working; we were passing cells on either side, where miners in coarse linen suits, filthy and black as chimney sweeps, were busy hewing coal by the pale light of their small lamps. The cells of the mine were of various sizes and shapes; in some the miner could stand erect, in others, he lay on the ground. It was an incredible sight. The arrangement was more or less, I thought, like the cells in a bee-hive, but also like a dark, gloomy passage in an underground prison, and like a row of small weaving looms, and even rather more like a row of baking ovens such as peasants had, and yes, of course, like the partitions in a crypt. The water leaked through in some, and the light of the miner's lamp made a curious effect, reflected as in a stalactite cave. What a vision! Each cell was a complete image, a framed imagining, a rendering of reality complete in itself, and yet linked to another and another all the way across as far as I could see. So you can see how it was beautiful. It was the first beautiful thing I had seen that day under the earth; I wished I could somehow capture what I was seeing and take it home with me—to show Pa, who says, "Why would you go to such a place?" and to show you, who say "You are not the same any longer"—to illustrate to you, to grab you by the hair and show you, *to rub your eyes upon it*—what this place is at its heart. Because there was no question that this was what I was looking at: the heart of the Borinage, beating red through the darkness.

I must keep trying to describe it. For the most part the first cells were fairly large, some miners standing erect, some standing stooped. A few men worked at the coal face with their picks, while a few others worked to get the coal away from their feet and onto the tub, which was then removed by the haulage boys and girls, pushed to the passage where the horses hurtled by. It got increasingly warm as we went along; some of the miners were stripped to their pants, and I could see their skin glinting with sweat in the light of the lamps. I was amazed by the organization of the underworld, the immensity and function of the working world around me, a beehive, as I say, and a teeming anthill with men instead of ants. In one cell, men stood in water nearly waist-deep. How was it possible? How much more than this could a man endure? A cage with a bird in it hung from a wire; the sight of it gave me a start, and I stopped, staring. Paul explained that the birds were there to warn the men if the gas grew too dangerous for them to stay in the cell. "If the bird dies," he said, "then the men know to get out quick."

If the bird dies? This logic rankled me. The bird, in effect, was waiting for its death. Did any of the miners care for it? There were birds in cages in many of the cells, and all of the birds were silent. What is a bird for, if not to sing or to fly? An army of silent birds in cages, waiting for death. I could look at the men, Theo, but from the sight of the birds in their cages I had to look away. Remember that story that Uncle Cent used to read to us when we were small, the one that Father used to forbid him to read but that we begged him for again and again? A Flemish fairy tale, I think, the one with the creature men who lived in the sea and collected the souls of drowned fishermen in cages? All those years fascinated by that story, Theo, and I never knew what a soul in a cage could look like until I went down in that mine.

Paul stopped to inspect various elements, scolding the men for shoddy timbering jobs where the wood was leaning and cracked, strained and surely in danger. Each time he stopped, he would tell me to wait, and then he would explain what he saw. Even I could see that the men were in danger if they didn't prop up more wood to keep the cells from collapsing, but they grumbled that the company didn't pay them for timbering, only for coal. "Well," was Paul's answer, "you can't collect your salary if you're dead!" Then he erupted into coughs, which seemed to be aggravated by his mood; when he was frustrated, he could not hold them back.

There were only a few miners ahead of us by the time we reached the tunnel where we descended from the gallery. It was a tunnel about the size of the big chimneys of the Brabant farms; I thought immediately of being a boy and peering up inside of the hearth to where I could see the sunshine. But there was no sunshine there; the chimney led only deeper into the darkness. A ladder was stuck on the side and we climbed carefully down. Paul instructed me to hook my lamp to a buttonhole on my coat, for I needed my hands for climbing the ladder. The rungs were wet and muddy; cold water dripped onto the back of my neck and slipped under my collar. It was as if we were descending into a bog.

At the bottom, there wasn't room to stand anymore, so we crawled on our hands and knees. Paul, crawling before me, called back to me, "I'm sorry for this! I'm taking you to the *maintenages* that are farthest away from the exit. I hope it is all right! If you're going to come down here you may as well see it all!" He couldn't see my face and so was concerned, I think, that I might be horrified by the depth of our journey but unable to express it. I wasn't, but I was amazed: I thought I had seen the mine, and that no part could be deeper or darker or more frightening, yet there we were crawling even farther.

I couldn't answer him; I couldn't come up with words; I could only dumbly follow. But my senses were completely alive. The mud beneath my hands was music, it was an ocean, I was controlling waves and landscapes with each plunge of my palm. I felt every drop of water that touched my skin, icy cold pinpricks on my skull and neck. One knee forward, one palm forward, one knee, one palm, this was how we made our way through the passage. I tried not to think of the weight above us, of how far under the ground we were, of how many hundreds of ways I could die down there, of how far a trek it was to get out. Every time I moved forward, I could see Paul's foot in front of me for a brief second before it disappeared, and I tried to concentrate only on that. The flash of a boot, cold water in darkness.

That was how the world was: There was no space for thought, no room for past or future, for doubt, talk, concerns. Only your hand in front of you, a foot disappearing, the thin light of a kerosene lamp. Darkness, darkness, and nothing to see, and yet somehow—and how can this be?—it felt like being blind was making everything clearer. I thought of Angeline, and comforted myself that she was elsewhere in the mine, higher up, where she might be able to breathe freely. I imagined for a while that Paul's foot was hers, and that I was following her, like in that fairy tale Uncle Cent used to read us, down to the bottom of the sea.

We continued on; I lost track of time. Every few minutes we'd have to flatten ourselves against the wall as a tiny cart was pushed through the passageway, pushed by younger and younger boys and girls, struggling to keep the cart on track without tipping over. The cells on that level were even narrower than the ones above, and getting narrower and narrower still. There were men crouching and sitting, lying on their backs, using only their forearms to swing their picks. There were no voices, only the sounds of the work. Rats scuttled by with no fear; they approached and nosed at our sweating arms, then turned and meandered away. All of the miners down there were naked, as the heat was well beyond any human notions of shame. They were coated black and swimming in sweat. If I could have spared the energy to contort my body in such a small space and remove my clothes, I would have.

The coal face extended for quite a ways off the passageway, inclining up like a flat, wide chimney. Peering into the darkness I could see the faint glow of lamps all the way up the slope, their lights tiny ghostlike flickers, throwing into relief a brief glimpse of an arm or a mustache, a shoulder or a knee, or a pick hitting the face. When a piece of coal fell off, there was a quick glint, and then the darkness swallowed everything.

Soon the cells were so narrow that in order to get up the coal face the miners had to drag themselves by their elbows, and they could not turn their bodies all the way over. They wedged themselves into the rock like dogs trying to fit into rabbit holes, with no fear of getting stuck. Once in place, in order to get at the coal they had to twist and contort, their arms over their heads and their picks slanted, so that when they knocked off a piece it would fall to the plank below them rather than just on their heads. The temperature only got hotter as the seam slanted upward, and the more coal that collected beneath the miners, the more the ventilation was blocked from reaching them. At the top

the men were caught like grapes between the grips of a vise. I
was at the bottom and not even moving, and I could barely stand
one more instant of the heat and the dust and the water that
constantly dripped from overhead. How was it possible that
these men worked down here all day long?

We were down for about six hours before Paul took pity on
me and we made our way out. I didn't complain, but I felt sure
Paul could tell how I was suffering. In the last cells the air was
terrible: When I breathed in, it seemed to ignite the dust in my
throat, I had to swallow again and again to settle what I imagined was a raging fire that lit up my insides all the way into my
nose and made my eyes water. Paul inspected the men's lamps
and showed me how they were glowing blue, which indicated
that there was gas in the air; he chastised them for working in
these conditions, arguing they should leave for a day to have the
bosses clean the air out. Decrucq was in that particular cell, it
turned out, for I heard him call out, "Fontaine, you know the
mine can't kill me!" The other men grumbled that they couldn't
afford a day without pay.

The shadows danced and grew; they became menacing and
then they disappeared when I looked at them; they were there
and then they were not there. I saw a hand and I heard the noises
of scraping in the darkness, of men grumbling and sighing, men
sweating. There was a black ankle and then there was a rock. All
was darkness, all was flickering fire. Inside my body was a mine
filled with soot; inside my body was darkness, darkness was all
we were, all of us, darkness. Coal. I tried to grow my eyes in
their sockets, I thought if I could make them bigger that perhaps
I could overcome the darkness, but of course there was no escape. I fixated on the flickering flames through the gauze in the
lamps, for they were the only concrete things I could see, though
after a while they were no real comfort, for they would not stay
still. I would not complain; I would not permit myself to want

out; this was how these men lived. As the mariners ashore are homesick for the sea, notwithstanding all the dangers and hardships which threaten them, so the miner would rather be underground than above it.

I was peering through the darkness, trying to use the dim halos cast from the blue lamps to discern a particular chin, an eyebrow, the hook of a nose. It was of sudden and dire importance that I know who the people were that were toiling before me. I had to identify them, Theo; I had to reveal them in their work and danger. I slunk toward them, feeling a desperateness, a compulsion to see. The lamps cast a light that was in itself a kind of shadow, so that all the men I glimpsed were unreal, men made out of wax and mud. They would have surely moved away from me if there had been room—a few gasped with surprise when I came close to them and then grumbled for me to move away.

I was making a list in my head, a kind of census. Hubert Aert, Joseph Trouls, Nim Parling. Who knew these people were down there, Theo? It felt in that moment like the whole town was there, mothers and fathers and boys and girls and babes— they were laboring there for a world that had forgotten them, carving out pieces of darkness in darkness so that others might have a light for their suffering. Now, writing this, after what has happened since then, I can see that such a census was necessary; that work is a laying down of life as much as on a battlefield. And I was there. I saw them, Theo, and I knew them and will remember them all until I die. I might grow old and daft, I might even forget one day that I had a brother, and that he deserted me, but I will never forget those faces, or how hard I had to look to discern an eye, a cheek, a chin.

I was still moving around, peering into the darkness like some kind of deranged explorer, when I heard a voice next to me that had the effect, in that underground inferno, of making my skin turn to ice.

"Monsieur Vincent, is that you?"

It was Angeline, Theo; I was sure of it from the sound of her voice, although I could not quite make her out. Angeline, who I had thought was in the upper part of the mine, who I had imagined was free to move her limbs and breathe better air! There she was next to me, in that place of extreme derangement, asking me if I were me.

I could not answer her. I panicked. I turned to move away; I had to get out of there. I struck my arm against what must have been a haulage cart. "Paul," I croaked into the darkness. "Paul!" My throat felt like two hands clasped tightly around a piece of string. "Paul!"

"I'm here," I heard him say. "Follow me; we're on our way out."

I couldn't catch my breath the whole way back, even when we got to where the air was cooler and we could walk once again; the panic was still plaguing me, my heart beating fast, and the sound of that gentle voice—*Monsieur Vincent, is that you?*— echoing in my mind. We walked for what seemed like forever along the big main passageway, the air growing cooler and cooler, carts and horses hurtling by us constantly, boys shouting orders and galleys opening up off the right and the left.

Theo, do you remember when we were boys and I used to tell you that if you looked down the inside of your mouth that you could see all the way down into your stomach? I remember the two of us standing face-to-face, one of us opening wide and the other peering in, holding up the lamp to get a better look. I want you to look inside me now, just like that. How am I different now? How have I changed? Look! Inside me is the machinery of the mine, the cage dropping down that shaft, the thick passageways with the blind horses hauling rumbling carts through, the big cells and then the ladder down to the smaller ones and then down still more to the darkness, the heat and the blindness and all along the hands scraping at the walls, scraping away the refuse of the walls and hauling the discharge away, and those canaries all around, carts rolling on wobbly wheels carrying coal, and then, there at the very bottom, Angeline with her barely blue light.

Do you see, Theo? What do you see?

Monsieur Vincent, is that you?

We stopped at the stable while Paul had a coughing fit, and in the darkness I came up close to one of the horses and laid my hands on his mane. The hair at the top of his neck was coarse and long, it fell down over the side of him, and I ran it through my fingers and thought of Mother brushing our sisters' hair in the sitting room while I sat and looked on. I always wished I could have hair like theirs so that I could experience that treatment, our mother touching a part of me so gently.

I laid my forehead against the horse's shoulder and breathed in, and the horse breathed out quickly and shook his head, snorting loudly and stamping his foot, a gesture perhaps of pleasure and perhaps of annoyance. I didn't care; the beast was alive. His hair against my face was warm and soft, and I felt it slowly rescuing me. I held on to the horse tightly, as if we were on a sled hurtling down a hill.

I felt such love for that horse in that instant, and for all of the creatures toiling in that strange underworld, countless people moving and sweating and carting, the birds in their hanging cages, and Paul behind me, leaning on the rock and spitting onto the earth, the other horses breathing loudly into their hay. I felt I could hear it all, the small noises in that magical place thunderous and deafening; they moved through me, along with all the innumerable bodies, human, bird, beast, insect, rat. We were all in the darkness together and we were all alive.

That's it, Theo! We are all in the darkness, and we are all alive.

•

December 20
Petit Wasmes, the Borinage

Dear Theo,

After going down in the mine, I saw everything in the Borinage differently. Finally I knew where life really took place: it
was not in the village, though this may be where the miners slept
and very often where they died. The villages look desolate and
lifeless and forsaken, and then I understood why: The heart of
the place was underground. Decrucq once said something to me
about toiling in a hole in the ground only to be buried in one at
the end of one's days; the distance isn't very far from those cells
underground to the cells a man's body lies in for the rest of time.

In March, after the visit to the mine, I moved out of the Denis house for good, preferring my hovel once and for all to their
home of comfort. Can you understand this? To me, it was as
clear as a mathematical equation: I simply could not sleep in a
home like theirs while men were naked in those mines with those
flickering lamps, while men and women, my sisters and brothers,
were coming home from that terrible underworld to dinners of
potatoes and maybe a leek. I capitulated to Father when he came
to visit, but I could not do it again, not after what I had seen.
Another man could have, perhaps, Father and his colleagues,
maybe even you could have, but I could not.

Madame Denis pleaded with me; she told me that the miners knew I was a good man, that I had nothing to prove, and that
times had changed since the days of Jesus Christ. I could not
explain to her that I was in need of a different sort of comfort, a
sort that could not be found under a quilt or with a warm bath.
I remembered what Father said when he was here, but this was
no sacrifice, this was no altering of station. It was not a punish-

ment; it was not an eccentricity, as I am accused of again and again. It was an honest act of fellowship, an act of love. How else can I explain it? Why does no one understand? I thought at least you would understand. I wondered when you would come to visit me, and how I could possibly explain all that had happened since we had last seen each other. I thought that when you finally arrived, you would see it as clearly as I.

I stuffed the holes in my shack's walls with sacking to keep the wind out. I bought myself a month's worth of coffee, cheese, and bread. Then I gave the rest of my salary to Madame Decrucq, so she could buy her children warm clothing. Whatever money I had from then on would no longer be for me. The spider and the mouse were happy to have me back. I asked Paul Fontaine if I might have one of the canaries from the mine—perhaps one that was too old to serve its purpose properly. He brought me one in a wire cage; it had only one leg, though despite a few years underground it was still a bright yellow. It was the strangest thing, this bird, for it was almost always silent; I would stand in front of its cage and coax it with my finger, trying to make it sing.

After being in the mine, I felt a new fever to try to capture what I saw; nothing could touch the darkness, of course, but I quieted the impossibility of capturing the mine by trying to draw everything else. I took my pencil and paper with me nearly everywhere, sketching what I saw: women carrying coal home from the slag heap, goats eating carrots while tied to a post, a little boy chasing a chicken, the trees standing sentinel by the mine fence. I admit there were times that I missed my duties—a sermon or a Bible class or even a scheduled visit to a parishioner— because I was out sketching and lost track of time. The sketching quieted my mind and occupied my hands. Some nights I was up all night trying to perfect an image that I had begun during the day, and although I sometimes threw these drawings into the fire in disgust, there were still more of them that I kept, neatly stacked in a pile near where I slept. I was seeing so much that I felt I could not capture in words. I would start letters to you and tear them up in frustration, all my words seemed so pedestrian, so inadequate, and so I would think instead of what drawings I would send you: Alard in his cap and jacket, Madame Denis cooking a stew. But the drawings frustrated me no less than the torn-up letters, for I couldn't do them right, either.

I dreamed of pictures—I did then and I still do now—like the ones I used to see all day in the galleries in The Hague and London and Paris. Those galleries were so much the same, paintings crawling across the walls and ceilings, hanging from every spare inch of visible space, paintings covered in brown paper and leaning on one another in the back storage room, prints and drawings and sketches piled in boxes and drawers, organized by artist and subject, with brown cards dividing them. And though I came to feel suffocated in those galleries, selling the same cheap prints day after day to people who wanted the least expensive and least inspired images to hang on their walls, pretending that their choices were good when behind me was a Maris or a Mauve overlooked on the wall, smiling through my teeth when they looked at a print I loved and called it "sentimental," though I came to hate my days in the galleries, I see those rooms before me now. There are no pictures in the Borinage, and I have been starved for them as if they are food. All those beautiful pictures, I see them in my mind, all those gilded frames, squares of life in color and fine line hanging on the wall.

I was thinking today of Millet's picture *The Evening Angelus*, the one we spoke about back when I was living in London. I remember when I first saw a print of it—one of the Germans I stayed with before I moved to the Loyers' brought a copy of it to a café where we were all having lunch. He laid it right down on the table in front of me, and I nearly lost my breath. That was "it," as Mauve says; that was poetry, that was beauty. A woman and a man bent gently over a bassinet in a field, the sun setting softly behind them, lighting their vigil in peaceful hues. I had admired Millet already, but that might have been the first time that I understood him, or truly felt his power. It was like I used to feel as a child, looking at the Weissenbruch print Pa kept over the mantel; I would be a boy in that landscape rather than a boy in our house. And it was like that, too, with that Millet print— suddenly I was standing on that field, the sun setting before me, and I could hear the murmurs of the child in that bassinet, the soothing coos of its mother standing over it. That was it; that is it.

Everything belongs to the world of pictures. Everything we see.

•

December 27

Dear Theo,

It snowed here last night; the world is white again. I am reminded of what this place looked like a year ago, when I first arrived, and remembering my awe that a landscape could look like this, all white and black, so beautiful and so full of stark contrast. It is as if the very land here expresses the state of life.

Not too long after I went down in the mine and then moved out of the Denis house, Angeline's father, Charles, was injured in a firedamp explosion. He was carried home from the mine by the black cart pulled by the white horse, a sight ubiquitous in the village, a sight of dread and fear. When the miners' wives heard the cart coming, they approached it wailing and weak-kneed, carrying babies and with toddlers clinging to their skirts. They called out to the cart as it came down the lanes, "Who is it? Who is it?" They turned from where they were gathered at the water pumps or ran from the factory store and clustered around the cart, elbowing and pushing and peering inside to see who it was that was being carried home.

I didn't know it was Angeline's father until I went to visit the house. It was the third explosion in as many days; the miners were on edge and frightened. I heard about the accident and saw the horse and cart returning from the mine; I ran to the group of remaining women who stood in the lane, sharing in their relief that the injured was not one of their own. When I reached them, I had to stop and catch my breath, placing my hands on my knees. One of the women leaned over and asked if I was all right. She put her hand on my back and then pulled it away, exclaiming over how thin I was. "Pastor Vincent!" she exclaimed as I stood up, and shook her head at me, making a tsking sign with her mouth. "Look at you! Do you think you are a miner? Why do you starve yourself? Why do you not wash your face?"

I looked at her blankly. I did not know how to answer her; there was no time for questions like that. How could I give adequate words in the face of the constant arrival and departure of that white horse? I had lost track of what I looked like. Surely a man's appearance was the least important fact of all?

Inside the Dubois house, I found Charles lying naked on his bed, facedown; the back of him from his waist up was charred black and swollen, ridges of skin snaking up his shoulders and the back of his neck, slipping under what was left of his hair, a handful of wisps at the base of his skull. He must have taken the explosion entirely from the back, for his face against the pillow was intact, only the very edges of it disfigured.

His women surrounded him, his wife and two daughters, both of them still wearing their clothes from the mine, covered in soot, though their faces were clean. They did not look up as I came in, and I did not see that one of them was Angeline. There was a washtub near the bed with the habitual film of dirt floating at the surface. The women were gently lowering compresses soaked in oil onto the remains of the man's skin; in the dim light of the lamp near the bed I could see his eyes scrunch tightly closed as the cloths touched him. The pain must have been unbearable. The women touched him gently, and his wife and one of his daughters wept silently. At the base of the bed stood a boy of about fifteen, who seemed paralyzed. He looked on at the women working on his father as if he were watching from a great distance.

I stood by the bed for a minute or two before any of them looked up. The room was filled with love and concern, every inch of space taken up with tenderness; when I breathed in, the care filled my lungs and crawled under my fingernails. I stood in awe. There is no limit to how people can love one another.

One of the women looked up from the bed, and then I saw that it was Angeline. For a moment our eyes met in surprise. Recovering, Angeline said, "Pastor Vincent," and then, quietly, "Mama, Monsieur Vincent is here."

Her mother turned to me with tear-stained cheeks. "Oh, Monsieur Vincent," she said, "thank you for coming." She held out her hand, which was slick with the oil from the rags, and I took it in both of mine. "Madame Dubois," I said, "God bless you. Your husband is a brave man, and he will come through this trial."

I didn't know if I believed it, Theo, but I knew it was what she had to hear.

She shook her head. "This family has already been through so much, Monsieur Vincent." She looked at Angeline, who kept her eyes on the bed, and for a moment I thought I felt the presence of another man in the room, the fiancé who had died in the mine. Then Madame Dubois looked at her son, still standing at the foot of the bed. "That mine just keeps taking and taking; when will it give back to us?"

Angeline's father lay still on the bed. I imagined I could hear the hissing and popping of his skin, as if it were a piece of meat frying in a skillet. How could I say to these people that the Lord works in mysterious ways? How could I tell them that this was God's will, their husband and father lying helpless on that mattress with his skin charred and sizzling? I thought of Father, tending to his parishioners all those years ago, telling those suffering people that it was God's will. I used to get so angry at him when I was a boy, listening to him say those things, and there I was, frantically trying to say the same thing.

I remembered the Reverend Laurillard, whom I had seen in Amsterdam the year before—such an impressive, capable preacher, who always seemed to know just what to say to address his congregation. I tried to conjure him, to think of how he might respond to Madame Dubois, but it was no simple thing. "Madame Dubois," I said, "the Christian life has its dark side, and it is mainly men's work. This world is incomprehensible. Is there anything that happens that we can understand? We must be as God made us, sorrowful yet ever rejoicing. In the next world . . ." I stopped. She was looking at me, Theo, looking me straight in the eye, her husband lying behind her. I could not say it. For a long moment I stood there with my mouth open, struggling, and then I gave up. "I don't know, Madame Dubois," was all I could eventually manage. I shook my head and looked away from her. "I don't know."

Later that night there was a knock on the door of my hut. I had never had a visitor; I opened the door with surprise, expecting Father perhaps, or you, I hoped, and then was even more surprised when I saw that it was Angeline. "Hello," she said shyly. She could barely meet my eyes. "I'm sorry to bother you. I hope it's all right."

"Of course!" I said. "I was just reading. Come in, please."

We sat on the floor by the hearth. I had only one chair, and a rickety old table that I had taken out of one of the abandoned miners' cabins in the village; I offered her the chair, but she said she preferred the floor. Together we watched the bird in his cage; I had taken to calling him Cricket, for he reminded me in a way I cannot explain of summer evenings in Zundert, the crickets singing and the birds chirping their last songs for the night. He watched us, in turn, quietly, curious.

I had to remind myself that Angeline was only seventeen. The Borinage ages people early, and I could see it in Angeline, who had been through more than many. Women at twenty-five in the Borinage have already spent years in the mine and then birthed five or six children. They are used up and spent, hollow and sagging, and there is no second birth for them. But sitting in front of the fire in my little hovel, I could see that Angeline was just a girl. Her skin was perfect and radiant, her features unlined and fresh, but nonetheless her face carried such pain. It is always difficult to see someone so young struggling to bear such weight.

"I just didn't know who to talk to," she said after a time. "I needed to get out of that house, but I didn't want to be alone."

"I understand," I said. "You're always welcome."

We sat for quite a long time in silence. The fire crackled and hissed, and I thought of her father's skin in the dark hut, his burns lit up in patches of shadow.

"He's so quiet," she said about the bird.

"I know," I said. "Paul brought him back for me from the mine. I guess he's not used to living aboveground. Isn't that so strange for a bird? He has let out a few chirps since I got him; I'm hoping to learn what he likes. This is Angeline," I said to the bird. "Say hello! Hello!" Cricket was quiet, but he was listening.

Angeline stood to inspect the bird in his cage, standing before it quietly for some moments. "See the feathers on the bottom of the cage?" she said without turning around. "This bird is molting."

"Really?" I stood up and joined her at the cage.

"Yes," she said. "That is probably why it is quiet. When birds are molting, they often don't sing. He might start to sing in a few months, when the molting period is over. Unless," she added, "this bird is female. Female canaries often don't sing much at all."

"Oh!" We looked in together at Cricket, who stood on his one leg, looking back at us calmly. "How do you know all this?" I asked her.

"My father bred canaries for a while when I was a child. We used to raise them until they were old enough to go down in the mines. I used to help him take care of them, clean out their cages and things like that. My father loves birds." She stopped, as if thinking about her father was dragging her elsewhere, somewhere she didn't want to go. She turned and sat down again before the hearth and was quiet. I joined her on the floor and waited for her to speak again.

"Monsieur Vincent," Angeline said after a while, "will you tell me about other places?"

I was confused at first; what kind of places did she mean? Was I to speak as the pastor and tell her of Heaven, promise her a future life beyond this one of suffering, or ought I speak to her as a mere man? As I had with her mother, I thought carefully about how to answer her. I tried, Theo, I tried to answer the way I thought Father might want me to. I was quiet for a time, and then began: "Perhaps when we long for other places, we are in fact longing to reach the Lord, for there is a house of the Father in which there are 'many mansions,' and 'Blessed are the poor in spirit . . . Blessed are the pure in heart,' who long to reach them."

She looked at me then with patience but shook her head. "I don't mean heavenly places," she said, "just anywhere, just some-place other than this. You've been to other places, I assume, to Brussels, to Paris? I've never been away from here. What are those other places like? What is it like where you are from?"

Then I understood: She wanted images. She wanted visions to replace the ones in her head, visions of joy rather than of suffering, visions of a wider world than the one that confronted her here. My heart broke open for her then.

That night, a ritual began that continued in the evenings for a few weeks. I started slowly and haltingly; that first night I showed her the prints on my walls, and one of them was *The Road to Rijswijk*, by Weissenbruch, which you gave to me, and so I told her about the day that we had walked along that canal in The Hague and drank milk at the old mill. "The sails," I said to her, realizing only as I spoke how difficult it was to describe them to someone who had never seen anything like them, "well, they were huge, probably each one the size of one of your smaller slag mountains, and they were slowly revolving, turning around and around one another in a beautiful slow white dance." She sat cross-legged in front of me, holding the print in her hands, her eyes wide and attentive, as if she were a child and I were reading her a storybook full of magical details. I imagined shrinking down that print, Theo, so I could place it on her tongue, so she could swallow the image like the sacrament that it was.

Nearly every night after that, she arrived at my door, terribly shy at first, as of course I was, too, for what was it exactly that we were doing there together? But we always soon forgot ourselves. I told Angeline about Zundert, about you and me in our bed in the room where the flag flew from the window, about the garden in the back with the magpie nest, all greens and purples and blues, about the fields and heath and rivers that we explored as boys. I told her about London, about the parks and ginger beer and the women with parasols of a thousand colors and hundreds of people on horseback; I told her about Amsterdam and its canals, all the little side paths that I walked along, linden trees, interwoven and Gothic. I told her about Paris, the houseboats parked on the quays, the books and prints for sale along the riverbanks, and how you could walk and walk and walk forever and never reach the end. I told her about walking along the ocean in England, watching the fisherman trawling with their nets, the waves washing up beautiful shells and smooth rocks that I then tossed back, the heads of seals poking up from the depths, the way that the sound of the surf calmed my heart. So many images, everything I had ever seen was transformed into beauty in that hut with Angeline. She was hungry for color, Theo; she was hungry to live. She was hungry for detail, for reality, for this world, not for any other.

"If only one can remember what one has seen," I said one night, "one is never without food for thought or truly lonely, never alone." I said this, and then I thought perhaps it was wrong, for Angeline had seen almost nothing outside her tiny village. "I'm sorry," I said, "that was insensitive, wasn't it."

She looked surprised, her eyebrows raised, and then she smiled. "Was it?" she asked.

"You asked me to share with you things I have seen, but not to brag, and not to proclaim that I am a happier person because I have seen these things. I am sorry; I get carried away."

She was amused, looking at me almost as if I were a child. It was a look I often saw on her face when I knew I was becoming too animated in my description of a particular place or thing—a look of patience, of bemusement. "Thank you for your sensitivity," she said, "but really there's no need for it. I feel that way about what few beautiful things I have seen in my life, too, and I am not sorry you said it."

I nodded. "Good," I said. "Well then, I don't take it back."

She laughed. "Monsieur Vincent," she said, shaking her head, "there is so much more to you than the people here know." She said it not with judgment or even with wonder; it was just a simple statement, as if she had looked out the window and said it had begun to rain.

Yes, Theo, I was confused about my behavior. Never before had a woman been so interested in me, so attentive and quizzical, so present, and Angeline was not just any woman, but a wounded and sensitive young beauty. Angeline had a sweet and thoughtful soul, and questioned everything she encountered, so that whenever we stumbled upon the subject of theology, she probed me with well-articulated queries that I could not always answer. "But why?" she often asked. "But why?" And *why*, I soon learned, is not a word easily answered by Scripture.

I did not tell her of my failures; instead of telling her that I had dropped out of my theological studies, I let her think that the study I had done in Amsterdam was what led me to the Borinage. The change from art dealer to preacher was a natural one, I told her, a choice I had made because my soul was not fulfilled by the selling of prints to the public. I did not tell her of my dismissal from Goupil's, nor of my brief stint at the school in Ramsgate or my job in that wretched bookshop in Dordrecht.

I was aware of a certain molding of my story so that it sounded crafted and planned, a series of forward steps along a road rather than a series of stumbles. My conscience pulled at me as I watched her accept my tale without question; why wouldn't she believe me? But of course what I was telling her were terribly close to lies. Yes, I wondered whether I was falling in love with her. If so, what could happen then? I thought of Father shaking his head, and I wondered what you would say; if this were true, if I loved her, I would lose my appointment for sure. But there were times when I looked at her in the dim light and knew I did not care. After she left, ducking out of the hut with a shy bow, I would punish myself, pacing back and forth across my dusty floor and castigating myself, furiously shaking my head to shake free the part of myself that needed her to see me as other than I was. It was confusing, to be so utterly yourself with someone— I shared more of myself with her than I had ever shared with anyone else, except you—and at the same time to feel you were hiding who you really were. Some nights, I felt no torture about this; other nights, I made myself go out and lie down in the snow until I nearly froze. Yes, I thought of writing you, but I did not know what to say.

You will no doubt be thinking of Eugénie Loyer, remembering how tortured that whole affair was. I thought of her, too, very frequently in those weeks with Angeline, worried that I was making a similar mistake, thinking that Angeline might have any interest in me when in fact she had none. I knew that if you were there, you would remind me of Eugénie, remind me of those nights in London after she told me she was engaged, and to the man who had slept in my room before me; I had to sleep in that bed for a few ugly weeks before I could leave to come home, imagining his body in those sheets next to mine; how could I forget it? It was enough, remembering that time, to encourage me not to get too close to Angeline.

Charles Dubois slowly recovered and began going out again, walking some distance just for exercise; his hands were still weak and it would be some time before he could use them for his work, but he was out of danger. There was an outbreak of typhoid and malignant fever, which gave the villagers nightmares and made them delirious. My days were filled with visits to the sick—I gave them my money and my clothes, all but the one set that I wore on my back. I moved from bed to bed, attempting to comfort and bring warmth, but I was growing weaker; I was not eating much and my nights were filled with vivid and terrible dreams. I was sick, too, but with something other than what ailed the villagers. One day, one of the miner women, whose husband and three children lay feverish in two beds pushed together in the back of her hut, placed her hand on my shoulder and turned her eyes on me with pity. She, Theo, she pitied me! "You don't look well, Monsieur Vincent," she said. "Perhaps you ought to go home and rest." She offered me a coffee and a crust of bread, neither of which she had to spare. I nearly fell to my knees right there in her hut; I wanted to crawl under those beds and die there.

My evenings with Angeline were what I gave to myself. I allowed myself them as if they were nourishment, as if she were food. Often, I sketched while I was with her, for there were so many images from the day that I wanted to capture. A few nights, I tried to draw her, sitting cross-legged before the hearth; the drawings were never right—in one she looked anonymous, as if she could be any woman at all; in another she was leaning back on her hands and so her front looked like an animal, as if it were unconnected to her arms. None of them captured her. I had to ask her permission, with some humiliation, to try again.

I was still doing the evangelical work as best I could, despite my own growing fever, brought on by overwork and lack of food and the cold in my hut. The outbreak of sickness in the village had put an end to our Bible meetings, and I was presiding over far too many funerals. I stopped giving sermons, too, for I felt my time was better spent with the ill miners and their families.

The miners were still mostly kind to me, despite the increasing frequency of strange looks cast my way and the children who hid behind their mothers' skirts when I came near. I was still trying to hold our school lessons, though fewer children were attending; no one told me why, but I suspect it was the parents who kept them away. One day, I arrived at the salon and found only Alard there, sitting alone on one of the chairs and looking out the window. "I think it is only me today," he said sheepishly when I stepped into the room.

He never asked me why I had moved out of his parents' house, though I could tell he didn't understand. He often looked at me with a puzzled expression, as if he was trying to make out just who I was. I didn't mind; he was trying to understand me, which is more than most people have tried to do. That day in the salon, I didn't read to him from the Bible, but instead began to read him Dickens's *Hard Times* from the beginning—I had just finished it, and was pleased to share it with him. I have spoken to you about Dickens before, I think, and so perhaps you know how I feel about him—he is one of the clearest writers there are. Alard, while he listened, was enwrapped in the story, and I loved to see him so.

I thought of all those nights with Gladwell in Paris, up late reading the Bible to each other. How lucky he is, Alard, that he will never have to go down inside that growling beast, the mine.

There was a miner who was notorious in the village for being an unbeliever; his name was Louis Desmet and he was a blasphemer, one of these sorts of men that spoke in torrents against God as a way to prove that He did not exist; why, his argument went, if He was so powerful, didn't He strike him down when he disobeyed His commandments? He was a terrible drunk, a burly, reckless man, who had once been married but whose wife had run away from him and from the Borinage in the middle of the night. He had a mustache that curled down off of his lip and just touched the base of his chin; he must have worked hard to keep the rest of his jaw clean. I avoided contact with him for a long time, not only because of the looks he gave me when I was near him, the way he spat on the ground close to my feet and muttered pointed words, but because I had no need to occupy myself with people who had no interest in me when there were plenty of other villagers who were welcoming. But recently I had heard he was sick, and I knew the time had come for us to encounter each other. I had visited every other sick person in the village; why should he be an exception?

He must have been tipped off that I was coming, for as soon as I approached the doorway to his house, I was greeted by a volley of abuse, he didn't want me in his house spreading God, he hadn't invited me, no rosary chewer was welcome in his house. His words were mixed with coughing and spitting and accompanying groans. This man was no one to fear in his present condition.

"Monsieur Desmet," I said, ducking into the darkness, "I assure you that I am no 'rosary chewer.' I don't even own a rosary, and never have."

There was something about the force of his disbelief that gave me confidence. I don't know exactly what his experiences had been before this with religion, but clearly they had undone him, and it took some time before he would even lie still in my presence. His infirmity helped, unfortunate as it was, for if he had had his full strength, I'm sure he never would have allowed me in his house in the first place.

I sat on a wooden chair near to his bed and let him exhaust himself. A few candles were burning; his hut was tiny, just the one room with the bed and a wooden chair, and along the wall a sink, a basin for bathing, and a small stove. "Throw all you want at me, Monsieur Desmet," I told him; "I will still be here. I'm not here for any reason except to be with you, to listen and talk with you, that's all."

For hours, he abused me, he abused the Church, and he abused himself. He hated the world, he hated himself, he hated the bed he lay on, and he hated me. He rolled and writhed and spat into the bucket next to his bed with furious force. I sat next to him and said nothing. His abuse was infectious; I could sense its poison entering me. The dark of the hut was thick with it, it was as potent as the smell of liquor that bled out through his skin. The hatred swirled and swam through the air; the longer I sat there, the more sure I was that I could see it, the tail of it dancing and taunting me, approaching my mouth, my nostrils, my eyes, entering my body through any available way.

This was it, I told myself, this was my test; here it was. My own hatred was easily reached. I saw it there, in Desmet's hut:

my own anger, my own disbelief. We were in the dark together, he and I, with all of our demons and all of our doubt, all of our misdeeds, all of our regrets and shame and fury.

In a moment of quiet, Desmet turned on his side, away from me. I heard my own voice whisper, "Fire proves gold, and temptation proves the righteous man." It was a quote from Thomas à Kempis's *The Imitation of Christ*, that book you know I love, and I heard it hiss out into the air as if it were coming from someone other than me.

Desmet's response was a grunt.

"All you have to do," I said slowly, quietly, as much to myself as to him, "to show God that you are worthy is to resist temptation. 'It is no great marvel if a man is fervent and devout when he feels no grief.' If it were easy, there would be no need for belief."

Desmet roared up in his bed like a tidal wave. "NO!" he screamed at me. It was as if he were a monster and not a man, so complete was his anger, so dark his form in the hut. "Don't speak to me of belief," he hissed. "Get out of here, rosary chewer, and let me die in peace."

My heart was leaping in my chest, dodging the poison from side to side. What would Father do if he were here? I wondered. The poison would not enter him; at least that much is sure.

"There is no deed that is unforgivable," I said to Desmet. Where were these words coming from? They came from me as if I were reading them in the air. "We have all done things we are ashamed of, Monsieur Desmet, all of us. God does not judge us based on the deed, but on the intent of the doer. 'Man looks on the outward appearance, but the Lord looks on the heart.'"

"Let him see it," he mumbled from his bed. "Let him see my intent. Leave me, rosary chewer. Leave me to my God. My intent is to die."

With those words, all of the air left the room; it became difficult, and then impossible, to breathe. I gasped; I leaned over and put my head between my knees, but there was no air to find. Desmet lay turned away from me; he would not speak again. A painful noise was growing in my ears, a cold headache, piercing like an icicle, in my mind. I saw that I had a choice: stay there and die with him, or leave the hut for air, and live.

Would I have been less a failure, Theo, less an idler, if I had sat next to his bed all night and all the next day, until he died? Perhaps. But I am sure that I would have died, as well. I chose, brother, I chose to live.

I will carry that man's death on my back my whole life.

●

January 3, 1880
Cuesmes, the Borinage

Dear Theo,

What happened next is hard for me to write about. I am aware of an impulse as I sit down to write to you—an impulse to lie.

The last time Angeline came to my hut was a night of perfect calm; late April, peaceful spring, and then the end arrived like a storm.

That night, Angeline was more pensive, and she spoke more about herself than she ever had before. She was so beautiful, sitting there with the light from the flickering lantern on her, her face looking into the hearth. Cricket let out a few peeps when Angeline arrived; Angeline lit up at the sound of him, and she crouched to peer into his cage. I let her open the door and stick her hand in and he climbed onto her finger. She held him for a few minutes, and then she let him go and turned to me. "I dream of it, Monsieur Vincent," she said. "I dream of getting out of here. I always have, ever since I was a girl, but I never allowed myself to think that it could be anything other than a dream, something unreal and unreachable. But lately, since I've been talking with you, I have started to want it more than ever. Why can't it be? Why? Why can't I, too, see the Amsterdam canals or the horseback riders in London? Why not me?"

She sat on the floor and looked out the window. Cricket stayed in his cage, perhaps feeling as helpless as I did. I held my tongue, my breath caught in my chest. She did not look at me.

"No one I know has ever gotten out of here, but that doesn't mean it can't be done." She paused again and was quiet for a few minutes. Then she spoke again. "When I saw my father after the accident," she said, "when he was lying there so helpless and unable to move, I felt so strongly that I needed to escape that I thought I might suffocate right there and then, falling down at the foot of his bed."

She spoke of Jens, her fiancé, and how she had thought the loss of him might kill her, but it did not, and so she must be stronger than she had thought. She said, nearly whispering, her head turned down, "Maybe you will think this cruel, but I wonder sometimes if his death might not have been the thing that set me free. It is not lost on me that it was his belief in God that led me to begin attending your services, which then led me here, and to your stories. And it is the stories, I think, that have led me to want to escape."

" 'The bud may have a bitter taste, / But sweet will be the flower,' " I said. She didn't ask me to explain the reference but merely nodded, as if she understood.

Understand, Theo: I'm still not sure what it was I felt for her. It was not what I felt for Eugénie, piercing and tortured, or for the prostitute Anna after her. It was not what I feel for Anna, our sister, or for our mother, or even for Lies and Wil. It was something altogether different. Every time we were together, I was trying to figure it out. I'm trying even now, imagining her sitting before me, the lamplight flickering on her face. How strange, to feel such a mystery in a person who sits before you! It was as if she were not real, as if she were a woman come from a dream. But then again, no, because there have been times when I have shared my space with people long dead or when I have dreamed while awake; this was different from that, too. She wanted to see; she was looking to me to fill her mind with images. I felt a responsibility toward her, a longing for her but an admiration, too, and a responsibility. She would never have left me, Theo, not like you have.

That night, we sat and talked for a while, and then a silence fell on us. We often shared silence in our evenings together; unlike most people, Angeline didn't make me feel any pressure to perform for her. Silence can be as natural as a blade of grass, and when it arrived, we let it stay. It was such a comfort to be with someone whom I could be myself with in this way. It felt as if we had known each other for much longer than a matter of months; as if our souls knew each other, if that's possible, from other lifetimes, other planets. Often, when there was a fire burning in the hearth, we would sit and gaze at it together, watching the simple, unending drama of the flames unfold.

After a long time, I looked to her and saw that her eyes were on me. How long had she been gazing at me like that? My heart began to flutter and I could feel my face blush; I was happy that it was dim in the hut and she could not see my color. Something large and unnameable passed between us then; I don't know how else to describe it. There was a presence in the room with us, and then it was in our bodies, and then, as we gazed at each other, it was in the space between us, suspended as if on a bridge. I was mesmerized by her gaze, I could not look away, at the same time that everything inside of me screamed for me to turn from her, to break whatever spell was being cast. A trap was being laid at my feet, a gaping mouth full of sharp teeth that would close over my flesh as soon as I took a step. The pull toward the trap and the pull away were equal in strength.

"Time for a portrait?" I managed, immediately regretting my words. Why had I broken the glorious silence in which we had been held? I was a coward to have stepped off the path of possibility the silence had contained. She blinked, and a certain presence came back to her face. "All right," she said quietly.

I suppose I have never been great with women. I admit to a certain fear where they are concerned, a feeling not unlike being in a body of water where you can't touch the bottom.

I sat before her with my pencil and paper and tried, clumsily, to capture her. The light from the lantern on the floor near us cast a warm glow onto Angeline's face, leaving half of it in shadow. I do not know why she wanted to be there with me— feverish and dirty and frenzied, with only one set of clothes to my name—but there she was, and I was grateful. My hand was shaking a bit as I sketched her; I felt out of control and confused, sensing a strange energy in the room with us, something from that earlier moment that still lingered. I had drawn her many times before but had never felt nervous while doing so. My lines were shaky and I went over them again and again, building the outline of her, cross-legged, her skirts pulled over her knees and tucked under her, her face half in shadow, gazing alternately at me, at the hearth, and at Cricket's cage, with a tiny hint of a smile. In the drawing, her head grew slightly too large for her body— the proportions were off—and yet as I watched the image grow I thought it was somehow fitting, accurate, for her face was the most interesting aspect of her. I had drawn her many times before, yes, but I had never felt that there was life in those other portraits—they were all simple studies for the portrait I made that night. The light cast shadows onto her arms and her skirts; her hands, resting on her knees, were patient and delicate despite the soot permanently caked under her nails.

Cricket had crept out of his cage and was hopping around the sill on his one leg, still not quite ready to fly. "Look at him!" Angeline squealed, overjoyed to see him exploring his world. I wished I could capture her face when it looked so delighted.

The drawing wasn't done when I put it aside, but I had reached my limit for the moment and knew that if I kept the pencil moving I would begin to do damage to whatever truth I had managed to set down. "Monsieur Vincent," Angeline said after I had laid the paper to the side and closed Cricket's cage, with him safely back inside, her voice a near whisper, "Can I stay here with you tonight?"

My face must have passed through a number of expressions in response to this. Was I surprised? I thought I was, though now I wonder. Of course some part of me felt I must say no to her request, but how glad I am now that I did not give in to it. I could not speak, but merely nodded to her in assent.

We lay down together on the straw. I pulled my ratty blanket over us, embarrassed at the way it smelled of dirt and animals. We did not put our arms around each other; I put all my will-power into holding myself back. I thought of her as a baby bird, in need of a nest, and commanded myself to be a better man than my instincts wanted me to be. It had been such a long time since I had lain down with a woman, and my body had trouble understanding what my mind did—that Angeline was different from all the rest.

She lay curled into my body, the back of her lightly touching my front. I breathed shallowly, not wanting her to know how my heart was dancing, how I could feel my pulse in my neck. I could smell her skin, natural and earthy, and something sweet in her hair. I breathed her in, happy to have the scent of her; I could have lain there forever with that scent in my nose. I could feel her breath against me, and spent what felt like a long time trying to align my breath to hers.

After a time, I don't know how long it was, she reached behind her and found my arm. I gave it to her readily; she pulled it over her side and held on to it, as if it were something that might keep her in place. My hand, which she held, felt as if it had become detached from the rest of me; it was an object floating in space, anchored only by her slightly damp palm and quiet fingers.

My mind was calm, more so than it had been in months, perhaps even years. I lay there next to her and all I was aware of was my breath, and hers, and the pleasant sensation of my hand being held. Her hand was around my wrist, her fingers gently touching my palm. The lantern was slowly going out, but still it cast dim flickers of light across us, and the room seemed to glow faintly. I imagined that the light was aligned with our breathing, too, and so it seemed that the dancing shadows were a part of our communion.

Even as I write this, the beauty of it gets away from me. I am trying to stay here, trying to conjure it back by giving it enough words, trying to see it as clearly as if I were still lying there. But I can't help feeling as if my words are not enough. Are you seeing it as it was? If a great master were to paint this moment, if the brushstrokes were placed just right, would that be a better way to translate the power of it? I am not sure if that would suffice, either.

Perhaps I just don't want to get to what comes next. I would happily stay forever, if I could, in the flickering shadows of that night, lying next to the breathing Angeline, Cricket safely in his cage on the windowsill, and not get to what comes next.

We lay together that way until dawn. When she left, I sat up with the rising sun and finished the drawing I had made of her, finally feeling there was some life in it.

Theo, when we were boys, sometimes I would get confused as to whose body was whose. You would do something, throw a stick or run across a field, and I would be confused, just for a moment, whether it had been you or me who had done that thing. Did you ever feel that way?

The truth is that even now, sometimes, it is hard for me to understand that it was me who did a particular thing, who lived through a particular moment, who witnessed a particular sight. Perhaps this is in part what these letters are—a way to prove to both of us what I have been through, so that I can believe it was really me.

1880

It is nearly dark when he stops by a small pond where swallows are feeding. They are diving and plunging, lunging and twisting and turning, swooping low toward the water but never touching it, their bellies missing it by barely the width of a feather. They cross one another and circle back, disappear into the trees at the water's edge, and then turn and come again toward the center of the pond. The air is filled with the sound of their turning, their tiny twitters and chirps. At first, Vincent imagines that it must be some sort of dance they are performing, a mating ritual, or perhaps an expression of joy; then he realizes that they are eating, catching the insects that have appeared in the first cover of night. He steps closer to the water and the birds fly around him. They hum and swoosh, a few of them barely missing the edges of his jacket. Whoosh, whoosh, he holds his arms out and stands still while the birds move around him. He closes his eyes and imagines that he is a tree, a perfectly still living thing. Fellow creatures with hearts and minds and desires swoop around him, brush against him, oblivious to his presence or his goals, uncaring about his thoughts and achievements and failures. They are letting him partake; they are all sharing space on the earth. It is a moment, he thinks, that no man could reproduce.

He thinks of being down in the mine, all the bodies sharing space in the underground darkness. He remembers how it felt to be at what he thought was the bottom, and then to climb down, and farther down, and farther down still, with no light but those flickering flames sometimes turning blue. The birds moving around him now are just as busy as those bodies digging at the earth back in mining country; even now they are scraping out its insides, pulling out its guts and discarding them in mountains; they are just like these birds, just like the earthworms below him where he stands now. It is all the same: creatures doing what they do, creatures making work, creatures feeding and working and being themselves.

He opens his eyes. He thinks perhaps Angeline is in the body of one of these birds; perhaps it is her wing that is brushing against him now, or now, or now. Perhaps that is Angeline who swoops across the pond in a dramatic arc, heading toward the water with incredible speed, then ducking and turning at the last moment. He smiles at this notion, and turns from the pond feeling buoyed by the rush of the birds, the fellow creatures engaged with life, but a mere few minutes past the pond he feels a cloud move back over his vision and his mind grows dark. He feels a pang of such despair that he sinks to his knees. This is a fool's errand that he is on; he is walking to nowhere, a wretched scarecrow dressed up like a man with a purpose. What does he think he will find at the end of this walk? His brother has sent him no letters for almost a year; what does he think will be accomplished by going to see him, by taking him his letters? And what in God's name will happen then?

He remembers the feeling he had when he went to the Borinage: it was as if he had been standing in front of a glass case with a treasure locked inside for almost four years, being told no and no and no every time he tried to reach it, and then one day the case was opened and he was allowed to reach inside. It was the first time in his life that he had ever felt like maybe he might be good at something, maybe he might know what he was meant to do, how he could be himself and bring good to the world at the same time. He knew his path would be different—he couldn't be a preacher like his father, he couldn't get the theological degree and wear a suit and tie and say things he did not believe, but still he could bring God's message to the poor, even only as himself, as the mere Vincent.

He remembers Angeline, in Bible class, asking him something about the text they were reading, and the way that his answer dissatisfied him, the way that her probing question made a rope in his stomach start to twist. He remembers the man in the village, Monsieur Desmet, who died alone and without God; wasn't his death just the same as all the others? Louls Hartmann, the hulking man who walked before Vincent in the mine shaft, dying with his insides exploded on the long yard of the terrible hungry mine—was he any more secure than Desmet was, dying in the warmth of his bed, his body intact? He thinks of his father, telling him that God wished him to be who he was: *If God had wanted you to be a miner, He would have made you one.* A man was not supposed to live like another man; a man was not supposed to prostrate himself beyond the level that he was already prostrate. The pair of reverends in his hut, standing over him with their disapproving faces under their top hats, making those noises with their mouths: *tsk tsk tsk*, as if he were a piece of fruit gone bad.

He gets to his feet and starts to walk again. They had a cat once when he was a boy—a stray that wandered over to the parsonage and would not leave, appearing every day and mewling desperately at the door until one of the children came outside. Eventually they convinced their mother to let the cat inside, where it swished happily across the living room, rubbing its body against all of their legs and hands. Anna suggested they call it Roo, a name that quickly stuck. Roo lived with them for only a few months, and then one day she didn't return from her afternoon wanderings and was never seen again.

One day during those months Vincent came across Roo in the garden in back of the parsonage with a mouse clamped between her jaws. The mouse's body was limp and hanging from the corners of her mouth, and Roo looked up at him as if she were carrying a prize that she would share with him only if he were lucky. He did not touch the cat then, merely shooed it away to go do its terrible business where he could not see. But that evening, when Roo came back, he sat with her in the front room and prayed over her, one hand on her tiny head, asking God to forgive her for her trespass and to take away all desire for murder from her heart. He concentrated, his eyes shut tight, fervently aiming his prayer to the sky. Wasn't that the way prayers were heard? When he released her, he felt sure that she swished away from him with a new lightness, a sense of relief at being forgiven. He was seven years old.

He thinks of this now, remembering the lightness and relief, the feeling that a prayer could fix something, that it was that simple. He mourns for that simplicity; he wishes to have it back with all of his soul. In his head everything is so confused, and at the end of the long trail of puzzlement is yet another question mark, for what can a man make of his life if he is so perplexed?

He is alone. He sees the sweep of the countryside; he imagines the horizon extending out past where he can see to other villages and fields and rolling heaths and eventually to oceans and ships and men in other lands. The earth is moving with human life and activity and he is alone on a road, his mind roiling in chaos, in awe at the grandeur and cowering at the fact of it, the incredible pressure, the challenge of being alive. How to be equal to the task? He does not belong to the birds. They have one another; what does he have?

He hears her voice, again and again: *Monsieur Vincent, is that you?* He doesn't know.

1880

Dear Theo,

In 1755 there was an earthquake in Lisbon, Portugal, that nearly completely destroyed the city and the surrounding areas. Forty minutes after the initial earthquake, there was a massive wave, and for days afterward fires raged. Nearly 100,000 people are said to have died.

•

Dear Theo,

A seventy-three-year-old convicted murderer named James Legg was hanged in 1801 for his crime. Three Royal Academy of Arts members convinced the surgeon at Chelsea Hospital to let them have the body after death. They wanted to use Legg's body to study the physiology of the crucifixion of Christ, which they thought had been depicted all wrong in popular artistic renderings. The men erected a cross near the sight of Legg's hanging and affixed the corpse to the cross just as Christ had been affixed. When the body, still warm after death, had cooled, the men made a cast of it, so they could study it; they also, then, flayed the body and made a different cast of it without its skin.

•

January 10

Dear Theo,

Sometimes I am visited by our dead brother, Vincent, the one who died the year before I was born. I have never told anyone this. He comes to me, Theo, I see him, and sometimes he speaks to me.

•

January 10

Dear Theo,

Why is it easier to tell you all of these things than to tell you about the explosion? I will tell you about anything else; anything that I know, even things I don't, I will tell easier than this.

The explosion was two days after Angeline stayed the night in my hut.

I didn't think there was anything worse than what I had already seen in the Borinage, but I was wrong.

The sound of it was a clash of thunder thicker and more ominous than any I had yet heard. I felt the tremor in my hut; the earth beneath me turned to liquid for an instant; it rolled as if in the wake of a boat. Then all was still. I instantly descended into dread. Outside my hut there was sure to be death and destruction and suffering the likes of which I had not yet experienced.

In a moment I heard the breaker whistle blowing from the mine. I ran toward the sound with a churning stomach and tingling limbs, and met many others running toward it, too. Many women were already crying, anticipating that the tragedy they had been waiting for daily was surely upon them at last. There were men running also, their faces fixed and stern, though their eyes were wide and their speed gave away their fear. Who was it they had lost this time? What kind of destruction would they find, and how far would it reach? It was a run of only a minute or so, but in the minds of each of us there was the conscious crossing over from before and into after.

As we came within sight of the mine we slowed our speed, for the vision before us was fresh with darkness and evil. There was a column of dense black smoke climbing to the sky from the center of the mine, where the pit was; the blackness had erased the sun. The air was thick and choking and rife with the sound of ominous crackling and snapping. Through the smoke I could see that the wheel at the top of the pit, that giant piece of machinery that helped to move the cages, was on fire, the flames reaching through the smoke as if they, too, were suffocating and desperate for escape. The buildings surrounding the pit were damaged and charred, their windows blown and hanging, flapping like pieces of cloth. One of the buildings had half collapsed, as if it had been brought to its knees.

It was a vision of Hell. It was more than a vision; it was Hell materialized. Hell has been raised, Theo, I saw it with my own eyes. On the ground approaching the mine there were the bodies of injured men, legs broken and skin smeared with char and dust and blood. Men were shouting and wriggling and squirming, using their elbows, their hips, their shoulders, even their chins to inch themselves farther away from the pit. Some were not moving at all. Scattered among the bodies were severed limbs—a hand, a forearm, a thigh and knee, a calf and ankle and boot, pieces of flesh both recognizable and not—mere objects now, bloodied and ragged, where a few minutes before they had been part of a man's identity, part of how he loved and lost, part of the body he had awakened with that morning.

All was chaos, all was terror, all was noise and dust and flame. Where to run? Whom to tend to? The landscape was awash with need, and I was only a man with two hands. I staggered from man to man, this one with blood rushing from his ear, this one with an elbow bent the wrong way, bone torn through skin like paper. I bent to hear requests and pleas, murmuring words of succor and support, quickly learning that without supplies there was nothing at all I could do.

A man with a mustache lay with a hole in the center of him. He was seemingly intact and howling, but when I drew close to him I saw that his center was open as a window. He fumbled with his insides as if they were clothing overflowing from a bureau drawer. But he had only his hands, and they were not enough. He did not seem aware of me or of anything else beyond his task. For a moment, I could do nothing but stand over him, paralyzed with shock and fear, my eyes fixed on those desperate hands. Through the man's fingers his insides oozed; his hands were solid objects grasping at a hole full of snakes. They were butterflies, those hands, butterflies fluttering over an expanse of living quicksand.

I was mesmerized; the color of the hands was a pale shade that was quickly darkening, saturated by blood, dyed from the inside and the outside. I was a monster, standing over the man and gazing at him, watching him die. I was a monster, but I could not stop; I felt horror that was so complete that it stripped everything away save for my eyes. The man died within a minute or two, his hands growing limp and sinking ever so slowly into his body. Man is made in the image of God, Theo, which is also the image of grief, of terror, and of fire.

Behind the man with the hole in his stomach was a man whose legs were severed. As I approached I saw that it was Louls

Hartmann, the man who had lumbered before me down the passage in the mine when I went down. He whimpered like a child. I took off my shirt and tore the sleeves from it to tie around Hartmann's thighs. He had already lost so much blood that this was most likely a futile act. Blood was pooling around him, the puddle creeping toward his chest. He was sputtering but making no words. I tied the sleeves tight, praying that I could stem the flow. I told him he was going to be all right, feeling a liar and not sure Hartmann could even hear me. His eyes were bulging and full of awe, as if he were watching Heaven approach.

Men and women were arriving with stretchers, planks of wood, horses and mules, anything they could find that might be able to transport bodies away from the mine. In the blur of faces I saw Else and Hubert Aert, their faces twisted, Jan Gilmart lifting a stretcher, Paul Fontaine bending over a man in the dirt. The Denises were there, all of them except Alard, whom they must have made stay at home. I called out to a boy leading a mule— the man without his legs would easily fit on the back of his beast. The boy came toward me, but when he saw the body at my feet he hesitated and then shook his head. "It's no use, Monsieur Vincent!" he said, and moved quickly on, for there was no time to pause for the dead. Louls Hartmann was gone: his chin on the earth, his eyes still wide and staring, but his soul departed. I paused a moment, then bent to remove my sleeves from his thighs. I used them on someone else.

•

January 12

Dear Theo,

How do you represent horror? How do you speak about your nightmares? If you know everything about how things should be, then tell me how to do it. When you are dreaming something horrible, you wake up in your bed and the dream disappears—sometimes as slowly as a fog burns off in the sun, but nonetheless eventually it is gone. The horrors that you see when you are awake do not disappear. When a man is burned in a fire, his skin turns to putty and runs like sand. I know this because I saw such men, such flesh. In the aftermath of the mine explosion I saw a man's face drip off of him, his skin a kind of liquid that pulled away from his eye, which stared up at me, unblinking and dead, like the eye of a fish.

Have you ever seen anything like that, Theo? Have you? Has Father? Has Mother, or Anna, or Lies? Do you think the men of the evangelism committee have seen such things? God sees such things, Theo, God sets them in motion and then lets them live, those moments, those images—they live on inside those of us who see them. What have you seen? What lives in you?

•

January 13

Dear Theo,

I started a letter to you about the explosion that happened here in the days soon after it happened, but I could not get my words to touch it. I still can't. Now I wish I had told you about it, or more than that, that you could have been with me to see it. If you had been here with me, then you probably would not judge me so harshly, for you would see that my time here has been anything but idle. If I am not the same any longer, it is because of what I have seen. If Father had been here for that, would he have picked up his Bible and run into the destruction to recite verses? Put any of the reverends in a scene like that and watch what they do. If they stand on a cart meant for bodies and raise their voices to the suffering herd, and if that is what you would have had me do, then I think it is best that we no longer speak, for then it is surely you who has changed, and not me.

•

Dear Theo,

It wasn't until much later that I learned the fate of Angeline.

I did not think of her. I did not worry. My brain was full but empty. In the hours after the explosion I thought of no one and nothing, only the particular flesh before me, blistered and ragged, and how I could soothe it, how I could tear my clothing into smaller and smaller strips and apply them to that skin. I ran from house to house and gathered olive oil from pantries and hot wax from candles, drenching the last of my clothing in this mixture and applying the linens to scorched and rippling skin.

Skin was divorced from bodies, from personalities and names; my vision was focused on pieces of people, as if these patches of wound were canvases of fine art. I didn't know what I was doing, whom I was tending, the need was so great and so constant. Now when I think of it, I suppose that somewhere inside I assumed Angeline to be all right, to be somewhere among the rest of them, overwhelmed and exhausted and running from place to place. My brain was filled only with the sounds and images. It was as if thought were a sin, in that sea of need, as if to think of anyone in particular would be to ignore all the others, to raise one need above the others, make one body more worthy than another. A few times people tried to give me relief. There was a hand on my shoulder, or Mrs. Denis with a look of concern, saying, "Vincent, slow down, have a rest," for I had been running nonstop since the explosion, and was that a day ago? Two?

But with every bandage I laid, every hand I held, every brow I wiped with a damp handkerchief, I fought the constant and gnawing presence of the conviction that nothing I was doing was of any use. Some of the miners expected prayer from me; they expected comfort in the form of assurance of the next world, of God's plan, of all the usual declarations of Christian faith and goodness in the face of horror. But with every crippled man and child I saw, every broken piece of flesh, I found my mouth was more and more set tight. How could there be any comfort to be found there? I was angry and growing angrier.

After three or more days, Charles Decrucq had still not returned from the mine. Hannah was beside herself; she sat by the entrance of their hut and could do nothing but stare absently in front of her and wring her hands. I felt sure that he would return, and I told her this, but she seemed not to hear me. Her boys threw themselves into the rescue mission, spending the day at the mine, where men were digging slowly toward the tunnel, where they thought they might be able to reach whoever was trapped, if there were any survivors. There were rumors that the rescuers had heard shouts and tapping from inside the tunnel. The boys thought that perhaps they, being small, could wriggle into passages that grown men could not enter, so they hung back and waited for their moment. They supplied the digging men with fresh tools and lamps refilled with kerosene, and remained there through the night.

I was coming back from a trip to the mine on what must have been the day after the explosion. The sky was a gentle pink, unearthly, like the sky before a storm. I stopped on the trail between the mine and the village and turned, looking around me. To the west the sun was disappearing fast; the sky darkened by degrees every few seconds, a visible and invisible change: pink to mauve to nearly purple, a beauty complete and indifferent, as breathtaking a sunset as I had seen in weeks.

I often watched the sunset in the Borinage, having discovered early on that it was one of the few opportunities to see bright color, particularly in the winter months, which seemed to last forever. Perhaps because of the drabness of the landscape, or the chemicals in the air, the sunsets were often spectacular. I'd watch them up by the Denises' house, or on the fence by the mine, enjoying the contrast between the heavenly delights and the earthly toil. That evening, though, I saw something else written in the sky: The sunset was a taunt, it was a pair of eyes looking down and laughing. I stood for a moment, looking at the streak of deep purple turning to red, and I felt only rage.

As I turned back to the path, I saw Madame Dubois, Angeline's mother, who was hurrying toward the mine. Immediately it rushed over me: Angeline! Where was she?

Her mother looked haggard and drugged, her face drawn and pale. "Madame Dubois," I said, stopping before her. I had no words to follow those.

"Any news, Pastor Vincent?" Her tone was pleading and desperate, and I knew then that some part of her family was lost. I blinked, and a silent cry shot through me: Lord, not Angeline.

"They're still digging," I said, and then my throat knotted against my words: "Who is missing?"

She looked at me with great sorrow and, I felt sure, with pity and a flash of anger. How could I ask her such a thing? How could I not already know the answer? Her eyes filled with tears. Her mouth opened to speak and then she closed it again and shook her head. She covered her mouth with her hand, looking at the ground, the tears spilling over her eyelids and falling to the dry earth. I reached out and rested my hand on her shoulder. I knew, of course, what she would say; maybe I had known it since I first felt the tremor in the earth. Maybe all of my frenzied fever in the last hours had been so that I would not have to be confronted, like this, with what she was about to say, and with what I already knew.

"Both of them," she whispered, her eyes still lowered. "Both of my girls are gone."

•

January 26

Dear Theo,

There is something that ties me to this earth; there is more than something. I want to declare this and let this be. A good Christian would take comfort in his unworthiness, perhaps; a good Christian feels this unworthiness and offers it up to God. Thomas à Kempis says in his *Imitation of Christ*, "Learn to be unknown and be glad to be considered despicable and as nothing." We are to despise the world, we are to withdraw from earthly things, we are to consider ourselves unworthy and as nothing, and in so doing we are to grow closer to God; we are to surrender, we are to ascend to the kingdom of Heaven. Presumably there is a point in all this struggling where a man can let go, where he fully surrenders his own will, and this is the point at which he begins to find peace. But I have never been able to find this place. Always at the end of my writhing and cudgeling there is a string that holds on, holds on, grips this world so tightly that it cannot be severed save, I suppose, in death, and who really knows if even then. And there is always a voice in me that says that God does not disapprove; that loving the world is a way to God as well. Do any of us, really, have any purpose here except a passing through on our way to the next world? And if not, why all this beauty, why all this pain, why even the sense of hatred that curls my hands into fists and sets my teeth against one another as if they were enemies?

It is only some days that I don't feel confused about this.

The woodpecker digs its beak into the bark. His beak is like a drill; he pokes violently at the tree. It seems arbitrary, but it can't be, for he comes up with a grub. What I mean to say is that what seems aimless is not. And perhaps a man should trust his instincts. Somehow I feel that there is a purpose to this writing, that at the end of all these words there is something to find, a grub to discover in the grass. Perhaps if I look closely enough at what has passed, I will find in the prism of it the seed of what comes next. Did you think you could come visit and learn anything in a few hours, in a day? When you've visited for a life already and learned nothing?

I am trying to get to a place where it does not pain me to say what I mean. It is hard to tell this story; I hope that much is clear. Here I am, months after your visit, and I have not reached the end. My words are fighting with my anger and my hurt wants to turn away from you forever. I approach the page again and again. I want to explain; I want not to have to explain.

·

Dear Theo,

One day not too many months ago, in September perhaps, I was sitting by the entrance to the Marcasse mine with pencil and paper, sketching what I saw: a thin tree, the men coming out of the gate.

Across the yard I saw a miner making his way to the pit. He was an older man, bent and shuffling, reporting for another day of work, his body carrying him through its routine as it had for so many years, a vessel to bring him through his day and what more? He was wearing the regulation linen work clothes and a vest made of burlap sacking, and as he moved across my line of sight I saw that there was something written on the back of him. Already, before I saw what the word was, I was pleased by this, and thought for a second that it might be my imagination, for if my mind had its way there would be words on all of our backs.

What would the word be if I were inventing it? I stood and moved a few steps closer, peering after him to see my own mind reveal itself, and when the word came into focus, I staggered back. Written across the old man's back as he made his way to the yawning mouth of the mine waiting to swallow him was this word, clear as water, in red capital letters: *FRAGILE.*

The man moved across the ground with his label, "Fragile," and the earth swallowed him, and it would have been so no matter the word on his back.

I spoke of that man to everyone who would listen, but when I described him to other miners, they nearly always looked at me with confused expressions: Yes, so what? It was as it has often been with me: I open my mouth to explain what I see and it is as if what comes out of me is a flurry of bees. People turn their heads and swat at their faces in confusion; they run from me, because why would you stay near a man who carries a beehive in his mouth?

•

February 6

Dear Theo,

Decrucq was recovered alive from the earth; Angeline and her sister never were. Decrucq, the man who claimed that the mines could not kill him, was proved right once again. The mine wanted the flesh of young women more than the tough old bones of a man hardened by its own air.

I lay in my hut as if I, too, were dead. Though it shames me to write it, I must tell you: Our baby brother Vincent appeared, wearing a shimmering nightshirt, hovering near the ceiling, waiting for me to address him. He did not speak. It had been at least a year since he had visited me—the last time was in Amsterdam, near the end, when exhaustion had a hold of me and I knew I could not go on. Please do not think I am mad for seeing him; I could, of course, not tell you about him, which might be more sane, but if I am to tell it all, if I am to trust you with it, he was there.

I thought of you, in a gallery in Goupil's, so far from me it was as if you were across an ocean. The phrase from Michelet repeated in my mind: "We are today what we were yesterday."

After a week or so, Decrucq back in his bed and tended to by Hannah, the rescue party gave up, backed away from the mine with their picks and shovels, and added the names of the missing to the names of the dead. Angeline Dubois and her sister, Francesca, lights in their eyes, skin like rosy petals, extinguished somewhere below the surface of the earth, swallowed back into the original dark womb. No one looked for them anymore; their mother would never see their bodies to wish them a proper farewell; there could be no burial because their burial had already occurred. Were they together when they died? Did they clasp each other's hands in the darkness? Did they share a moment of peace or fellowship before the end? Were they crushed quickly, or was death prolonged, air slowly diminishing, delicate bodies twisted awkwardly in spaces not meant for bodies? I imagined every scenario: timbers entering flesh, ladders bent and crumbling, visitations from Heaven and Hell. Angeline's death became the vision that I lived inside of.

Madame Denis brought me food, ducking into the dark of my hut and clucking over me. When I could not respond to her, she left me milk and warm bread on a tray. In my delirium, I did not know that I ate.

Hubert Aert came to my hut one morning just past dawn to tell me of the strike. I don't know how many days I had been lying there; when Hubert knocked, it was the sound of someone alive knocking in the depths of the earth.

It must have been sometime in May. I was delirious from hunger, and the absence of sleep had turned all my waking moments to a dream. Baby Vincent hovered by my ears and whispered to me: I was no good, I had killed her because I had touched her, because everything I touched went wrong. I no longer knew what I believed in, and without this I no longer knew anything. If a man knows nothing, he is lost.

Cricket the bird lay dead on the bottom of his cage; I do not know if he died of natural causes or because I had ceased to feed him.

I lay on the floor as if in a grave, and Hubert said my name again, and again, and consciousness began to return to me; in confusion I began to perceive the light in the room, streaming through the dirty window onto the floor near my feet, I began to understand that the man now crouching near to me was not an apparition. Hubert placed his hand on my shoulder; his palm was rough but warm and with it came a charge of life. When Lazarus was summoned, did he have a choice but to respond?

"Monsieur Vincent," Hubert said again, and this time I heard him. "We need your help."

I was in no position to help anyone. My spirit was more broken than many of the miners', for I was supposed to be in a position to aid them, and instead I had given away all I had. I had nothing left. No spirit, no clothes, no money, no food, no warmth, no comfort or belief or assurance, no answers. It was Hubert who was helping me and not vice versa.

But when Hubert said, "We need your help," again I felt my soul rise up. I shook my head against my visions and focused on Hubert's face. He was real; he was alive. He helped me to sit up and he told me about the strike. The miners were angry. They were desperate. Explosions had been happening more and more, and this last one had devastated the village; the company's inspections of the mines were not adequate.

"They are ignoring the dangers," said Hubert; "the company is putting our lives in danger and offering us no compensation in return." While the rescue teams searched for survivors in the mines, while the mines were closed, no wages were paid, and so on top of their grief and their suffering, the miners were now also hungry. Even Madame Denis could not make bread anymore. The company was now ordering them back to work. They had given them nothing, though it was, of course, not the miners' fault that the mines were unsafe. What could they do but strike?

In my time in the Borinage I had seen the miners come close to a strike more than once; sometimes it seemed they were always on the verge of a strike. Conditions never improved, and there was never enough of anything—food, money, coal—and striking was the only commodity the miners felt they had, though it wasn't much of a commodity at all. When they went on strike, they suffered more than anyone: Their food dwindled and disappeared; their meager ration of coal was retracted; they had nothing to do but confront the reality of their situation, which was that they lived in houses that were owned by the very company they were up against. Without their enemy, they were even more lost, even more nowhere and no one.

I could see from Hubert, though, that this strike was different. He sat next to me on the floor of the hut, the rectangle of light from the window creeping closer to us, slowly covering his boots.

"What is the limit of what a man can stand?" Hubert whispered, and even in the dim light I could see his eyes were shining with tears. His words were all of action, but all he was really speaking of was sorrow. He was a representative of a group of people felled by grief and by desperation. Striking was the only way they could manifest that they were still human.

My suspicions were confirmed later that day, after Else Aert fed me bread and a few cups of black coffee, and Hubert took me to the strike meeting in the salon. My legs were weak as we walked down the hill toward the building, but I dared not show my limp. As we approached the building, I could see the crowd. People were pouring into the building and standing in clusters outside, chattering and shaking their heads and fists. Everyone who could walk was there—Decrucq, though his sons were there on his behalf, had had to stay behind in his bed—and when I managed to push my way into the room, I saw Paul Fontaine was at the front, holding up his hands and fielding questions as if they were tangible objects that he could push away.

I wasn't sure what I was doing there. I knew nothing, least of all how a man should gamble with his livelihood or honor his pain. I was not the same man I had been a few weeks before—or perhaps I was just the same, but with a new fear that when I spoke, it would be as hot air that came out, dangerous and deceptive hot air that could help no one.

Paul saw me in the crowd and called for me to come stand with him. I thought of Angeline, her quiet smile, which gave me such confidence, which showed me how she was listening to me, that my words were gifts that were given and received. I tried to picture her in the crowd, watching me with her brown eyes under her scarf, encouraging me to be the leader that I once dreamed I was. What would she think of this strike? I was sure that she would think it sad, the desperate gesture of a population drowning in despair, a people with no means of escape.

Paul looked to me to say something. " 'In the midst of life we are in death,' " I began; " 'of whom may we seek for succor?' " But I could not answer my own question; I felt no interest in its answer. I dropped my hands.

She was gone. I stood next to Paul and all my words died in my throat.

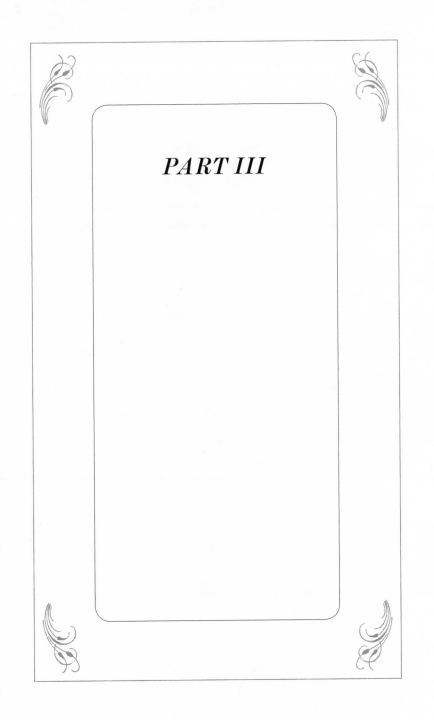

PART III

1880

May 14, 1:00 p.m.

He is delirious with hunger, and starting to hallucinate. He dreams of water and a feast of rosemary chicken, succulent drumsticks in both his hands. Paul Fontaine walks beside him, carrying a mining lamp; Charles Decrucq lies in a pit by the side of the road, his skin slick with mud and his lamp burning blue. Angeline stands before him in her mining clothes, covered in dust; Angeline hovers before him, cross-legged and with a shy smile, her head just a bit too big for her body. Alard holds his hand and swings it with each stride, but when Vincent looks at him, he is gone.

He starts to lose time, shifting between moments near and far.

He is a boy. He is lying on the thin rug before the hearth in Zundert with a pencil gripped in his hand, so tightly that it makes a groove in his palm. He hears no sound, only the scratch of the pencil over the parchment, the dark stroke over the page.

His family is there, he can vaguely hear the sound of them talking over the noise of his concentration. It is a joke for them, how they can say things to him and he won't hear them; they can insult him and poke him with their shoes and he will not respond. He is never very good at doing more than one thing at once, but this is a disappearance, so they have told him, as complete as if he has fallen through a hole in the floor.

The image his hand is molding grows before his eyes; a line turns into two, turns into a shaded corner or a shortened face. He is drawing a frog, an elephant, a beetle, the fireplace itself. It is his hand that is making this thing, his hand is growing an object that is not an object, but how can his hand do such a thing? It is his brain, it is a pencil, it is his hand, it is the parchment paper itself, stained with growing streaks of black. His head lies on his arm; he is at eye level with the paper. He sketches the lines on the paper but feels the shape of each line as if it is being carved onto his arm.

But as the image develops, so does his hatred of it. There is unease from the start, a twist in the lowest part of his stomach, not unlike what he feels as Christmas approaches each year. The image is a root that could turn into beauty or poison. And as the drawing emerges, becoming more a representation and less a collection of disconnected lines, the unease, too, gains definition. The hand cannot stop itself, the lines continue to expand and marry one another, but he resists what the hand is doing: The shading should be darker, the pencil is inferior, the face looks like an apple and not a face at all. The image looks nothing like what it should. He hates the pencil; he hates the paper; he hates his hand.

He digs the pencil deeper and deeper into the parchment; he hates the drawing and he wants it to disappear, and yet he can't stop himself. The image grows, the parchment rips, and the lines grow angry and distorted. He scribbles over it, then sits up and tears it in two, and then four, and then a hundred pieces, and throws them into the fire.

He is ten years old, in his father's church, listening to his father preach about sin. The concept is one Vincent has always known—the word is a part of his world, and has always been—but hearing his father at the front of the church speak of the sinners among them, he knows suddenly and without doubt that he is being spoken to. His father is speaking to him, from the pulpit; his sermon is directed at his second firstborn son. A sinner! So that's what he is.

He feels relief, a sense of recognition, a sharpening of vision as when a steamy mirror is wiped clean. At the same time there is shame, hot and relentless, a tightening in his stomach and groin such that he immediately feels he has to relieve himself. His face flushes; his ears are on fire. He wants to hide under the pew where his family sits, block his ears with his hands so he can't hear any more. What do you do when you are labeled, when you see yourself clearly for the first time? He sits quietly, his face burning, his hands in fists on his lap, his legs crossed, until the service is over.

Back at the parsonage, his mother preparing supper, he sneaks out of the house and dashes down the lane, running quickly to the nearest empty field. Behind a barn, he sinks to his knees, breathing heavily. He doesn't know what to do. He is still wearing his church clothes, the long shorts coming just to his knees, his socks and black leather shoes, which are now scuffed and probably ruined, another thing he has done wrong, another reason to repent. He will be in trouble just for being here, for having sneaked out of the house, for thinking the wrong thing during his father's sermon, which his father will never say was about him. He has ruined his clothes and, no doubt, his family's meal. He bends over, touching his forehead to the grass, breathing in the smell of dirt and grass, taking a few blades into his mouth. He is a sinner, that is what he is. When a person is a sinner, is there any way to change? He is surprised to realize that he is crying.

He rakes his fingers through the grass behind the barn, harder and harder, tearing up the soil in clumps, feeling the dirt press in under his fingernails. It is not enough. He brings his hands to his skin and rakes the dirt across his legs, using his fingernails to scrape ruts in his skin, watching with a strange detached wonder as the dirt mixes with his blood and makes lines across him. The

pain is both close and far away. The ruts light up his skin, the fiery
sting of them clearing the clouds in his chest, relieving the pressure in his bladder. It is what he deserves. There is less, now, to
be ashamed of.

It is late November in the Borinage, four months after his dismissal. He is back in Petit Wasmes, a ghost returning to the scene
of his death.

This is where he died: These huts, these chickens, these goats
scampering away from him, these are his murderers. People peer
out from behind dirty curtains; he can see their grubby hands as
they shoo him away. Chickens flap their wings as they run, trying
to show him that they are strong. He runs after them, shaking
his head and flapping his arms like wings. Noises come from his
throat that he has never heard before. He runs after the chickens
and he is no longer human, he is a bird that cannot fly. His feet are
claws, his arms are flightless wings, his feathers ratty and ragged.

Three boys are gathered at the end of a lane, and they are using a stick to poke a goat that is tied to a stake in the ground. One
of the boys wears pants that are tattered and frayed; all three of
them wear shirts of coarse linen, surely sewn by their mothers.
Vincent slows to a stop in front of them. For a minute or two they
just look at one another. He can see the one with the torn pants is
the leader; he is deciding what nature of foe Vincent is.

"What are you looking at?" The boy sneers. His mouth turns
back like a dog's does when it growls. The baring of teeth is a
sure sign that they are not friends.

Vincent takes a step closer to him and snatches the stick
from his hand. "Hey!" the boy says. The others shuffle their feet
uncomfortably.

As if he is blind, Vincent swings out with the stick. The
boy jumps back. "Are you crazy?" he squeals.

"You are goats," Vincent says. He jabs the stick at the boy.
"Poke," he says, as he jabs with the stick. "Poke, poke."

The boys run from him. "He's crazy!" yells the one with the tattered pants. When they are a safe distance from Vincent, the boy picks up a rock and throws it. It misses, though it was strongly thrown. One of the other boys throws another—it hits Vincent's leg. Pain blooms like a flower on his shin.

Without thinking, he picks up the rock that hit him and hurls it right back. He is a boy, too; he is back in the village in Zundert, running from the peasant boys who will not let him play. These boys have been after him his whole life; he is finally ready to fight back. His first rock misses; he picks up another and throws again. Women are coming out of their huts, wondering what the commotion is about. The boys start to run. One of the boys has been hit, and runs now with a limp—"He's crazy! Just run!"—and in their retreating forms Vincent sees that one of them is Theo, his brother, who has become his enemy. He hurls another one, as hard as he can; the women are running after him now; he has only one second to see the rock land just to the left of his brother. He missed.

When night arrives, he lies down between two haystacks; his body is heavy and still as a log. He has no memory of the last few hours of walking. He has been washed there by a tide, delivered by waves and then left, driftwood on a shore. He breathes in the smell of hay and earth, sweet and musty, a comforting odor, not so different from the scent of a man, but sweeter and more tangible, a smell that can be held and tasted on the tongue.

He is a log; he is still and slowly decomposing. His eyes are closed. His body—its bark flecked with crevices, nooks for grass to grow and beetles to crawl in, its landscape a heath of moss and mud—is a planet of its own kind. His body is a planet, a harbor for living things. But in the midst of life we are in death, a phrase he thinks of so often, and knows from the inside: Inside him there are planets living and dying, just as the whole of him lives and will die. Even as he lies there on the damp ground beneath two haystacks, the time of his life is ticking away; he is a log decomposing and returning to the earth. He is living and he is dying; both are true. Next to him is a baby in a nightdress.

Images crowd him—a Jules Breton painting, *The Rainbow,* with a little boy pointing back into a dark storm toward the arc of color and the slim opening of light at the horizon; Alard, laughing with Nathen, laughing with Smoke, inspecting a fallen bird's nest with a broken egg; Theo, turning his back and boarding the train; Theo, with his top hat next to him on the table, eating an egg; two horses, one of them blind; Angeline, standing by her father's bedside, the candlelight flickering on her face; a man with his insides hanging loose, trying to stuff them back in with his hands. A sketch is on his knees, growing in the firelight: It is Angeline, her skirts tucked under her, lamplight hiding half her face in shadow, the outline of her thick and seeming to raise her off the page, and she is beautiful. Reverend Pieterszen from the evangelism committee is standing in his doorway, holding the sketch of Angeline, gazing down at it as if he were reading a newspaper. His mother is in front of the grave with his name on it, her shoulders heaving with sobs.

A thunderstorm rolls in; the night is lit up in flashes and explosions. Rain pours off of him, it clouds his vision, he cannot see, and then in a flash of light all is as bright as day. The water pours off of the farmer's barn behind him and he thinks of the hulk of Noah's ark, as it would have appeared in the darkness of the Flood by the light of a lightning flash. "Stop this, Vincent," his mother screams over the storm. He yells to her that he cannot hear her, though he can.

He remembers Alard, a few weeks ago, sitting with him in the salon, his face confused and fearful, his eyes wide; Smoke the cat had disappeared, and Vincent was weeping, his face streaked with dirt. "I am mourning!" he yelled. "Our friend is gone; she is gone, Alard! We are mourning!"

Theo! How can I show you all that is in my head, all that I have seen? Theo, can you hear me?

He crawls to the haystack to his right and tries to get close enough to it that it might shield him from the rain. He nuzzles close up to it and breathes into the hay. A lightning flash lights the night, and in the moment of light he sees a spider clinging to the hay a few inches from his face. The spider treks along, seemingly unperturbed by the weather. Where is it off to? He pulls himself up and peers at the insect. He is impressed with the spider's temerity—for the insect, the length of the haystack is an enormous way. The spider crawls, eight legs working in tandem with ease, a strange creeping magic show. It is a marvel, he thinks, that such a creature exists.

With a quick movement, he covers the spider with his hand. He feels the insect crawl onto his fingers, and thinks of how it must be startled, the world suddenly changed, the new surface of these warm fleshy things. The spider is moving, unperturbed, exploring.

He brings his hand to his face and tosses the spider into his mouth. For a second, he feels it throw itself around in there, and then he swallows it.

He lies back and lets the rain fall onto his face. His body is hot and tingling, energized as if he were still moving. The night lights up again and again in flashes of bright, unearthly light, so he can see everything plainly, in a clearer light even than daylight. He can see everything, there, from his position on the earth in the rain. He feels an incredible growing power, as if, were he to move, he might crack open the whole world.

1880

Dear Theo,

Sometime in very early July, we held a memorial service in my hut for those who had been lost in the explosion. Yes, it was late, but I couldn't bring myself to host it any sooner.

I had had nothing but coffee for days and days. Look at me, Theo, I am not ashamed, not anymore: I had only a few coarse coal sacks draped around me for clothes. I was unshaven and starved, feverish and delirious and filthy. My lips were dry and cracked, my face streaked with shades of brown and black. I lay back on the straw in the corner of my hut while the miners came in and surrounded me. There were not many of them, but to me it was a crowd.

It was early evening and the light was dim; my lantern hung from the rafters near the door, but it hardly gave more than a glow. I kept forgetting why the people were there, thinking I was dreaming, then realizing that they were waiting for me to speak. I squirmed and resisted, left myself and came back, struggled and calmed myself a hundred times in a minute. The bodies darkened and turned to creatures; they were molded and wax, they were black stone, they were shadows, nearly a hundred shadows hovering and swaying in my hut, looming over me, dancing, a hundred versions of our brother Vincent, judging me, a hundred versions of myself, of you, of the bird Cricket, whom I had buried outside my door, of Father and Mother. Their heads shook, their fingers wagged, their eyes burned. It was a nightmare, I was dreaming, there were a hundred tired souls staring down at me and waiting for me to save them, to heal their hearts; it was a task I was not capable of. But wait, this was no nightmare, these were my friends, my gentle and sorrowful friends, my starving friends. They looked to me as if I were God, waiting for me to deliver answers. But where was God? I had lost Him.

I propped my head on my hands and began to speak. My voice was quiet, and many of the miners crouched to hear me. "My friends," I began, "we are gathered here today to mourn together for the loss of our friends, those who were taken from us and swallowed in violence by the mine." It was difficult for me to get the words out. My mind was interfering with my mouth; I had to concentrate on each word before I said it so that I would not merely speak nonsense. "Preachers say that God works in mysterious ways," I said, "and this is true. We often don't understand the ways of the world, for there is much to the mystery that we simply cannot comprehend. Only one thing we know for sure, and that is that we loved those people whom we have lost, and they did not deserve to die."

"My friends," I continued, pushing the words out, "man is a serious being. There is a string in the heart that accords to the voice of sorrow, and impressions of grief take the strongest hold of the mind. There is a time when cheerfulness gives place to melancholy, and when the house of mourning is better suited to the soul than the house of mirth. This, I think, is one of those times, and I am so happy we are all here to experience it together. For whether we think of it or not, death approaches. Every path in the world leads to the tomb, and every hour has been to some the last hour. We have learned this already, these last few months, mourning our friends who were struck down so cruelly.

"Preachers say that the lesson of death is that we will rise again in the next world; Scripture says, 'the dust returns to the earth as it was, the spirit shall return unto God who gave it.' Preachers say that we should let the grave speak to us, teach us lessons of purity and lead us away from our vanity in this world. This is what I am supposed to tell you, that our suffering will be relieved in the next world, that it is God's plan that we should suffer in this world so that we can go in glory to the next. But the truth is that I wonder about this as much as you do. What is this world, if it is just for passing through? Is it true what the preachers say, that we are not to cling to this world, not to cling to those we love? Friends, I admit it! I don't believe this. I want to cling to this world with all of my strength; I want to cling to all of you, to this place, to the people whom we lost. Friends, we are alive! We are alive, which means that we can still see this world, which means that we can still appreciate its beauty. I am not living for the next world, not now, no; I am living for this one. I want to do justice to the world I am in right now. I am moving toward the grave, yes, as are we all, but I am paying attention to every step along the way."

The bodies in the room held me, Theo. I could feel them holding me with their attention, with their presence and their weeping eyes. I started again, feeling I must go on for them, "Friends"—and at this, there was a commotion at the door, and the miners parted. In the doorway stood Reverends De Jong and Van den Brink, two of the members of the evangelism committee. They were finely dressed, in black coats and top hats, more funereal by far than the miners. Their faces wore expressions of shock.

"Welcome, Reverends," I managed to say after a moment. I was too weak to muster surprise. Much of me still thought I was dreaming, and the arrival of the reverends made some sort of strange sense. I addressed them: "We are conducting a service for the fifty-seven people who perished in the explosion in the Marcasse mine. Now that you're here, perhaps you'd like to offer some words of comfort to these good people?"

Of course they would do no such thing. They cleared their throats and tried to shake off their disgust; they mustered the professional stance they favored before potential believers. They waved their arms and demanded private audience with me, despite my inadequate protests, shooing the miners out of the hut as if they were crows. They believed they held jurisdiction over any roomful of people; any collection of hearts was theirs.

I am not sure why the reverends came to the Borinage. Maybe it was the letter I sent to Brussels that roused them, although they gave no help to the people while they were here. Maybe they wanted to come in person to tell me that I had been dismissed. Later, I thought it hard to believe that they would have given me another chance had they found something different upon their arrival, but perhaps they told themselves as much.

I was dismissed. The reverends called me "un-Christian" and "savage." They chastised me for attempting to have any kind of a service in such a hovel as that little hut, and they decried my state, my weakness, and where, oh where, were my clothes? They shook their heads and spoke to each other more than they spoke to me. Their French was rapid and I was exhausted. I could not bring myself to care much at all about what they said or what judgment they passed. As I lay at their feet, their shiny black boots in my line of vision, I tried to conjure the time when I would have cared. It was so recent, but I could barely bring it to mind. They spoke at me, they spoke above me, they shook their fists and their heads. At some point, without my noticing, they disappeared.

My probationary period was up, my services no longer desired. I was not surprised. I had tried to show them that their love was the same as mine, but I failed.

The official letter came to the Denises' house. "The absence of certain qualities," the reverends wrote. "Lacks a talent for speaking." They praised me for my "devotion to the spirit of self-sacrifice," but this was not enough to "render the exercise of an evangelist's principal function." They granted me three months to look for another situation. Even the word *situation* was strange to me.

Function is the word the reverends used. A man is supposed to have a function, just like a scythe or a hoe.

Madame Denis brought me a clean shirt, underwear, and a pair of pants belonging to her husband. She also brought me a piece of soap, which I used to scrub myself, standing in a basin of water as hot as I could stand it.

All of my movements were languid; it was as if I were moving through molasses. My limbs felt heavy and difficult to move, as if they were new to me, as if I were learning how to use them. As the water ran off my body, I looked down at it and barely recognized it. When I arrived in the Borinage my body was robust, it had strength I could rely on, and I knew it as my own. In less than a year, it had dwindled to something I no longer knew. I was barely more than a skeleton: There were my hip bones, my knobby knees, my ribs pushing through my skin as if they wanted to reach the air. A man does not know his skeleton like he knows his body; he can have a distinct birthmark, freckles, a patch of ruddy skin, a suit of reddish hair that covers him, but his skeleton must look the same as any man's. If he were shown a group of skeletons, could he identify his own?

It frightened me, the confrontation with my body in that warm basin. I moved the soap gently over its contours and crevices, scrubbing only just enough, scooping the water from the basin with an old metal cup and pouring it slowly over the skin to wash away the suds. I knew it was my body because I could feel the warmth of the water, the steam that rose up into my eyes, the way that beneath the layer of dirt the skin was soft and pink and alive. As the dirt fell away and I saw the rosy pink rise through the skin of my sunken stomach, my thighs, my arms, I felt tears rise into my eyes. To whom was this body sacred? No one would care for a person if he did not care for himself. It was another failure to add to the list. Through the blurring of my tears, I saw our brother Vincent hovering next to me, his body warm and rosy and plump, forever healthy. When I reached for him, he slipped away.

After the bath I shaved off the growth of months and saw my face in the small mirror over the sink. Without the fullness of the beard, my face was long and narrow. My cheekbones sat high on sunken cheeks, my eyes low valleys among steep peaks. I stared at myself for quite a while, trying to find myself in the image in that mottled mirror. Always before it had been others that I lost a hold of—other people, other ideas, other notions and professions and convictions. This time, I had lost myself. These are my failures, Theo; I lay them before you to judge.

And then, just a mere month later, you arrived. Before your visit, which I had been dreaming of for months, I walked to Brussels to see Reverend Pieterszen, who had always been the member of the evangelism committee who was the most supportive of me. A fairly punishing walk in the hot summer sun, though an invigorating one. Pieterszen looked at my drawings and praised them, found me lodgings in the Frank home in Cuesmes, and sent me off with a pair of new boots, a train ticket, and the encouragement to keep going, to find my own path despite my lack.

Now that you know a bit of what I have been through in this place, can you imagine how I longed to see you, how I yearned to commune with the brother who had always understood me when no one else did? I couldn't tell you about this place in a letter; my words could not do justice to it, to Angeline, to the horror of the explosion, to the wonder of the people, Decrucq and Paul Fontaine and the little school, the slag heap, the sunsets, the mine.

I couldn't tell you about it, but I thought we would have the time to talk in person. When you arrived, you were different—you, Theo, not me, for as much as I may have changed, as much as I had seen, I still, after all, wanted to talk to you and to be seen by you.

•

March 1

Dear Theo,

Not even a man's words can always represent what is in his mind. A man is always choosing his words, in charge of his narrative, free to omit what he wants to, to invent and to twist. I write you of the past, and yet I do not share the present.

It is March here now, seven months since you came to visit. A cover of snow is still on the ground from the last snowstorm; there have been many storms here lately. Still I have heard nothing from you, and except for that first letter that I mailed you, you have heard nothing from me. But all these months, I have been speaking to you. The letters are piled in the drawer of my desk here in Cuesmes. Why haven't I mailed them? What am I waiting for?

I fear that you will read them and it will not matter. I fear that you will judge me no matter what, that I have lost your fellowship forever. I fear that I deserve this, though at the same time I am sure I do not.

•

Dear Theo,

For Christmas this year I shared supper at the Decrucq house; it was the first time I had been in their home since before my dismissal in July. I saw Hannah Decrucq one morning a ways back after visiting with Alard in the old salon; she must have thought me a fright, for I can think of no other reason for her kind invitation. I had to force my legs to carry me there; I felt sure I was no longer welcome in the miners' village, and did not wish to face my shame on that day of all days.

On my way through the village to the Decrucq house, I kept my head low and prayed that I would not be recognized. A few children I passed knew me for sure; they stared, as children are wont to do, betraying to me the reality of their parents' whispers of my name. What has my reputation become, in the months since my dismissal? As the months pass, I feel more inquiring eyes, more and more people wondering why I'm still here—or, if they don't know me, who I am and what I am doing in this place.

Who knows what is being said about me now. A rock landed near me after I passed some children in the village, and I dared not turn back. Children can be the cruelest of all, but everything they know they learn from adults.

Decrucq himself came to the door and boomed his greeting as warmly as ever. "Vincent!" he practically shouted, and I winced at his volume, though I was grateful for his extended hand as he pulled me into the hut and shut the door behind us. "Great to see you, lad!" he exclaimed. "Come in, come in." He ushered me into the middle of the room, where the table was set. His limp was more pronounced than ever—it seems both legs are deficient now. I hadn't seen him since those dark days after his rescue from the collapsed mine, and I was happy, though by no means surprised, to see him recovered so fully. "Oh, my friend," he said, his hand on my arm, "you are too thin, too thin. Hannah, we must fatten up this man!"

Just being in their home was a trial, a battle against the ghosts of my hopes and expectations and, in the very presence of Decrucq, the absence of Angeline. The room was dim, as ever, the shadows from the lantern and candles trembling into the darkness. Though it smelled wonderful—they had somehow managed to find a goose to cook—and the whole family was there, the parents and their four children, two of whom had spouses and children of their own, I was still, despite all, reminded of death, and that these lovely people were not my family.

"It was a terrible business," Decrucq was saying. "I thought for sure I was going to die down there that time."

"Father," said his eldest daughter, Marie, holding her youngest child on her lap, feeding it spoonfuls of mashed potatoes, "let's not go over this again."

"They don't like it when I speak of it," Decrucq said to me with a familiar wink. "I don't blame them, but also I think it's important not to forget."

"Why not?" exclaimed Hannah, coming toward the table with the goose, steam rising off of it. She slid it onto the table and everyone looked at it. "It's in the past. And you will not be in such danger again. I think forgetting is exactly what you need to do." She handed him the knife to cut the bird.

He stood and began to carve. His right hand was twisted awkwardly, so he held the knife with his left and a fork in his right. Yes, I have been reading much Shakespeare lately, but Decrucq made me think of Falstaff, somehow both a joker and a wise man. "That's right!" he said. "Vincent, I have news. I have been appointed foreman of the Cuesmes mine. We are moving at the end of the month."

He kept cutting but looked at me for my reaction. I was silent, as I had been for nearly all of my visit. Decrucq, a foreman! Perhaps some of us are rewarded for our trials after all.

My eyes must have given away my surprise, for he laughed. "I never thought I'd see the day, either," he said. He shook his head. "They must have figured I would cause less trouble at this point from aboveground than below."

"Or maybe," said his eldest son, Jan, a miner himself, "they are simply rewarding you for all of your hard work and sacrifice."

"That doesn't sound like them." Decrucq laughed, and everyone joined in, even me.

It was a delicious meal, and there were moments when I forgot my circumstances and felt true comfort with the Decrucqs, so different from our family, so informal and warm and with concerns so different from ours. I felt privileged with them, and envious, too, a familiar combination of feelings. They did not ask me about what I had planned, about what path I would take, because these were not questions they ever asked themselves. Decrucq, I could tell, wanted to ask me about what I had been doing, but he did not. I was here, at his Christmas supper, and I did not preach to him of God: I am sure this told him enough.

Neither did I ask him about Angeline. At the end of the evening, I said good night and thank you to Hannah and the rest of the family, and Decrucq walked me out of the house and down the road a ways, just past the end of the houses. He claimed he needed the exercise, and I was grateful, for being with him would protect me from any unwelcome encounters with children and their rocks. We walked along in silence—both of us, I am sure, thinking of the explosion, though neither of us mentioned it. What was there to say? I wanted to ask him if he knew how Angeline had died, though of course that was as silly a question as any of them. The chances that they were near each other when the explosion happened were next to none. What was it that I was really looking to know? Nothing that he could tell me, surely.

"It's truly great news, about your promotion," I said.

He nodded. "Yes, Hannah is very happy. We will have a proper house, and I will have to go down into the mine only every once in a while."

"Did Fontaine help, you think?"

He laughed. "Oh, I'm sure of it. He insists that he didn't, but I have no doubt that he did."

"We will be neighbors again," I said.

"Indeed!"

I thanked him again for having me to his home, and we parted ways at the end of the lane.

Does what goes on inside ever show on the outside? Someone has a great fire in his soul and nobody ever comes to warm themselves at it, and passers-by see nothing but a little smoke at the top of the chimney and then go on their way. So now what are we to do, keep this fire alive inside, have salt in ourselves, wait patiently, but with how much impatience, await the hour, I say, when whoever wants to will come and sit down there, will stay there, for all I know?

•

March 25

Dear Theo,

I have been to France and back, a walk of a few days. I went to see Jules Breton, the painter; he lives in Courrières, just over the French border.

I find that I do not want to write to you about it. I don't know why I went, what I was hoping to find, but suffice it to say I did not find it. I turned back without seeing him, feeling a fool, and am now back in Cuesmes just the same. Another useless, fruitless journey, nothing gained except a stuffed-up nose, a rumbling cough, and some blisters on my feet.

•

Dear Theo,

There is a cat here, I have named him Smoke. He is nothing but fur and bones; when I touch him, I can feel his skeleton. He is missing a toe, and his left eye is sunken and blind, a bleached-out blue, the color of a robin's egg scrubbed with steel wool. One of his ears is ragged and bloody, a jagged mountain range of crusty skin. He is so old, he seems to have lost most of the ability to clean himself; he tries, sometimes, but it never lasts long. But he still arches his back at the touch of my fingers.

When he walks, he is halting and slow, as if he is made of metal and needs oil, as if his parts don't quite fit together. When he is outside, he moves a few steps and then he rests, licking his sore paws, shutting his eyes to the sun. Then he is on his feet again. I watch him on his slow journeys until he is gone from view.

Alard said he is the cat version of me. We sat together yesterday, the three of us, in front of a fire that Alard made. Smoke has taken to Alard, too; he prefers to sit in his lap more than in mine. I told Alard it is because he has more warmth in him; he is a like a warm patch of grass in the sunshine, while I am like a thin and barely standing tree. Alard gave me a look that showed he was pleased with what I said at the same time that he thought it strange.

We lay on the floor and drew pictures together, while Smoke lay curled in a ball nearby. It is such a joy to draw with Alard, for though he had not done it much before he met me, he has that insatiable child's imagination that only needs to be set loose before it runs and jumps. I can't help but think of you while we draw, remembering all those sessions at home in Zundert on the rug before the fire. Alard and I drew animals that we are afraid of. Alard combined a tiger and a wolf, and I admitted it was a terror to behold.

"Who do you think would win in a fight?" Alard asked me, sitting up with his legs crossed. He pointed to one of his drawings and then to the other. "The tiger-wolf, or the lion-shark?"

"Does the lion-shark live on land or in the sea?"

"It can live on both!" He pushed my shoulder with his little hand. Smoke lifted his head and looked at us, annoyed that we were making so much noise. "Of course!"

"Well, in that case it's the lion-shark for sure," I said, and smiled at him.

I am not drawing much right now; I only do so with Alard. When I try on my own, a feeling of uselessness and fatigue descends. Alard encourages me, and when I am with him, I feel the old need tug at me.

•

April 19

Dear Theo,

The other day Alard asked me to tell him about you. I didn't know whether to tell him about the version of you that was my friend, the only one who has understood me, or about the you who has disappeared. He has a brother who is exactly as close in age as we are, and I don't want him to know that brothers can ever disappear. No boy should know that. I wish I didn't have to know it, either. I changed the subject, if you want to know, because it hurt me too much to talk about you.

•

April 25

Dear Theo,

Smoke the cat has gone. He left one day and hasn't come back. Another thing I loved that has disappeared.

•

April 29

Dear Theo,

I have decided that I will come to see you. There are too many of these letters, now, to send them through the mail. Perhaps it is time that we see each other again, that we talk again as brothers. It has been a long time since we wrote to each other as we used to, but I am not ready to give up hope that we can be close to each other again. I will deliver this story to you, I will return the money that you gave me, and though we may not forgive each other, I will at least once again shake your hand.

1880

At dawn, the sunlight a stripe of possibility on the horizon, he rises and continues on. He is delirious with hunger, his body creaking and aching with every step. His boot, the one bolstered with cardboard back in Burigny, has given way again, so his bloody sock is visible through the toe. He limps on, determined. His mind is a sieve; images, memories, snippets of language rise up and float away; he cannot hold on to a thought; he is merely two legs, a torso, and a vessel through which words and colors can pass. Next to him, the baby Vincent continues to float, but he has been reduced to a few words. *Step*, he says, *step, step, step.*

After a few hours, he has reached the outskirts of Paris; the road begins to form into a lane more traveled, and in the distance he can see the tall buildings and the plumes of smoke that mark the city. He is getting close. His nerves, accordingly, are dancing and clamping, little spikes of electricity shooting through his limbs. He clenches and unclenches his fists and shakes his wrists; his hands flop and shake and still they tingle as if they are falling asleep. He slaps his face to keep himself alert and in the present. His knapsack over his shoulder has grown heavy, though there is very little inside it, only words, really.

He carries the money that his brother gave to him in August, untouched, still in the envelope in which his parents passed it to him. What had they become to each other, that he heard nothing from him for nearly a year and was passed fifty francs through their parents as intermediaries? He will give it back. From now on, he wants to earn all the money he is given, be it from his brother or anyone else.

Delirious, he walks on. The streets are busier now, dark carriages rolling past him and women clipping by on dark high heels. He stumbles and trudges and shuffles, feeling as if he is seeing everything through a glass of water or a thick mist; he is walking through a dream. When was the last time he was in Paris? In 1876, before he left Goupil's for good, and when Harry Gladwell was still in his life.

He is not sure if the dream is now or the dream was then. What he sees before him now—the cobbler on the corner, polishing a man's shoes as the man reads a newspaper, his feet up on a wooden box—is it any easier to believe than the images that flood him? Baby Vincent floats alongside him, rests on his back. Baby Vincent shouts for him to look at a baby in a carriage, pushed by a woman in what looks like an identical bonnet tied under her chin.

A woman and her child sharing an outside table at a café are as familiar to him as if they are his kin; he smiles at them, but they look up at him in horror, and he realizes that he must have the look of a monster, a man returning from a war. He walks on, thinking that he must stop somewhere to clean himself; he must gather himself together somehow before he arrives at his brother's door.

In the dim water closet of a poorly lit pub, he splashes water onto his face and squints at himself in the mirror over the sink. He blinks and slaps his cheeks, trying to restore himself. Between one blink and the next he has the face of a baby, and then the face of a man. His cheeks are drawn in and sunken, his beard ragged and dark. He tries to scrub off the dirt of three days on dusty roads, thinking of his brother's face when he sees him at the door. When the dirt comes free his skin is pink and mottled, protesting the sudden attention.

There is not much he can do about the state of his clothes or his boots. He hits himself all over, the dust rising off of him in clouds that make him cough. The leather of the toe of his boot is now completely loose and flopping with every step. He remembers the kindness of Bertha and James at the pub in Busigny; perhaps this place will have more cardboard for him to slip into his shoes.

Back out at the bar, he takes a seat and says, "Coffee, please" to the bartender. They are the first words he has spoken in almost two days, and it surprises him that his voice sounds as it always has. He has a few cents left from a farmer the day before who took pity on him and gave him a few pence as well as a hard-boiled egg in exchange for a sketch of a wheelbarrow. The bartender brings him the coffee in a thick ceramic mug, which he puts both of his hands around gratefully. He sits there, his back against the bar, looking out into the room. His body is exhausted and grateful to be stationary, his legs faintly tingling as they relax. His mind is quiet; he sits there, sipping his coffee, enjoying the bitter taste of it so thoroughly that he is barely aware of his surroundings at all.

The room is small and dim, with only a few tables around the bar and a pool table in the back next to a fireplace. The afternoon sunlight comes through the dirty windows in muted arrows, cutting across Vincent's field of vision in strange golden screens that cast themselves onto and illuminate the surfaces they touch in fine detail. The room is paneled in wood and smells of earth, musty and close, like the miners' huts. It is lunchtime, he realizes; a bearded man in shirtsleeves eats a cut of meat with potatoes at one of the tables. At another table, a different man, with a large and circular bald spot and a bushy mustache that curls over his cheeks, eats a baked potato and slurps from a cup of soup. There is no noise save for the men chewing and the bartender tinkering behind the bar, setting down glasses and cleaning them with a white rag. On the pool table in the back, a cat is methodically swishing its tail back and forth, back and forth, silently, as if it might do so until the end of time.

Vincent's stomach growls as he watches the men eat, and the movement in his body stirs his consciousness. His coffee is warm against his palms and he sips it, slowly waking his body and his mind. He feels peaceful and relaxed; he is not thinking of his mission, of where he still must go, of the possibility that it will not turn out well. His body, in movement for days, has come to a stop, strangely, perfectly, in this room. He sits and watches the men slowly eat, a swirl of insects dancing in the cut of sun. Perhaps this is where he has been traveling to, these days, all those footsteps; perhaps this has been his destination all along. The men seem not to notice him as he gazes at them; they are perfectly peaceful in their solitude, sharing a meal with their parallel thoughts.

He remembers the visit he made in July to the Reverend Pieterszen. When he arrived at Pieterszen's house, Pieterszen's daughter came to the door. She was maybe seven, wearing a pink frock with lace around its edges, a ribbon in her hair, and no shoes. Her eyes went from Vincent's waist, where her gaze was level, up to his face and down again before she gave a terrified shriek and turned and ran from the door. Children always see more than the rest of us can, he thought; had he been a tramp, come to her door for charity, no doubt she would have received him with warmth. He thought instead that she could see straight through, beyond his appearance, to his anguish and confusion and doubt; it was that—not his rotted shoes, matted hair, or the hungry angle of his cheekbones—that made her scream.

Pieterszen came to the door soon after, his arm around the girl. When he saw Vincent, his face at first was heightened with confusion, his eyebrows furrowed at the sight of such a filthy creature at his door, and then his expression melted into softness and warmth.

"Vincent!" he said, "How lovely to see you! Come in, please, come in." He stood to the side and gestured widely with his arm into the darkness of the hall. His daughter looked up at him with fear, as if he had invited in a bear. "Don't worry, Roos," he said, "it's my friend Vincent come to see us!"

After supper, he and Pieterszen sat in Pieterszen's study with cups of coffee. Vincent's body refreshed and his mind somewhat restored, he was able to take in the room as he couldn't when he first arrived; there were prints covering the walls, as well as a few studies in ink and watercolor that were clearly Pieterszen's own. Vincent stood and moved around the room, examining them. Landscapes, primarily, many of them by Pieterszen's favorite painter Schelfhout and his student Hoppenbrouwers, as well as a few portraits of peasant women and clergymen. The studies that seemed most recently hung were of a particular figure that Pieterszen was struggling to get right—a woman sitting somberly on a stool.

"It's my wife," Pieterszen said from behind Vincent, answering the question he had not asked.

Vincent smiled. "I was just about to ask."

"I can't get it quite right. I'm beginning to think it's because I'm too close to her; perhaps I will never be satisfied with her portrait. I paint her, and the image is accurate, but there is something missing."

Vincent stood back from the wall and looked at the studies of Pieterszen's wife. There were three of them, and they were very much the same. In each of them she wore an expression so blank that it was as if her face erased itself; you would be looking at her and already forgetting that you were doing so. It was as if she were a representation of the human race rather than a member of it.

Technically, however, the paintings were nearly expert, just as his landscapes were. If Vincent had not just sat at table with his wife, he would not have found anything to be missing in the painting, but would only have wondered at the represented woman's vapidity. He wondered of Pieterszen's work just what he wondered of his hero, Schelfhout: Could perfection be a flaw?

Pieterszen was clearly a serious artist. Vincent knew he was in the presence of someone who understood the world of pictures. This was why he had come.

"Reverend," he said, "would you take a look at the drawings I brought with me?"

Pieterszen looked surprised. "I'd be honored," he said.

Vincent brought them to him. That little package that he had lugged all that way, so meager in his hands as he laid it in Pieterszen's. Why had he brought it? What strange impulse had made him tuck it under his arm and come here? He needed to show them to someone, to show someone what he had seen, what he had been through.

Pieterszen opened the little package and looked through the drawings very slowly, taking time to examine each one. Vincent stood over him and watched the drawings pass through his hands, reliving them in his eyes: the men leaving the mine; the wives bending under their sacks of coal; the landscape in winter, with its black trees over white snow and the gray slag heap looming; the studies of Angeline's father, of Madame Denis, of Angeline herself. Angeline! Hair pulled back, cross-legged beside the lantern, little smile, frenzied outline, head just a bit too big; looking at it, he felt his whole body tremble, hearing the sacred silence of that night in his hut, and seeing her body now crushed somewhere underground.

Pieterszen didn't speak until he had looked through them all. Then he lifted his head, to find Vincent anxiously hovering. "Well, Vincent," he said, "I can see that these drawings have been born out of deep love. I can see that you have a keen eye, and a respect for representing what you see with absolute honesty."

Vincent sat in the chair opposite him. "Thank you," he said, barely able to get the words out.

"I wonder if you've had any training?"

For a moment, Vincent thought he meant in evangelism, and he felt a flash of rage. But this was not what Pieterszen meant. "In drawing?" Vincent shook his head. "No."

He nodded. "I thought not. Your perspective is amateur, and there's a rawness to your figures that needs work."

Vincent nodded. There was no question about this. They were crude, shoddy studies, barely anything more than scribbles.

"But I do see something in these drawings, Vincent," Pieterszen said. He rose from his chair, leaving all the drawings on the seat but one, which he brought with him to prop against the wall, near the studies of his wife. It was the drawing of Angeline.

"I don't really understand it," he said, standing back from the drawing. "Somehow you've captured something in this drawing that I haven't been able to capture in so many attempts at painting my wife! Your technique is crude, and you've drawn this woman, I'm sure, nothing like what she actually looks like. Yet there is something here, something I can't quite identify. I feel like I understand something about this woman." He was talking at the wall, as if he were addressing the drawing itself. He paused. "I can't figure it out," he said.

Vincent remained silent. The idea that he might have succeeded in capturing anything at all of Angeline before she left the earth stole his speech.

"Well," Pieterszen said, still addressing the wall, "it's character, I suppose. Your drawing lacks precision, but it has *personal-*

ity. My painting presents a perfect picture, but I've removed all the individuality."

He took the drawing off the wall and came back to his chair. He was smiling. "I daresay I could learn a thing or two from you, Vincent my boy."

Just before Vincent left the house the next morning, Pieterszen handed back his drawings, but he kept the one of Angeline in his hands. "Might I keep this one, Vincent?" he asked. "I'd like to study it."

He thinks of this now, remembers the elation he felt when he left Pieterszen's house, wearing the boots that the reverend had given him, the ones still on his feet now, worn-out and torn; that feeling of hope, crushed so soon after by Theo's visit and the awful visit to their parents' house. Now he feels a sudden burst of clarity: the scene in front of him is a palette of browns and a swath of golden yellow; it is Rembrandt's *The Holy Family in the Evening*, the golden light illuminating the travelers, the lonely men at their meals just as holy as the painted family beneath the window lit by the sun. It strikes him with force, the scene in front of him taking on a sudden and definite holiness; he looks around him with pleasure and awe. The room begins to sparkle, to tingle and glow. He sits there on his stool with his coffee and feels a surge of love: for the men before him, for the quiet bartender behind the bar, for the room itself, the supreme pleasure of being there. This is God, he thinks, right here. This is life; this is my life. I am witness.

He takes out his paper and sketches each of the men, sitting at their tables, clutching their forks and spoons, the cat on the pool table, and then a still life, the items in front of him on the wooden bar: mug, beer tap, bartender's rag. The drawings are composed simply, the subject at the center of the page, each one a simple rendering of what he sees, and he is pleased with them. When his mug is empty, he allows the bartender to refill it, nodding at him as he does so. There are no words in this pub, he thinks. This is a sacred, wordless place.

He has the address written on a torn piece of paper that is folded into four squares and resides in his pocket. This address, just a few words and a couple of numbers, represents where his brother has been all this time. Vincent has it memorized by now, having stared at it for many long hours in his room in the Borinage, trying to imagine the place it represented, trying to imagine his brother's life without him.

Before he leaves the pub, he asks the bartender how to get to his brother's house. The bartender tells him; it is still an hour or so from where he is now, but he is grateful to have a little more time to himself.

He steps out of the pub into the afternoon sunshine. He feels a far more coherent man than he had when he arrived just an hour or two before; it is as if his outlines have been restored, his body once again visible and in human form. The coffee has given him some energy, and he feels a renewed vigor in his legs, which still ache but are no longer crying out in pain. In his excitement inside the bar he forgot to tend to his feet; they will carry him nonetheless.

He walks. He walks past vegetable stands and boys with newspapers and little girls selling flowers out of large baskets, past crowds of people at outdoor cafés, past parks and along the river, where thin boats float gracefully and women with white gloves and hats tied under their chins with ribbons laugh with their heads thrown back. It has turned into a beautiful day, and all of Paris is outside to enjoy it.

He passes by a gallery: in the window, unknown landscapes, seascapes, women in bathing dresses by rolling waves, a dog playing in the surf. Pieterszen would like these paintings, he thinks. Would Theo?

He thinks of the letters in his knapsack: Will they make a difference to Theo? Will they explain anything to him? He remembers Theo's visit so vividly; he remembers how his mouth clamped shut over his words, how he could not answer Theo through his cloud of fury. *You are not the same any longer.* He hears the phrase again and he feels his face flush.

What will Theo say when he arrives at his door? What will he see, about everything, that Vincent cannot see? He tries to think as Theo might: If their places were reversed, would he feel a failure?

But Theo, Vincent thinks, would never have gotten to where he is. Theo is too composed, too sure of himself, too much of the world in a way he will never be. Vincent travels toward him, not exactly sure why, drawn toward his brother as if toward a sun.

From down the street, though he has never been there before, Vincent knows which door is his brother's. At the far end of the block of row houses there is one with a blue door. His heart beating fast, a lump in his throat, his face flushed red, he approaches slowly, and sure enough, under the third doorbell is a brass plate that reads T. VAN GOGH.

Theo, at the Rijswijk mill, milk dripping down his chin. Theo, standing before the train in his top hat. Theo, at the family table on Christmas Eve, his hand over his face as he laughs at something forbidden that Vincent has said, his eyes twinkling with mirth. Theo, in their bed in Zundert, their knobby knees lined up, their feet one after the other, Theo's smaller and more dainty, Vincent's like ugly flesh-colored frogs. At night, when Vincent woke up frightened, some ungraspable nightmare at the edges of his mind, the darkness in their room complete and total, the sound of Theo sleeping would calm him and return him to the earth. His body was there to grasp onto if he needed it.

He stands on the doorstep, his hand poised in front of the bell. He pictures Theo opening the door, his hair slicked back, a cigarette holder in his teeth, his top hat, shining and polished, obscuring his face. A man in a suit with his brother's face, the face of the boy on the pillow next to his.

Baby Vincent, hovering nearby, says, *Don't worry. No matter what, I'll be your brother forever.*

He presses the bell.

He waits.

There is no answer.

He stands at the door for what seems like an age, presses the bell again, looks out over the street. Theo does not arrive. The brass plate screams, *T. VAN GOGH*, but his brother is not there.

His heart slowing, he trudges across the street and sits on the stoop of a different building, watching Theo's door. Of course this was a possibility, but he never considered it. Where is Theo? Here Vincent is at his door and still he is not here. A sinking feeling begins in his bones; he really has lost his brother forever. The gap between them is too great; there is no amount of walking, no number of letters that can bridge the distance. He has come here in vain, a fruitless search, just like all the rest. His brother does not need him, so he must not need his brother.

But then, what of the money that Theo has given him? He puts his hand into his jacket pocket and fingers the envelope with the money in it. A strange gesture, to be sure, giving Vincent money just after that terrible visit, and through his parents' hands. Theo had never given him money before. If it were truly a gesture of support, he thinks, Theo would have enclosed some word, some acknowledgment, some direction as to how the gift was meant. Without that, he cannot see it as apology, or even necessarily as support. Probably he just didn't want their parents to have to dish out any more of their own funds, that's all. Perhaps he instructed their parents not to tell Vincent whom it was from, and they disobeyed.

Still, the money is here. He touches it; it is real. And if Theo wanted no more connection with his brother, he would not have given him something he can touch.

A man in a dark suit and a top hat hurries by, and for a moment Vincent's heart leaps, but it is not Theo. Just a man hurrying back to his office, Vincent imagines, after a comfortable lunch at home. With this thought, he realizes—of course! Theo isn't at home because he is at Goupil's. How could he not have thought of this?

For a long time he sits there, thinking of what to do. If he waits here, eventually Theo will come back, and he can save himself having to walk the mile or so to Goupil's. He doesn't want to see the people who work with Theo, Vincent's old boss and his old colleagues, who will no doubt look him over with contempt and think him mad, think him strange, think he has failed at one more thing, and think they were right to dismiss him those years ago. They will give him those looks. He can see their faces now, their eyes roaming over him, their smiles set and made of bitter glass.

The thought of this makes him restless; he gets up and strolls quickly to the end of the street. On the corner there is a café, a line of outdoor tables nestled under an awning. A few well-dressed people sit with coffees and newspapers. Crossed legs, creased trousers, brown leather shoe dangling, hand tapping tablecloth: He takes in the details as his glance sweeps over the street. Across from the café is a cigar store. He can see a few men inside with dark hats; a stream of smoke trickles out the door. He crosses the street and looks in. He is often able to think better with a pipe; it helps him with his spirits, helps him to concentrate. He peers in the store window, trying to make out the dark shapes moving inside. Two men come out of the store, wearing bowler hats and smoking cigars, and glance at him with contempt: another street person with his dirty hands against the window, hungry for a smoke but unable to pay.

He turns from the window and a woman is there, holding an open box with a display of golden apples neatly nestled in rows. A thick strap attached to the sides of the box is around her neck, and she wears a long dress with a lace trim in a worn and faded purple. Vincent looks from the apples—so burnished and still!—to the woman's face. She has large, dark eyebrows and a mouth painted red, but when she smiles, her teeth are brown and crooked. "Apple?" she says to him.

He stammers, embarrassed. "I don't have any money," he says. She nods and begins to turn away. "But I could pay you with a drawing, if you might accept that," he finds himself saying. "I could do your portrait?"

She turns back to him, smiling again. "I don't think my boss would appreciate that," she says.

He nods. "Of course. It was a silly idea."

Still she stands in front of him. "You are an artist, then," she says, "are you?"

He lowers his eyes, suddenly embarrassed. "I . . ." he stammers. "No, I just . . . I don't know . . ." He wishes to flee, but his feet are rooted. "Never mind," he says. "Thank you."

He turns and hustles away from her, turning the corner back toward Theo's door, feeling her eyes on him. When he is out of her sight, he stops and stands on the sidewalk, breathing quickly, his heart suddenly pounding.

He does not move, simply stands there. The world moves around him: men in hats, women in dresses, a boy in short pants chasing a tiny dog with huge ears. Clouds, above him, roll across the sky; he looks up, and it is as if the buildings are swirling, as if even the buildings are moving around him as he stands still. He closes his eyes, and the sounds come at him: the clip-clop of a horse's hooves, the click-click of a woman's shoes, a snip of conversation—"Yes, she told me she was going to do it right away"—a birdcall, a bell, the sound of a distant train. When he opens his eyes, the blue of the sky, the reddish brick of the buildings, the yellow of a woman's skirt are painfully bright; it seems as if all the colors on the street have sharpened and are converging before him. Everything is piercing and prickly, everything burnished as if it has been polished; there are too many colors, too much movement, too much to take in. It is all too much, suddenly, and he cowers, shielding his eyes.

He moves with effort back to the stoop opposite Theo's door, keeping his eyes cast down. He sinks down as if into a cave. The space feels safe, the stairs and the doorway protecting him from the street; he sits with his eyes closed, breathing, and tells himself he can sit there as long as he likes. With his eyes closed, he still sees the street, its colors bright and burning, and he sees himself standing in it, a figure in dark, colorless clothes, a ragged shape cut from reality and inserted into a painting. In the shaded cool of the doorway, his heart slowing, he examines the image he sees behind his eyes, and it changes slowly, so the figure that is himself takes on form, and color, and slowly blends, the street becoming the background of the portrait of the man.

He opens his eyes. Across the street, next door to Theo's house, a woman washes a window, her hair covered in a white bonnet; above her, in a building next door, a different woman holds a rug out the window and beats it with a rolling pin. Puffs of dust rise from the rug; the woman keeps right on, the dust rising right into her face and hair. Vincent watches these women, his eyes shifting from one to the other. The window washer uses her whole arm as she swipes the glass with her rag. Her face is set in deep concentration and the sweat on her face catches the sunlight so that it sparkles. There are circles of perspiration under her arms; she wipes her forehead with her forearm and keeps right on. The woman with the rug beats the pin against it again and again.

The street, the women at their labor, the buildings framing

the scene, the sky: All of it is still shimmering somehow, infected with a keen sharpness, a fineness of line and angle.

For many long minutes he watches. He sees the women framed by the houses on either side, one in the top left corner, leaning out of her window, the other in the bottom right with her rag swept far away from her. It is a living, moving masterpiece that he is watching; it is holy, like the men in the bar, as holy as any sight he has ever seen. A perfect image, reality unveiled, souls revealed in their natural purity. Neither of the women so much as glances at him; they care only about their work. He thinks of Madame Denis in her kitchen, mixing ingredients in her big wooden bowl; men in a mining cell, sweat dripping from their noses as they peer at the rock for coal. He wants to bow before them; he wants to capture their image and show it to them, so they can see their sacredness with their own eyes.

Baby Vincent has gone silent.

How long will it still be before Theo returns? He imagines his brother coming down the street, his long strides, his confident gait. He imagines standing up before his brother, Theo seeing him in his dirty clothes, knowing he must have walked there from the Borinage, knowing exactly how far he has come. He watches the door, imagining his brother opening it and inviting him in, imagining following his brother into the house, his brother's back in his suit jacket, the back of his brother's head. And what will he find inside? Theo's rooms, Theo's life, the life he has made without Vincent.

In his mind, his brother approaches. "Vincent!" he says as Vincent stands to face him. He hurries toward Vincent and takes him in his arms. He smells of cedar and pine. "I worried that you were dead," Theo says into his ear. "Me, too," says Vincent in return.

He imagines the two of them in Theo's living room, the furniture pushed neatly back against the walls, a vase of purple flowers on the table by the window, a book turned facedown on the table next to the red armchair. Theo sits on the sofa, reading the letters that Vincent has brought him, and tears run down his face. "I'm sorry, Vincent," he says, "I didn't understand! I never understood. I've been a terrible brother. I know now all you needed was for me to listen to you, for me to believe in you, and I do." The two brothers embrace before the sofa, they are both forgiven, they part the best of friends.

Then they are by the door, in a dark hallway that leads from Theo's living room, by a table on which Theo has laid his keys and a tray with two cuff links. They are arguing, the vein on Theo's neck pronounced as a snake. "I don't know you!" screams Theo. "Who are you? What are you doing here?" He puts his hands on Vincent's shoulders, turns him around, and pushes him hard through the door. Vincent stumbles and falls to his knees on the step, but Theo does not stoop to help him, only throws the stack of letters after him, the pages fluttering out into the street, and slams the door.

He looks up at the women again. The woman with the rug is pulling it inside, beating the end of it a few last times before the task is done. The window washer has moved on to the next window, working as furiously as ever. He imagines himself standing and approaching her, and then he sees himself in her place: He is washing the window, he is pressing on the glass with his rag, moving it in quick circular motions, watching the streaks of water evaporate after the rag passes over. He can feel the sweat under his arms and dripping off of his nose; by his foot is a bucket filled with dirty water, a different rag floating at the top. He looks up and wipes the sweat from his eyes with his already wet hands; Theo is approaching from down the street, but he stops when he sees Vincent at his work, and just stands there, unmoving, taking it in. He has spent all day at the gallery looking at works of art, and now he watches his brother clean a window as if he is creating one. Vincent, after a beat, goes back to his labor, wishing to complete the task more than to greet his brother.

He blinks, returning to himself on the stoop. Everything on the street—the women, the windows, the roofs, the people rushing by—is softened suddenly, the angles gentle and warm, and each piece of it feels close and tangible, easy to grasp. He thinks of how he would describe what he is seeing to Angeline; how he could show it to her, make it a postcard that she could receive. Blinding blue of the sky with wispy circling clouds above the dark roofs, sharp white of the women's bonnets like blooming flowers against the weathered wood of the buildings, window washer with bent back over her bucket and rag, the tools of her labor. What would it take to be able to reproduce this holy image, to share the gift of being here to see it? It would take work to do it right, punishing work, the work of his life.

His body feels suddenly refreshed, as if he has just bathed in his filthy clothes. He must leave, now, before Theo comes home. He will not see him; he will not leave the letters. He will put to use the money that Theo gave him to pay for the train back to the Borinage, and when he gets back to Belgium, he will work on something to show to Theo, something that can explain what has happened to him better than his words ever could. The story he has told to Theo is actually only for him, Vincent, to understand, and now he does at last. Theo was right after all: Vincent is not the same any longer.

He will earn his brother's money, somehow, or he will die trying.

He picks up his knapsack, rises, and moves off the stoop into the street, away from Theo's door, the sun falling warm onto his shoulders.

Epilogue

Cuesmes, June 22, 1880

Dear Theo,

It's with some reluctance that I write to you, not having done so for so long, and that for many a reason. Up to a certain point you've become a stranger to me, and I too am one to you, perhaps more than you think; perhaps it would be better for us not to go on this way.

Without wishing to, I've more or less become some sort of impossible and suspect character in the family, in any event, somebody who isn't trusted, so how, then, could I be useful to anybody in any way? That's why, first of all, so I'm inclined to believe, it is beneficial and the best and most reasonable position to take, for me to go away and to remain at a proper distance, as if I didn't exist.

As molting time—when they change their feathers—is for birds, so adversity or misfortune is the difficult time for us human beings. One can stay in it—in that time of molting—and one can also emerge renewed; but anyhow it must not be done in public and it is not at all amusing, therefore the only thing to do is to hide oneself.

I am a man of passions, capable of and liable to do rather foolish things for which I sometimes feel rather sorry. I do often find myself speaking or acting somewhat too quickly when it would be better to wait more patiently. Now that being so, what's to be done, must one consider oneself a dangerous man, incapable of anything at all? I don't think so.

About a month ago, I came to see you, a walk of about three days. You don't know this because I arrived while you were at work, and left before you came home. Why? you ask. Well, I could see all the ways it would go, I could hear all the things you would say, and after playing out a hundred different endings I thought better of it, and returned to the Borinage with a new sense of direction.

For as much as five years, perhaps, I don't know exactly, I've been more or less without a position, wandering hither and thither. You would say, from such and such a time you've been going downhill, you've faded away, you've done nothing. Is that entirely true?

It's true that sometimes I've earned my crust of bread, sometimes some friend has given me it as a favor; I've lived as best I could, better or worse, as things went; it's true that I've lost several people's trust, it's true that my financial affairs are in a sorry state, it's true that the future's not a little dark, it's true that I could have done better, it's true that just in terms of earning my living I've lost time, it's true that my studies themselves are in a rather sorry and disheartening state, and that I lack more, infinitely more than I have. But is that called going downhill, and is that called doing nothing?

You ask: what is my ultimate goal? That goal will become clearer, will take shape slowly and surely, as the croquis becomes a sketch and the sketch a painting, as one works more seriously, as one digs deeper into the originally vague idea.

You must know that it's the same with evangelists as with artists. There's an old, often detestable, tyrannical academic school, the abomination of desolation, in fact—men having, so to speak, a suit of armor, a steel breastplate of prejudices and conventions. Those men, when they're in charge of things, have positions at their disposal, and by a system of circumlocution seek to support their protégés, and to exclude the natural man from among them. There's little fear that their blindness will ever turn into clear-sightedness on the subject.

This state of affairs has its bad side for someone who doesn't agree with all that, and who protests against it with all his heart and with all his soul and with all the indignation of which he is capable. Myself, I respect academicians who are not like those academicians, but the respectable ones are more thinly scattered than one would believe at first glance. Now one of the reasons why I'm now without a position, why I've been without a position for years, it's quite simply because I have different ideas from these gentlemen who give positions to individuals who think like them.

It's not a simple matter of appearance, as people have hypocritically held it against me, it's something more serious than that, I assure you.

Why am I telling you all this?—not to grumble, not to apologize for things in which I may be more or less wrong, but quite simply to tell you this: on your last visit, last summer, when we walked together near the disused mine they call La Sorcière you reminded me that there was a time when we also walked together near the old canal and mill of Rijswijk, and then, you said, we were in agreement on many things, but, you added—you've really changed since then, you're not the same any longer. Well, that's not quite how it is; what has changed is that my life was less difficult then and my future less dark, but as far as my inner self, as far as my way of seeing and thinking are concerned, they haven't changed. But if in fact there were a change, it's that now I think and I believe and I love more seriously what then, too, I already thought, I believed and I loved.

So you mustn't think that I'm rejecting this or that; in my unbelief I'm a believer, in a way, and though having changed I am the same, and my torment is none other than this: what could I be good for, couldn't I serve and be useful in some way, how could I come to know more thoroughly?

One who has been rolling along for ages as if tossed on a stormy sea arrives at his destination at last; one who has seemed good for nothing and incapable of filling any position, any role, finds one in the end, and, active and capable of action, shows himself entirely different from what he had seemed at first sight.

For I know this now: everything in men and in their works that is truly good, and beautiful with an inner moral, spiritual and sublime beauty, I think that that comes from God, and that everything that is bad and wicked in the works of men and in men, that's not from God, and God doesn't find it good, either. I'm always inclined to believe that the best way of knowing God is to love a great deal. Love that friend, that person, that thing, whatever you like, you'll be on the right path to knowing more thoroughly, afterwards; that's what I say to myself. But you must love with a high, serious, intimate sympathy, with a will, with intelligence, and you must always seek to know more thoroughly, better, and more. That leads to God, that leads to unshakeable faith. Someone, to give an example, will love Rembrandt, but seriously, that man will know there is a God, he'll believe firmly in Him. Try to understand the last word of what the great artists, the serious masters, say in their masterpieces; there will be God in it. Someone has written or said it in a book, someone in a painting.

In other words, I would be very happy if you could somehow see in me something other than some sort of idler.

Because there are idlers and idlers, who form a contrast. There's the one who's an idler through laziness and weakness of character, through the baseness of his nature; you may, if you think fit, take me for such a one. Then there's the other idler, the idler truly despite himself, who is gnawed inwardly by a great desire for action, who does nothing because he finds it impossible to do anything since he's imprisoned in something, so to speak, because he doesn't have what he would need to be productive, because the inevitability of circumstances is reducing him to this point. Such a person doesn't always know himself what he could do, but he feels by instinct, I'm good for something, even so! I feel I have a raison d'être! I know that I could be a quite different man! For what then could I be of use, for what could I serve! There's something within me, so what is it?

That's an entirely different idler; you may, if you think fit, take me for such a one.

In the springtime a bird in a cage knows very well that there's something he'd be good for; he feels very clearly that there's something to be done but he can't do it; what it is he can't clearly remember, and he has vague ideas and says to himself, 'the others are building their nests and making their little ones and raising the brood,' and he bangs his head against the bars of his cage. And then the cage stays there and the bird is mad with suffering. 'Look, there's an idler,' says another passing bird—that fellow's a sort of man of leisure. And yet the prisoner lives and doesn't die; nothing of what's going on within shows outside, he's in good health, he's rather cheerful in the sunshine. But then comes the season of migration. A bout of melancholy—but, say the children who look after him, he's got everything that he needs in his cage, after all—but he looks at the sky outside, heavy with storm clouds, and within himself feels a rebellion against fate. I'm in a cage, I'm in a cage, and so I lack for nothing, you fools! Me, I have everything I need! Ah, for pity's sake, freedom, to be a bird like other birds!

An idle man like that resembles an idle bird like that.

You may not always be able to say what it is that confines, that immures, that seems to bury, and yet you feel I know not what bars, I know not what gates—walls.

You know, what makes the prison disappear is every deep, serious attachment. To be friends, to be brothers, to love; that opens the prison through sovereign power, through a most power-ful spell. He who doesn't have that remains in death. But where sympathy springs up again, life springs up again.

And the prison is sometimes called Prejudice, misunder-standing, fatal ignorance of this or that, mistrust, false shame.

But to speak of something else, if I've come down in the world, you, on the other hand, have gone up. And while I may have lost friendships, you have won them. That's what I'm happy about, I say it in truth, and that will always make me glad. If you were not very serious and not very profound, I might fear that it won't last, but since I think you are very serious and very pro-found, I'm inclined to believe that it will last.

If it became possible for you to see in me something other than an idler of the bad kind, I would be very pleased about that. And if I could ever do something for you, be useful to you in some way, know that I am at your service. Since I've accepted what you gave me, you could equally ask me for something if I could be of service to you in some way or another; it would make me happy and I would consider it a sign of trust. We're quite dis-tant from each other, and in certain respects we may have differ-ent ways of seeing, but nevertheless, sometime or someday one of us might be able to be of use to the other. For today, I shake your hand, thanking you again for the kindness you've shown me.

Now if you'd like to write to me one of these days, my ad-dress is care of C. Decrucq, rue du Pavillon 8, Cuesmes, near Mons, and know that by writing you'll do me good.

Yours truly,
Vincent

Author's Note

I am deeply indebted to a number of sources in the creation of this novel: most notably Steven Naifeh and Gregory White Smith's excellent *Van Gogh: The Life*; David Sweetman's *Van Gogh: His Life and His Art*; Lawrence and Elisabeth Hanson's *Passionate Pilgrim: The Life of Vincent van Gogh*; Philip Callow's *Vincent van Gogh: A Life*; and the Van Gogh Museum's *Van Gogh's Imaginary Museum: Exploring the Artist's Imaginary World*. Irving Stone's 1934 novel, *Lust for Life*, was the inspiration for a few key scenes, as well as for the character of Decrucq as "the man the mines can't kill," and for the phrase "black Egypt," which, when Vincent uttered it in Stone's book, rang as true to me as if it were a detail from one of his letters. For knowledge of mines and mining life, I am indebted to Emile Zola's *Germinal* most of all, and also to Susan Campbell Bartoletti's *Growing Up in Coal Country*. Thomas à Kempis's *The Imitation of Christ* and C. S. Lewis's *Mere Christianity* were helpful in my understanding of Christianity. I used John Thomson's *Victorian London Street Life in Historic Photographs* for help imagining Van Gogh's life in London.

I relied heavily on the use of Vincent van Gogh's actual letters, and was lucky that the publication of the beautiful new translations, and the extensive website that accompanied them (www.vangoghletters.org)—the product of fifteen years of research at the Van Gogh Museum and Huygens ING—occurred while I was working on the novel. I used Vincent's letters (those from the Borinage as well as those from before and after) as my guides and touchstones, and have quoted from them whenever possible throughout the novel (the quotations are mainly from the earlier, 1958 translations, as that was what I had when the bulk of the novel was being written). I am also indebted to the extra texts included with both translations of Van Gogh's letters— the brief memoir and family history written by Theo's wife, Jo, is very moving, and all the supplemental letters and essays included with both editions were crucial.

The letters that serve as the prologue and the epilogue to the novel are both largely excerpted from Van Gogh's actual letters, the former from his letter of around August 14, 1879, and the latter from his letter of June 22, 1880, though I altered them with some editorial cuts and authorial insertions. These are the letters that began and ended the ten-month period where there are no letters between the two brothers, a silence that never again occurred between them.

Acknowledgments

Thank you to the Constance Saltonstall Foundation for the Arts and the fantastic Ucross Foundation, where I wrote large portions of the manuscript in inspiring countryside. Thank you to Simon Schama, in whose class this novel was born. Thank you, Maggie Pouncey, Karen Thompson Walker, Alena Graedon, Susanna Kohn, Tania James, Joel Pedlikin, Mary Beth Keane, Philip Pardi, Ephraim Rubenstein, and Mary Gordon, for careful early reads and suggestions that improved the book enormously. For believing in this book, understanding its vision, and working so hard on its behalf, thank you to my agent, Susan Golomb, and her team, Krista Ingebretson and Soumeya Bendimerad, and to my incredible editor, Eric Chinski, his assistants, Gabriella Doob and Peng Shepherd, and the whole fantastic team at Farrar, Straus and Giroux. It has been my great fortune to work with you all.

Huge gratitude to Chris Adrian, for generosity and brilliance beyond belief, and for understanding what I was up to in a way not even I did.

Thank you to my family, for everything, always.

And I need to reach beyond the grave to thank Vincent van Gogh, the man himself, whose life and brilliance in words and pictures provided the inspiration for this novel and afforded me a fascinating and ever-complicated home to live in for a number of years.